For Jim Kirby,

still the man I want to be when I grow up

Library of Congress Cataloging-in-Publication Data

Kirby, Matthew J., 1976–

The lost kingdom / Matthew J. Kirby. — 1st ed.

p. cm.

Summary: On the eve of the French and Indian War, Billy Bartram and his naturalist father travel into the American wilderness in an airship — pursued by a party of French soldiers and haunted by a terrifying bear-wolf — on a quest to find the lost kingdom of the Welsh prince Madoc.

ISBN 978-0-545-27426-5 (jacketed hardcover) 1. Bartram, William, 1739-1823 — Juvenile fiction. 2. Bartram, John, 1699-1777 — Juvenile fiction. 3. Naturalists — United States — Juvenile fiction. 4. Quests (Expeditions) — Juvenile fiction. 5. Voyages and travels — Juvenile fiction. 6. Adventure stories. 7. United States — History — Colonial period, ca. 1600-1775 — Juvenile fiction. [1. Bartram, William, 1739-1823 — Fiction. 2. Bartram, John, 1699-1777 — Fiction. 3. Adventure and adventurers — Fiction. 4. Voyages and travels — Fiction. 5. United States — History — Colonial period, ca. 1600–1775 — Fiction.] I. Title.

PZ7.K633528Los 2013

813.6 — dc23

10 9 8 7 6 5 4 3 2 1   13 14 15 16 17

Printed in the U.S.A.   23   First edition, September 2013

The text type was set in Book Antiqua.

The display type was set in The Youths Companion.

Book design by Elizabeth B. Parisi

THE LOST KINGDOM

MATTHEW J. KIRBY

Scholastic Press ~ New York

✳ CONTENTS ✳

CHAPTER 1

Spies

A muffled clatter startled me awake, and I froze in my bed, listening in the darkness. Through my open window, I heard whispers from down in my father's garden.

Deep voices. More than one.

I slipped to the floor, holding my breath, and crossed to the window. The moon had come and gone, the night over our farm as dark as it would get before dawn. But I could make out the edges and borders of the kitchen garden and the flower beds. And then I caught the waver of candle-light through the windows of my father's garden study. Someone was in there.

But not my father. Not at this time of night.

I leaned farther out the window, trying to hear, but a slight breeze rustled the trees and made it hard to understand what they were saying. I swallowed, a chill deep in my chest.

Who were they? Robbers? What did they want? What would they do to my family?

I turned to look at my little brother sleeping in his bed, undisturbed. And then I heard a creak on the landing outside my door, then footsteps down the stairs. I crept to the doorway and peered out, finding my father halfway down to the first floor.

"Father," I whispered.

He jolted. "Billy, what are you —"

"There are men outside." I stepped out onto the landing.

He laid his index finger against his lips and nodded. "Stay in your room."

"But, Father —"

"Do as I say, Billy." He descended the rest of the way and disappeared into the kitchen.

I hesitated. A part of me wanted to do what he asked, wanted to climb back into my bed and pretend I hadn't heard anyone creeping around in the garden. But the larger part of me worried about what would happen to my father and couldn't ignore the men outside. I followed him down the stairs. As I came into the kitchen, I saw him loading his rifle by the dim red light of the coals still smoldering in the fireplace.

He looked up. "I told you to stay in your room."

"But who are they?" I took a step toward him. "What do they want?"

"Billy." He set his powder horn down on the table. "You must return to your room. Now."

Why wasn't he raising the alarm? Rousing the family? I could run to my older brother's neighboring farm and be back with him in minutes. There was something my father wasn't telling me. "I'm coming with you."

"Absolutely not."

The sound of breaking glass came from outside.

My father cocked the hammer of his rifle and slipped to the door. He opened it slowly, letting in the sound of crickets and the night breeze. He raised the barrel of the gun, tucked the butt into his shoulder, and stepped over the threshold.

I followed him to the door but stopped short. In the darkness, I could almost lose his black shape stalking up to and then around the nectarine tree that grew by the house. Beyond him, the door to his shed hung open, and shadowy figures moved inside. When he reached the gate to his flower gardens, he paused and crouched behind the fence. He seemed to be listening.

That was when I caught movement to my left. A dark shape rose up in the kitchen garden. I couldn't tell, but I thought I saw a gun taking aim.

"Father, behind you!"

The shape dropped out of sight, but a man's voice shouted from where I'd seen it.

"Prenons la fuite!"

French.

"Nous avons été découverts!"

The light inside my father's study went out, and then

three silhouettes burst from the doorway and scattered. One vaulted the fence near my father and ran right past me around the house. My father gave chase, and I followed after him, my bare feet cold on the wet ground. I rounded the corner just as the stranger leaped onto a waiting horse, spun, and galloped down the lane.

My father rushed into the middle of the road and aimed his rifle, and I ran to his side.

As I reached him, he cursed. "Too far." And he lowered his gun. Then he turned to face me, and in the darkness, I saw his eyes grow wide. "Move!"

He lunged at me, knocking me backward, throwing us both to the ground as three more horses thundered by and vanished into the night.

I tried to get up. "Who were —"

"Shh!"

He held me down for several moments, listening.

I heard nothing but the sounds of our farm.

He sighed. "I think they've all fled." Then he stood, extended his hand, and lifted me to my feet. "Are you hurt, son?"

"No."

"Thank God." He shook his head. "I told you to stay in the house."

As we walked back around to the kitchen door, I thought about what had just happened, watching it all unfold again in my mind. Those men had not been simple robbers. They had only broken into my father's study, and they had fled even though there were four of them against us.

They had come for some other reason. Something they'd hoped to find in my father's work.

"What were they after?" I asked.

He didn't answer.

"Father?"

"Ask no more questions," he said. "You will return to bed, now."

"But, Father —"

"You may have saved my life tonight by shouting that warning. But that does not mean I approve of your disobedience. I would rather die than see you in harm's way. Do you understand? Do you realize that you might have been hurt? Even killed?"

I said nothing.

"Return to your bed, Billy. We will speak no more of this, for now."

"Yes, sir."

I left him standing in the kitchen doorway, still holding his rifle, staring out into the night. I trudged up the stairs, back into my bedroom, and collapsed onto my bed. I was cold. My body shook. And I knew I would never get back to sleep.

The next morning, my father put me to work drawing one of his specimens as though nothing had happened. We were in his study, the very place the French intruders had been rummaging, though my father had cleared away any sign of their having been there. I stared at the plant, pushing down all the questions I wanted to ask, holding back the fear, ignoring the cracks forming in my world, trying to focus my attention.

The plant had a mouth.

Many of them, in fact. The little green maws sat open, waiting, lined with pale green needles for teeth. They ate flies, and their jaws snapped closed as swiftly and surely as any lizard's. My father worked nearby. He packed the tender roots of another boring plant in black soil and then swaddled it in burlap, preparing it for the journey across the seas from Philadelphia to London. He appeared calm, as though the events of the previous night hadn't happened.

I cleared my throat. "Are there many of these plants out there?"

He didn't look up. "The small ones are common enough in certain regions."

"Is this a small one?"

"Yes." He took the plant he'd been working on in both hands, like a newborn, and gently dipped the root end in a pail of water, letting the burlap soak up all it could. "The larger specimens have been known to consume men whole."

My eyes widened. I imagined myself out in the wilderness and what it would be like to stumble across a plant that could eat me.

"Where did you find it?" I asked.

"The Carolinas." He paused, laid down the dull plant, and came over to me. He picked up a slender knife, looked at me in a way that said, "Watch," and he used the tip of the blade to tease the plant mouth into closing. He chuckled. "They call it a tipitiwitchet. It grows in poor, wet soil. Bogs full of sand and peat. Now, back to your drawing. Mr. Franklin will be here soon."

"Mr. Franklin is coming?"

"Yes."

I stared out the window, wondering if the visit had something to do with the robbery.

The nectarine tree swayed in the breeze. Honeybees the size of musket balls hummed about the flower beds, visiting each blossom in turn, spreading pollen and doing what they were kept for. Visitors from as far as England and France had come to my father's garden. Some had commented on its lack of order, the seemingly haphazard way in which my father had laid it. But Father said his plants were arranged according to nature's design, not for the amusement of bored and wealthy men: Plants that had been found together, grew together, living as neighbors in spite of their differences in color, size, or shape.

It was the nearest thing to Eden I could imagine, and it had always felt like the safest place on earth.

But not anymore.

I suppressed that thought and dipped my quill, then scratched out the first line. Then I sketched out another, and another, the broad, necklike shape of the tipitiwitch-et's stems. Line by line, I translated the details of the plant to paper: the fine, almost invisible hairs that lined the green tongues, the little bead of sweetness in the center, which I guessed to be what drew the flies in for a drink. I included every detail worth noting, and as I did so I started to think that perhaps I understood this plant.

Those hairs, for example. In the absence of eyes or a nose, those hairs seemed to be what alerted the plant to the presence of a fly and closed its mouth. So I sketched one mouth with a just-landed fly, its little foot tickling the hair, and I drew the mouth near it snapped shut, fly wings and feet splayed outward. And then something occurred to me.

"Is that why it eats flies?"

"Pardon?" my father asked.

"You said it grows in poor soil. Is that why it eats flies?"

My father leaned back and looked at me. "An interesting question. Share your reasoning."

I hesitated, waiting for the thought to finish forming, not wanting to sound foolish.

"Go on, son."

"Well . . ." I felt a squirm in my shoulders that turned into a shrug. "If the plant can't get the nourishment it needs from the soil, maybe it gets it from the insects it eats?"

My father said nothing. But he smiled.

"That is a sound conclusion," he finally said, coming over. He picked up my drawing. "Another fine representa-tion, son."

"Thank you, Father."

For a little while after that, we worked together, surrounded by my father's precious books and other oddities collected on his journeys. The massive, curved fragment of *incognitum* tusk, the bear-wolf claws, curious rocks and twigs, bird nests and wasp nests. I loved listening to the stories of how he came by each of them out in the frontier. And every time he left on one of his journeys, I would stand in the road, watching him grow smaller and smaller, wanting to go with him, hoping he would turn around and call to me to follow him. I wanted nothing so much as I wanted that.

But he never even looked back.

We packaged the remaining specimens within the special crates my father had designed, a variety of seeds for my father's subscribers in England and live starts and roots for a few ardent collectors who were willing to pay the cost. The tipitiwitchet got its own box.

"Does it ever make you sad?" I asked.

"What?"

"That many of these will die before they arrive."

He frowned. "I suppose. It is a waste, isn't it?" He set the lid on the last crate and hammered it in place with thin nails he held between his teeth. He stood up when he was finished, hands at his hips. "But do you not marvel at those that do survive? That there are gardens in England with Pennsylvanian plants growing in them? . . . My plants."

"John?" came a call from outside.

"We're in the study, Ben," my father said.

A figure appeared in the doorway. "Of course you are." And Mr. Franklin entered the room.

He and my father shook hands.

"You remember my son Billy."

Mr. Franklin turned to me. Next to my father, he appeared short and round. But he had a quality in his gray eyes, at once mirthful and sharp, that made it difficult to meet his gaze for more than a moment at a time. "Of course. Your father tells me you're growing into a fine young man, and now I am able to see that plainly for myself."

I bowed my head. "Thank you, Mr. Franklin."

He nodded and inhaled through his nose. "Ah, the smell of black soil. The shipment is in order, then?"

"Packed and ready," my father said.

"Good. I'll have my men load it onto the wagon. While they're doing so, you and I shall discuss . . . the other matter."

My father cleared his throat. "If it's agreeable, I'd like for Billy to join our discussion."

What? He had said nothing to me. But my heartbeat quickened with excitement.

Mr. Franklin paused and regarded me at an angle. "Oh?"

"Yes," my father said. "He was a witness to what happened last night. And I am considering bringing him on the expedition."

I nearly gasped.

"On *this* expedition?" Mr. Franklin asked.

My father paused. "Yes."

"We'll deal with that shortly," Mr. Franklin said. "But first things first. What did they find?"

My father looked around his study. "Some of our early correspondence on Madoc is missing. So is an early drawing of the ship. They knew what they were looking for. I can only conclude that our mission is known to the French and has been for some time."

What mission was he talking about? Who was Madoc, and what was this about a ship?

"We must change course." Mr. Franklin gripped his cane, his eyes hard. "You must leave at once. Ahead of schedule."

"I agree," my father said.

Mr. Franklin nodded. "I must get word to the others." He turned to leave.

"Ben," my father said. "There is still the matter of Billy. After the events of last night, and witnessing his bravery, I think it is time he join me."

My father thought me brave? I believed he'd been only angry with me last night.

Mr. Franklin pushed out his lips. "Persuade me."

I wanted to speak up, to assure him that I possessed whatever was needed. But I realized I would only hurt my chances if I did.

My father looked at me. "The nature of this journey is such that I will not have the opportunity to collect specimens according to my usual methods."

"That is true," Mr. Franklin said.

"Beyond his bravery, Billy has proven himself to be a talented artist, accurate and astute." My father picked up my drawing of the tipitiwitchet and handed it to Mr. Franklin. "He has been making such drawings for me for some time now. If I cannot collect specimens to bring back with me, I will need him at my side to record my discoveries in a way that will still profit my botanical studies."

"I see." Mr. Franklin looked over my drawing. "It is a worthy attempt. Quite remarkable, in fact." He wrinkled his brow and then pulled a piece of paper from an inside coat pocket. He unfolded it and handed it to my father.

"What is this?" my father asked.

"Just something I've been thinking about. Look at it and give it to Billy."

My father took a moment or two to examine the paper, and then he passed it to me. I saw what I supposed was a snake, though not a well-drawn one, divided into thirteen pieces. Each piece was labeled as one of the colonies, and beneath the image were written the words *Join, or Die*, suggesting the ability of snakes, when cut into pieces, to join back together again if left overnight.

"What is it, Ben?" my father asked.

"That, my friend, is us," Mr. Franklin said. "Whether Marylander or Pennsylvanian or Virginian, I have begun to believe quite fervently that if we colonists are to survive in this New World — with the French at our backs and the

Spanish at our toes, and never knowing if the Indian be friend or foe — we must recognize that our fates are shared. What happens to one of us happens to all. You're the artist, Billy." Mr. Franklin turned to me. "What do you think of my drawing?"

The idea was something I hadn't ever given any thought to. My family, me — we were Pennsylvanians. But what if we were also something else? Something larger. But I didn't want to say what I thought of the drawing. "Well . . . it might need a bit of adjustment."

"Is that so?" Mr. Franklin gestured toward the desk, where my inkwell and quill rested. "Show me how you would improve upon it."

I hesitated. "Mr. Franklin, I didn't mean —"

"Nothing to worry about, Billy," Mr. Franklin said. "I just want to assess your abilities."

So this was a test. And it seemed the outcome might determine whether I was allowed to accompany my father. My stomach tightened as I sat down at the desk. I placed a piece of paper in front of me and stared at it.

Mr. Franklin put his hand on my shoulder. "My snake, Billy."

I dipped the quill. How would I make Mr. Franklin's picture differently than he had?

Well, to begin with, I thought it needed to be more snakelike, with a coil and more curves. So I began drawing the slide and curl of a snake, adding scales and a tail and a forked tongue flicking the air. Then I drew lines where I thought it could be cut, but in my nervousness I misjudged and ran out of snake at eight pieces. I had failed the test.

I tried to cover it up. "It's all wrong, Mr. Franklin. I'm sorry."

But Mr. Franklin slipped it out from under my hands. He pulled out his spectacles and wrapped them around his ears, and then studied my drawing, rubbing his chin.

"I can try again," I said.

"Nonsense," Mr. Franklin said. "What you've done is quite good. I'll just make this headpiece represent all of New England together, and perhaps combine some of the others. It's a striking image. Thank you, Billy. I will print this in my gazette one day soon."

I was surprised at his approval, but I welcomed it. "Thank you, sir." And though my mother had always cautioned me against the sin of pride, I allowed myself a small transgression.

My father nodded. "Very well done, Billy."

And when he said it, I sinned a little more.

Mr. Franklin pulled off his spectacles and regarded me with narrowed eyes. "I think you may be right, John. Billy seems to have a keen eye, and a keen mind as well. I think he would be a valuable addition to our society of philosophers."

Society?

"Have you been persuaded?" my father asked him.

"I have," Mr. Franklin said. "But I think we should find out if Billy is willing to rise to the challenge." He turned to me. "Are you prepared to accompany your father into the frontier, lad?"

I stood up as tall as I could and was surprised to see that I was almost as tall as Mr. Franklin. "Yes, sir."

"It will be perilous," Mr. Franklin said.

"I am prepared," I said firmly.

Mr. Franklin nodded. "Then welcome to the expedition."

My father clapped his hand on my shoulder, and in my excitement, it felt like the only thing keeping me anchored to the earth.

"Thank you, sir," I said.

Mr. Franklin gave me a wry smile. "Don't thank me until you make it back home safely." He turned to my father. "Have you told him where you're going?"

"Not yet," my father said. "Until moments ago, he did not even know I thought to bring him."

Mr. Franklin nodded. "Then we should tell him, shouldn't we?"

CHAPTER 2

The Expedition

"**H**ave you heard of Prince Madoc, Billy?" Mr. Franklin asked.
"No, sir."

"He was a Welsh prince, and according to legend, he sailed from his kingdom across the seas and landed in the Americas nearly six hundred years ago. Centuries before Christopher Columbus or Jamestown or Plymouth."

"Is that true?" I asked.

"It would seem to be," my father said. "If the rumors can be believed."

"What rumors?" I asked.

Mr. Franklin sat in one of the chairs, leaning forward with both hands on his cane. "Several backwoods traders, and a few missionaries, have reported encounters with Welsh-speaking Indians out in the frontier, beyond the

Ohio Country. It would seem there is a lost Welsh kingdom somewhere out there."

"And we mean to find it," my father said. "That is the purpose of the expedition you are joining."

"Why do you want to find it?" I asked.

"Allies," Mr. Franklin said. "The French want the Ohio Country. Badly enough, I'd wager, that they will soon attempt to take it by force. War is imminent. If England can secure the support of Madoc's kingdom, between us we can squeeze the French out. This expedition is a diplomatic mission."

"And a scientific one," my father said.

Mr. Franklin nodded, his eyes closed. "Of course, John."

"Mr. Franklin?" I said.

"Yes, Billy?"

"What did you mean when you said I was joining a society?"

"Ah, the American Philosophical Society," Mr. Franklin said. "Your father and I founded it ten years ago. It is a group of philosophers, each interested in a different aspect of the natural world. Your father is the Botanist. We have a Mathematician, a Mechanician, a Chemist, and others. Each philosophical branch has a seat. We even have an Electrician. You will make their acquaintance soon enough."

"And what is your branch, sir?" I asked.

My father chuckled. "Mr. Franklin does what Mr. Franklin wants to do. His seat is . . . malleable."

Mr. Franklin tipped his head. "I won't disagree with that."

"And what does the Society do?" I asked.

"When we started," my father said, "we wanted to create a forum for sharing knowledge among the colonies. We corresponded with New Yorkers, Marylanders, Virginians. But within a few years, it became obvious that we needed to adjust our mandate."

Mr. Franklin cleared his throat. "You see, Billy, the Philosophical Society is now a secret society. It was once our custom to disseminate our discoveries and insights for the greater good of all mankind. But as the French and Spanish began to make threats against the colonies, we realized we had a much larger duty and purpose. So seven years ago we ceased operating publicly and became what we are today."

That aroused my curiosity. "And what is that?"

"Patriots," he said. "Philosophers and patriots."

My father agreed. "We use our knowledge and discoveries to secure the safety of the colonies. We protect them, though they are unaware of us."

As my father spoke, the image of him shifted in my mind. He grew in stature and mystery. There were things about him I didn't know, had never suspected. He had always been admired as a botanist, but I had no inkling that he belonged to this group of important men.

"The Philosophical Society," I whispered.

"Yes," Mr. Franklin said. "And now you are one of us, trusted with the knowledge of our existence. I hope our trust is well placed."

I swallowed. "It is, sir."

"Our enemies surround us," he said. "A fact about which you are now all too well aware." He turned to my father. "How soon can your team be ready?"

"We'll need at least a week," my father said.

"Let us hope that is enough."

Shortly after that, Mr. Franklin had my father's crates loaded onto his wagon and returned to Philadelphia. We watched him trundle down the lane, and then we went to work weeding in the upper kitchen garden. As I moved down the cabbages, I came across a spot where the produce had been trampled, the place where the French spy had crouched. I froze.

My father bobbed up and down along a nearby row of carrots, with clutches of weeds in his hands. When he saw me, he stopped and came over, then noticed the ruined vegetables. "It's all right, son." He put his hands on my shoulders. "They found what they came for. They won't be coming back."

"Are you certain?" I asked.

"Yes. You're perfectly safe. I won't let anything happen to you."

I wanted him to still think me brave. So I smiled and nodded.

He let go of me, and we went back to work.

"Having said that," my father lowered his voice. "Best not to tell your mother about the expedition just yet."

"She doesn't know?"

"She knows I am leaving soon. She does not know you're coming with me."

"Oh." If my mother decided she did not want me to leave, then I would not be leaving. "How will we convince her?"

"*We* will do nothing," he said. "I will speak with her when the time is right."

"Do you think she will allow it?"

"I will do my best to convince her."

Over the next few days, I spent a great deal of time with my father in the garden. "To help me, you'll need to know the proper labels of things," he said, and he began instructing me in the classifications of the great Swedish botanist Linnaeus, taken from my father's cherished copy of the *Genera Plantarum*. "You must first understand what is known if you are to recognize what is unknown."

He taught me the Latin names of plants, and the way he recited them, they sounded like a prayer. But as I repeated them to myself, they struck my core like an arcane incantation. *Rhododendron maximum. Ursa leguinium. Panax quinquefolium.* They felt to me like keys, the *real* names known only by a few, and with this initiation, I could now unlock their secrets and power.

But what I enjoyed even more about my time in the garden was making drawings. My father wanted me to practice. He gave me my own paper, ink, and quill, and a board that rested on my lap as I sat in the dirt and the mulch. Each day, I would simply wander until I found a flower, a shrub, or a tree that I wanted to know better, and I would spend the afternoon drawing and figuring it out.

"That's a beautiful picture," my mother said, two days after Mr. Franklin had come.

"Thank you," I said. "It is called *Kalmia angustifolia*."

My mother laughed, a gentle, flowering sound that belonged there in the garden. "You remind me of your father out here. But I prefer to call it sheep laurel," she said. "Its common name."

"Why?"

"Because that sounds like what it *is*, not what a group of botanists have decided to call it."

I looked at the Latin label I had written beneath the drawing. And below that I added *Sheep Laurel*. I looked up at my mother.

She gave me an approving nod. "Now we know what it is." Then she looked over her shoulder. "Your father has recently involved you a great deal in his studies."

I focused my eyes on the drawing so I didn't have to look into her eyes. "Yes, he has."

Did she know about the expedition?

"The two of you out here," she said, "lately, I suspect some conspiracy between you."

I looked up. Her mild expression unnerved me. "What — what do you mean?"

"Your father and the Society have done much for the protection of Pennsylvania."

"Society?"

She smiled. "Has he told you where you are going?"

I swallowed.

"Your father has determined to take you, hasn't he?"

"I, uh —" What was I to say?

"Your father is as easy to interpret as a Puritan sermon, Billy. And you are no better."

She knew. Of course she knew, and it was best to be forthright with her. My father had not spoken with her yet, so I resolved to ask her permission, myself. If I was old enough to accompany him, I was old enough to do that.

I laid my drawing board aside and got to my feet. "We are going in search of the lost kingdom of Prince Madoc."

"The Welsh? In the frontier?"

"Yes, ma'am."

She laid the flat of her hand against her chest, touching her neck.

I mustered the arguments for my case. "It is time for me to begin a trade, and I would like to follow after Father in his business. The journey will be dangerous, but I will be careful. I must go out into the world eventually, so —"

"Yes, you must."

"I must?" Her agreement surprised me. But I wasn't exactly sure what we agreed upon. "Are you giving me your blessing to go?"

"I didn't say that." She brought her hand down. "You are certainly old enough. And I know your father would do his utmost to keep you safe. I only wonder if this is really what you want."

That wasn't the objection I'd been preparing for, and I took a step forward. "It is what I want."

"You're certain?"

"Yes, Mother."

She looked down at the drawing I'd laid aside. "Your brother James is a farmer. Moses and Isaac run an apothecary in town. I've watched you for years as you've watched your father, and I just want you to know you don't have to follow his trail. You are like him in so many ways, but unlike him in others."

"I want to follow him."

My mother studied me, and I had the feeling that she didn't quite believe me. But a moment later she smiled. "Then I am pleased for you, and you have my blessing. You leave soon, do you not?"

"In five days."

She nodded. "Then your father and I must talk about preparations."

"He may be angry with me for telling you myself."

She laughed her gentle laugh. "How can he be? You told me nothing I had not already guessed."

The next few days passed quickly. We packed the provisions my mother worked hard to prepare. Hard biscuits, dried fruits, smoked and salted meats, though not in great quantities. We expected to do some hunting and fishing along the way. We also prepared several of my father's special crates for specimens. I remembered Mr. Franklin had said my father wouldn't be able to collect on this expedition, but apparently he planned to anyway. He filled another box with his tools and instruments, and one with my supplies: paper, bottles of ink, and a bundle of quills. All of this we loaded onto our wagon.

I hardly slept the night before we were to leave. Anticipation tossed me in my bed, and my younger brother's snoring across the room made it even harder to keep hold of the little sleep I found. I was awake when the pale light of the setting moon vanished from the room. I was awake when a brief rainstorm came through and broke the day's heat. I was awake for the screeching of a distant cat fight somewhere on the farm. I was awake when the first cock crowed, and upon hearing it I gratefully rose and dressed.

Downstairs, I found the kitchen empty and cold. I was the first one up, and in the dim dawn I coaxed the cooking fire back to life. I sliced myself some bread and spread it with butter from the crock. Then I sat near the hearth and held my bread out to let the flames breathe on my arm and melt the butter.

Something shifted above me, waking up the floorboards, and some moments later I heard footsteps on the stairs. I stood up, thinking to greet my father. But my mother walked into the room, still adjusting her house bonnet.

"Billy, you're up."

"Good morning, Mother."

"Your father will be down in a few moments." She tied on her apron.

When my father came into the room, he wore his gray wig, the one that made him look older and more distinguished. My mother made us a breakfast of mushed oats mixed with milk. But instead of honey or molasses, she sheared some rare sugar from the loaf to sweeten it. My father watched her, and I watched him watching her. Perhaps it was the firelight, but there was a glow in his eyes that he never had for anything or anyone else. Not even his plants.

"Both of you, eat," she said, busying herself with things that didn't need doing. She poked at the fire and then straightened the stack of firewood. She wiped off the table twice. And then she got out a broom and began sweeping even though I remembered my sister Lizzy doing it the night before.

My father left his food and went to her. He put one hand on her back and took hold of the broom with the other. He gently pulled it from her hands, set it aside, and then he gathered her into his arms. I looked down at my oats, a little embarrassed.

"Everything has been taken care of," he said. "James will tend to the farm, and Isaac and Moses said they would try to come out to help as business allows."

"That's not it," she said. "It never is. You know that."

My father sighed. "All shall be well. Haven't I always come home safe and sound?"

I looked up.

"But this isn't like your other expeditions," she said. "The dangers —"

"Are no greater nor worse."

My mother pushed back to arm's length and looked up at him. "That's not true."

"The dangers are merely different this time." He pulled her back in. "We shall return safely. You shall see."

They stood together for some moments. I stared at my food again, and for me the kitchen held an awkward silence. I was still hungry. I took a bite, and only after it was in my mouth realized that my chewing was the loudest thing in the room. So I just swallowed it all down whole.

A moment later, my mother took a deep breath and said, "It's time."

My father nodded.

"I'll gather everyone. You and Billy collect your things." She left the kitchen.

I got to my feet but then hesitated. My father looked at the space before him where my mother had been, arms at his sides. He appeared vulnerable in a way I hadn't ever seen him. I waited.

He stared.

"Father?"

His back straightened. "Yes, Billy. Let's be off." And he left the kitchen.

I followed him to the stable, and together we led out the horses and harnessed them to the wagon. My father pulled on his wide-brimmed hat and we went around the house to the lane, where my mother had collected my siblings. My father embraced each of them. "Mary, Lizzy, Ann. Be a help to your mother. Johnny, you help James when he asks for it."

I shook my brother's hand and hugged my sisters. Then I hugged my mother.

"Keep to your path," she said. "Whichever you choose."

"I will," I said. "I promise."

My father embraced her one more time and kissed her.

"Farewell," he said. "Come, Billy."

And with that, we climbed up onto the wagon and started down the lane. I knew the rest of my family would be waiting and waving behind us, just as I had always done before. I resisted the urge to turn and look back at them, and instead watched my father's forward gaze, intent on the horizon.

"Do you know that we always wave to you?" I said.

"I do."

"But you never turn to look."

"One good-bye is sufficient," he said.

I frowned, and he saw it.

"Partings are not a talent like your drawing," he said, his voice softening. "They do not get easier with practice."

His answer took me aback. All these years, all his expeditions, I had thought him cold and indifferent to our farewell ritual. But that wasn't true. A prolonged good-bye was simply that much harder for him.

I locked my eyes on the path ahead, chin high. I imagined my mother and my siblings behind us, and I felt their waves and smiles like sunlight on my back. Only this time, I was the one growing small and distant in the road.

CHAPTER 3

The Aeroship

We set off at a brisk pace down the Darby Road. A low fog still hung about the fields. But as we rolled along, the first full rays of sun charged in and drove the mist away. A mile down the road we arrived at the Lower Ferry, where we crossed the Schuylkill River. From there we drove to Cedar Street, which we followed east into town.

"Mr. Franklin asked us to stop by his home on our way to the ship," my father said.

I remembered the French spies had stolen a drawing of a ship from my father's study, and I assumed that meant we would be going by river into the frontier. But I wondered what about the ship made a drawing of it valuable to the French.

Mr. Franklin's house was grand, redbrick with two chimneys and carved marble casings around the windows.

It also had a curious metal spear stabbing upward from the tallest point of the roof. My father noticed it, too, and he asked Mr. Franklin about it after we'd been shown into the parlor.

"I call it a lightning attractor," Mr. Franklin said. "I installed it last autumn. If my house is struck by lightning, that metal rod will conduct the electrical fire safely to the ground and spare the intervening structure."

"Ingenious," my father said.

"Before long, I think all buildings will have them." Franklin paused. "But I did not ask you here to discuss fire prevention."

My father waited.

"John, I do not want to alarm the others, but I've told Cadwallader and I'm telling you. And I trust you to keep this quiet, Billy."

"What is it?" my father asked.

"Since the break-in at your farm, I called on a few spies of my own. It seems the French have a greater presence in the Ohio Country than we anticipated. Right now, there is a force of fifteen hundred *troupes de la marine* marching south through the valley, led by Captain Paul Marin."

"That name is familiar," my father said.

Mr. Franklin nodded. "He destroyed Saratoga seven years ago. He's a veteran, and he drives his men mercilessly. The Six Nations dare not oppose them, and any English trader they've encountered has been sent to Montreal in chains."

I listened, trying to appear both grave and unafraid.

But I was afraid.

"I was hoping," Mr. Franklin said, "that in light of this information, you would reconsider your opposition to bringing guns on the expedition."

"No." My father sliced the air sideways with his hand. "No guns, Ben. The *de Terzi* is a vessel of philosophy. Not a ship of war. She will keep us aloft and out of Marin's path."

Mr. Franklin sighed. "That is the hope. But it could also be said that you are flying our greatest invention right into the enemy's hands."

Flying? Had I heard him correctly?

My father folded his arms. "We won't let that happen."

"I trust not. But make sure she touches land infrequently and only when absolutely necessary." Mr. Franklin inhaled and rubbed his hands over his waistcoat. "I have to say that in spite of all the dangers, I wish I were going with you."

"As do I," my father said. "But you're a man of politics and business, Ben. Not a frontiersman."

I listened to them, trying to make sense of it all but feeling like I was missing a large part of the conversation.

"You're right, of course." Mr. Franklin tapped his chin with a finger. "Though, I do fancy those coonskin caps."

"You do realize the hat does not actually make the man," my father said.

Mr. Franklin smiled at me with one side of his mouth. "You might be surprised. But speaking of frontiersmen,

I've received confirmation that George Croghan is currently at Aughwick Old Town. You'll rendezvous with him there. If the winds prevail, the *de Terzi* will have you there within a day. After that, it's onward to the Forks of the Ohio."

It was afternoon when we left Mr. Franklin's house and took a circuitous route north through the city. "We keep the *de Terzi* in a quiet part of town," my father said. "Away from curious eyes."

Before long, we turned toward the wharves that lined the Delaware River and came to an immense warehouse. The street was indeed quiet. Deserted, even. As we pulled up, a broad-shouldered man in a white wig, with red cheeks, appeared in the low warehouse doorway.

"Welcome, John!" His wave had the sharp quality of a salute. "This must be Billy."

"Greetings, Cadwallader." My father brought the wagon to a halt and climbed down. I did the same. "Billy, this is Mr. Colden, the leader of the expedition."

I shook his hand. "It is an honor to meet you, sir." He had thick eyebrows.

"Pleasure to meet you, too, Billy. Mr. Franklin was greatly impressed with you, and I've looked forward to making your acquaintance." He turned toward the warehouse as several Africans emerged through the doorway. "My men will take care of your things, John." The Africans went to our wagon and unloaded the first crates.

My father frowned. "That won't be necessary. Billy and I will do it."

"Nonsense," Mr. Colden said.

But my father ignored him, walked to our wagon, and hefted a small crate. I did the same and followed my father through the doorway, where I almost dropped the box.

Inside the cavernous warehouse rose a mighty ship, the aeroship Mr. Franklin had been talking about. Her broad bow stretched high above me, elegant and fluid, and her length retreated into the shadows away from my view. Around her foremast she bore four massive copper spheres, each as large as a sail. Their glinting metal sang with the light they seemed to catch and wrap around themselves. Above those, she bore the English flag.

My father stopped ahead of me and turned back. "She is quite astonishing, isn't she?"

"She — she flies?"

"That she does."

I nodded toward the spheres. "What are those?"

"Vacuum balloons. We evacuate the air from them, which then provides the lifting power she needs. Like a bubble rising in water."

"Just leave the crates there." Mr. Colden had followed us inside. "They'll load them with the crane."

I looked up and saw a thick timber arm, draped with ropes and pulleys, swinging into place overhead. A few more Africans approached us. My father sighed and set down his crate, and I did the same. We went back out and brought in another load. Then another. Each time I carried a crate into the warehouse, I stole a glance up at the ship, at her sweep and line, her polished copper and varnished wood. I decided that she was one of the most beautiful things I had ever seen, the first of her kind.

On one of my trips back to the wagon, Mr. Colden leaned into me as I passed him. "Your father doesn't approve of slavery."

"No, sir," I said, breathing hard.

"I freed my slave years ago," my father said from behind us. "You should consider doing the same, Cadwallader."

I noticed the Africans were listening to us without looking up.

"You Quakers are always upsetting the natural order of things," Mr. Colden said with a nervous laugh.

"Slavery is decidedly *unnatural*," my father said. "A fact impressed on every soul from birth, including yours."

Mr. Colden closed one of his eyes partway, as though looking at my father through a microscope. "Yes, well. Be content that we granted your request and won't use any slave labor on the expedition."

"At least you granted me that," my father said. "Is everyone else here?"

"With the exception of Mr. Godfrey, yes. Kinnersley has been here since dawn. You should see the equipment he's already loaded on board."

"What kind of equipment?" my father asked.

Mr. Colden shrugged. "Electrical equipment, naturally, though I failed to recognize much of it. There were several Leyden jars."

My father put his hands on his hips. "I am uneasy with this."

"Your objections are noted. And now if you'll excuse me, I must see Mr. Faries regarding some final preparations. I'll see you on deck, gentlemen."

"Thank you, Cadwallader," my father said.

We exited the warehouse and met a young woman as she was coming in. She wore a blue dress and appeared to be about my age, pretty, with hair the color of ripe corn. Having just come from inside the dark building, I found myself blinking in the sunlight.

She curtsied. "Hello, Mr. Bartram."

"Hello, Jane," my father said. "I'd like to introduce you to my son Billy."

"Pleased to make your acquaintance, Billy," she said, and I felt a little heat in my cheeks.

I squinted. "Pleasure to meet you as well."

"Jane is Mr. Colden's daughter," my father said to me. "She assists him in his philosophical pursuits, much as you assist me."

She folded her hands before her at her waist. "Do you draw, Billy?"

"I do," I said.

"So do I," she said.

My father clasped his hands behind his back. "You've been helping your father today?"

She nodded. "I have."

"And have you had the opportunity to board the *de Terzi*?" he asked.

"This morning." She looked past us up at the warehouse. "My father showed me all around. She is truly a marvel. I only wish that I were coming."

"I know your father will miss you," my father said.

"It shall not be for long." She sounded as though she believed it.

"That is a splendid attitude." My father tipped his head. "Billy and I must see to our wagon. Good day, Miss Jane."

She curtsied again. "Good day, sir. Good day, Billy."

"Good day," I said, watching her go inside.

We drove the wagon to my older brothers' apothecary, where we said our good-byes to Moses and Isaac and left the horses and wagon for them to return to the farm. Then we walked back to the warehouse.

By that time, evening shadows had filled the streets up to the rain gutters. I lagged a bit behind my father, and as I rounded a corner after him, I heard the skip of a boot on the road behind me. But when I turned to look, there wasn't anyone there. A cold feeling settled in my chest, and a sense of dread slithered up my neck, the feeling of being watched and followed. I glanced back again at the empty street and then hurried to catch up to my father.

"Is everything all right?" he asked as I came up beside him.

I didn't want to confess any fear to him. Not now, just as we were about to embark. "Everything is fine." And I convinced myself that it was, that I had imagined it.

"Where does her name come from?" I asked.

"The ship?" he said. "From the man who conceived of her. Francesco Lana de Terzi. He lived nearly a hundred years ago but lacked the materials and ability to realize his creation. Thanks to Mr. Faries, whom you will meet shortly, we have now brought his vision to life. She'll make the journey to find the Kingdom of Madoc much easier and safer."

I still found something of the impossible in her. "She really flies?"

The corner of my father's mouth lifted. "Yes. She flies. As will you."

I understood the meaning of his words, but I could not imagine actually doing what they suggested. I was about to *fly*. How was that possible? Nervous excitement gripped my stomach and my throat, and quickened my pace to the warehouse.

Inside, Mr. Colden stood above us at the aeroship's bow. He waved to us.

"Come aboard, gentlemen!"

My father led me along the port side of the ship to a steep ramp, and we climbed it, up through the massive timbers that scaffolded the *de Terzi's* dock. And then we reached the peak, and I stepped onto the aeroship's deck.

I looked up at the copper spheres, and they were even larger from where I now stood. But apart from them, the *de Terzi* resembled any sailing vessel meant for water. She had two masts. One forward, around which the spheres appeared in orbit and a series of thick metal pipes grew like strangler vines. A second, taller mainmast jutted behind it. There was a small aft cabin, and two hatches leading below deck.

"What do you think, Billy?" Mr. Colden asked.

"She's mighty impressive, sir," I said.

"She is now. You should have seen her sorry state before Mr. Faries got hold of her. She's an old schooner, and she wore her age poorly. I didn't think she was salvageable." He tapped his foot on the deck. "But she has good bones. She's seen her share of seas and rivers, and now she's ready to ply the air. Come, let me show you."

Mr. Colden led me up to the forward parts of the ship.

"No carved maiden, nor hero, nor beast of legend for us," he said, and pointed to the prow. "Here is *our* figurehead."

The *de Terzi's* bow bristled with polished brass instruments: multiple telescopes of varying sizes and lengths, octants, barometers, a complex arrangement of wires, pipes, valves, and gauges, and many other curious devices for which I could not guess the uses. And along her deck, where another ship might have wielded cannons or cranes, the *de Terzi* bore periodic stations with yet more scientific equipment.

As my father had said, she was not a ship of war. Nor commerce. She was a ship of philosophy.

"Magnificent," my father said. "Even having seen her, she continues to inspire."

"That she does," came a voice from behind us.

We turned as Mr. Franklin walked up the deck toward us.

"Is everyone here?" he asked. "And is everything in order?"

"Everyone else is below," Mr. Colden said. "And we're almost prepared to leave. Mr. Faries is still completing his inspection of the flight systems, and we've a few more things to sort and secure."

"Well," Mr. Franklin said, "let's get to it. It is almost time for you to leave."

With that, we went below.

CHAPTER 4

Philosophers and Patriots

I *had expected it to be dim and gloomy below. But the space was* lit almost as well as the warehouse and the open deck above. I searched for the source of the light and found a series of glass lenses and bowl-shaped mirrors mounted along the low ceiling in such a way that they gathered the light coming down from the hatch and tossed it between them throughout the hold.

"You'll both need to choose a berth," Mr. Colden said, and pointed upship.

To the fore I saw our sleeping quarters. A column of bunks lined the hull to either side, with a row of hammocks strung between them. My father and I claimed two available beds with our satchels. He wanted a bunk, but I saw how narrow they were and chose a nearby hammock.

Mr. Colden then led us down past a bulkhead to the

middle of the ship. "And here is the *de Terzi*'s heart. We call it the Science Deck."

We entered a room crowded with several men. I spotted our crates among a stack of other boxes. Behind them, I saw a bookcase already carrying the weight of several volumes. In the center of the room, the foremast rose up through the ceiling, and from its base sprouted a ring of desks. Above each desk hung a bowl-mirror, reflecting light downward, but each had an oil lantern as well. A few larger work stations had been built into the bulkheads and hull, several of which had apparently already been claimed.

Mr. Franklin placed a hand on my arm. "Billy, I'd like to introduce you to the other members of your expedition."

He guided me to a station that bore a series of glass bottles, vials, beakers, and tubes, along with a few burners. Near it stood a young man who wore no wig and had long blond hair pulled back in a ponytail.

"This is Dr. Bond," Mr. Franklin said. "The Chemist."

The man shook my hand. "Call me Phineas. You're a member of our society, Billy. No need to stand on ceremony among peers."

"Thank you . . . Phineas." I looked to my father, but he did not seem to disapprove of the informality.

Next, Mr. Franklin led me to a much older man seated near the bookshelves. His wig had too much powder and appeared flattened, as though someone had left it under a pile of books. When he stood to greet me, his clothing gave off a whiff of the ancient and moldering.

"This is Mr. Godfrey," Mr. Franklin said. "He is our Natural Philosopher, and there is no one in all the colonies more well versed in ancient Greek and Latin."

"It helps that I was there." Mr. Godfrey's voice was stronger than I expected. "Or at least it feels that way to an old man like me."

I nodded. "A pleasure to meet you, sir."

"This is my station." Mr. Colden gestured toward a desk stacked with what appeared to be astronomical charts and mathematical tables. "I am currently our society's Mathematician. Though my interests also include the study of astronomy and botany. My daughter Jane makes drawings of my specimens for me."

"I do the same for my father," I said.

Mr. Colden patted my back. "Yes, of course."

Mr. Franklin looked around. "Now, let us see. Who is left?"

"I am Mr. Kinnersley," came a sharp voice from behind me. I turned around to greet an angular man with a small, severe mouth.

Mr. Franklin turned to him. "Ah, Ebenezer. Is everything arranged to your satisfaction?"

"No. But it will do."

"Mr. Kinnersley is our Electrician," Mr. Franklin said to me. "Studying the relatively new science of electrical fire. It can also be said that his generous financing allowed for the *de Terzi* to be built in the first place."

"A worthwhile investment," Mr. Kinnersley said.

The mention of this electrical fire intrigued me. I'd heard of it before. And the way my father talked, it sounded dangerous. I looked around the room. "Where is your station, sir?"

"I have my own quarters." Mr. Kinnersley's eyes flicked downship. "Near the stern. My equipment required it."

The blond man, Phineas, chuckled. "And your money paid for it, I'd say."

"What sort of equipment?" I asked.

Mr. Kinnersley perked up in a manner that suggested an excited bird. "Have you an interest in electrical fire?"

"I do," I said.

He clapped and rubbed his hands together. "Oh, the wonders. Oh, the possibilities. Do you know, I have used electrical fire to shock chickens back to life?"

"Truly?" I said.

Phineas snorted. "Chickens you first rendered unconscious with the same electrical fire, if I am not mistaken."

Mr. Kinnersley ignored him. "Perhaps I'll show you a Leyden jar, Billy. Once we're in the air."

"Mind you're careful, now," my father said.

Mr. Kinnersley flapped his hand. "Yes, yes, of course. You needn't worry, John."

That did not seem to appease my father. He stared at Mr. Kinnersley a moment longer before turning to Mr. Colden. "Which desk is ours?"

"You mean yours." Mr. Colden put his hand on my shoulder. "Billy shall stake out his own territory."

"My own desk?" I asked.

"Mr. Kinnersley said he had no use for one," Mr. Colden said. "So I think his should be yours."

Pride lent me boldness. "Which one?"

"That one." Mr. Colden pointed to a smaller desk against the mast.

"Thank you, sir," I said. "I shall put it to good use."

"I trust you shall," Mr. Colden said.

I retrieved my crate from the stack, as did my father and his fellow Society members, and we each unpacked and set up our equipment. My desk had a single drawer in which I stowed my bundle of quills and penknife, as well as my ink. I left my paper on the desk, ready to be drawn upon.

After the members of the Society had each arranged their desks to their satisfaction and shelved their books in the ship's library, we went further aft to the galley. There we found our store of provisions, to which we had all contributed, as well as a fine meal laid out.

"Gentlemen." Mr. Franklin spread his arms over the table. "Having seen the victuals on which you will subsist for the next few months, I took both pity and the liberty of providing this last meal before your departure tonight. Please, eat."

We sat and passed the dishes around: a roasted haunch of venison; wild turkey; meat pies of pork with a faint flavor of spice; pickles; and sauerkraut. I drank milk and cider, while my father and the others drank beer and wine. For dessert we had custard, tarts, and gingerbread. The galley warmed and the walls closed in, filled with laughter and charged with excitement.

I looked around the room and noticed a door downship of the galley. "What's in there?"

"That is my cabin," Mr. Kinnersley said, "which I shall show you at another time."

I nodded and went back to my plate. But my attention kept returning to the door, and I found myself imagining a world of electrical fire beyond it.

A few moments later, a young, slender man came into the galley. He surveyed the table quickly, but did not sit. "The ship is readied," he said.

"Thank you, William," Mr. Colden said. "Billy, this is Mr. Faries, our Mechanician, and the mind responsible for building the *de Terzi*."

I stood and extended my hand. Mr. Faries had a darting, cold handshake. "It's an honor to meet you, sir," I said. "The ship is incredible."

He bowed his head.

Mr. Franklin wiped his mouth with a napkin. "Eat, Mr. Faries, eat."

Mr. Faries looked at the table again, sighed, and sat. The portions he dished for himself were small.

"I bade farewell to Jane at the house this morning," Mr. Colden said to the room. "It was difficult. She was sorely disappointed that I wouldn't let her come."

This morning? My father and I had seen her at the warehouse that afternoon. . . .

"It was the right decision," Phineas said.

"And what about you, John?" Mr. Franklin asked. "Is everything in order with your family and farm?"

"James will see to things while we're away."

"Excellent."

Next to me, Mr. Faries quietly poked at his food. The man intrigued me, and I leaned toward him. "What of your family, sir?"

He opened his mouth, closed it. He stared at his plate. "A fever took my wife from this earth two and a half years ago."

"Oh." Shame flustered me. "I — I'm sorry, I didn't mean to . . ."

He shook his head. "Do not trouble yourself for it, Billy."

"A man your age needs a wife," Mr. Godfrey said. "When do you think that you will take another?"

A sad smile graced Mr. Faries's lips, but before he could answer, Mr. Franklin said, "Any sea captain will tell you that when the woman in your life is a ship, there can be room for only one. And the *de Terzi* is a very fine woman."

Mr. Faries nodded and seemed content to let Mr. Franklin's answer be his. But I could see that even with his aeroship he was lonely and sad.

The conversation around the table turned to politics and business, complaints about taxes and tariffs, worries over the Iroquois League and their alliances.

"You should all know," Mr. Franklin said. "We have

been asked to make an inspection of the trading post at the Forks of the Ohio River."

"Why is that?" Phineas asked.

"Because it is arguably the most strategic point of land in all of the Ohio Country."

"Will we be landing?" Phineas asked.

"Yes, Phineas, for a day perhaps."

Phineas nodded.

Whatever external luminescence the mirrors were sending below deck faded with the evening, and before we had finished the meal, we had to light the lanterns. But the lenses still reflected and made efficient use of the yellow oil-light, gilding everything below.

After we had all eaten our fill, Mr. Franklin passed around a bottle of brandy.

He stood. "Gentlemen, I regret that I must bid you farewell. But I leave you with a few words, the somberness of which I trust you shall forgive. For it seems inevitable to me that somewhere in the very near future, a conflict will erupt between England and France, very likely a war, fought on our soil."

War. The word chilled me and, it seemed, the room.

"Perhaps it will begin in the Ohio Country. Perhaps elsewhere. But in the coming conflagration, our colonies and our people are the ones who will burn, unless you succeed in your quest. To find the Kingdom of Madoc is to find our salvation in the wilderness. To find Madoc is to find ourselves." From his pocket he pulled out a drawing and held it up. *My* drawing of the snake. "Remember that you go not only to save Pennsylvania but also to save what these colonies might one day become if we unite."

Then he held his glass out over the table. The members of the Society all rose and did the same, forming a ring of crystal at the center. I extended my cup of cider and joined them.

"To you," Mr. Franklin said. "Philosophers and patriots and brave men all. It is my privilege to league with you. May the winds fill your sails, let the storms flee before you, and may you find what you seek in your journey across this land."

Glasses clinked and were drained.

"And now," Mr. Franklin said. "It is time for this historic expedition to get under way."

Up on the open deck of the aeroship, the warehouse yawned around and above us, an endless black void. Mr. Franklin shook hands with each of the philosophers and then mine.

"You're going out into the wild, Billy," he said. "It can change a man. Make certain it does so for the better."

"Yes, sir."

Mr. Franklin took a lantern from Mr. Colden and crossed the deck. "I'll open the roof!"

I turned to my father. "Open the roof?"

Mr. Franklin's flickering light bobbed down the ramp and then along the floor of the warehouse. It came to rest at a distant point, and a moment later I heard a far-off clang. Then a loud ratcheting sound chewed up the silence on all sides of the ship, followed by the squeal of metal and the groan of wood overhead. There was a deep and hollow rushing of air, like a breath over the lip of a bottle, and the void above split open. And as the gap widened, revealing stars and ribbons of argent clouds, the cold light of the night sky rushed in.

"Extinguish the lanterns," Mr. Colden said. "Mr. Faries, when you are ready, raise the *de Terzi*."

The moment had come.

Mr. Faries went to a broad podium at the helm that stood next to the ship's wheel. "Would you like to see, Billy?"

"Yes, thank you." I rushed to stand next to him, my heart pounding. The podium bore a series of levers, dials, and gauges, as well as a compass, barometer, and whirling speculum.

"Prepare for sphere evacuation!" Mr. Faries called to the ship, and then to me, "I'm letting the air out to create the vacuum."

He cranked a wheel, and a roaring hiss emanated from somewhere in the bowels of the ship. I leaned to look over the rail and saw a cloud of wind-stirred dust churning under us. And then the deck shifted beneath my feet. The whole vessel shifted.

"Prepare for elevation!" Mr. Faries said.

And then I felt the shift in my stomach, a lurch and a lift in my gut, and the scaffolding began to fall away by degrees.

First by inches, then by feet, and I realized it wasn't falling, but we were rising past it. We were floating in the air, with nothing but air between us and the earth we crawled upon. We continued to rise up through the warehouse, among the rafters, and then out of the open roof.

Philadelphia spread out around us, gray peaks, black streets, and here and there a glowing window. We hovered at what I guessed to be the height of a great cedar tree, or a clock tower, looking down on a world I recognized but had never seen from such an angle.

"Clear?" Mr. Faries asked.

I noticed the dark shapes of two men running through the street below us. I remembered the earlier sensation of being followed. The spies at our farm.

Mr. Colden said, "Clear."

My father came to stand behind me, both of his hands on my shoulders. "You will enjoy this," he said.

I was about to point out the two men to him, but then —

"Prepare for flight!" Mr. Faries threw a lever.

The hiss of air increased beneath us, and the *de Terzi* heaved and leaped straight upward. I nearly lost my footing, but my father held on to me. The wind tossed my hair and stung my eyes as we rose and rose and rose. The city receded and shrank, until it looked more like a charcoal map of a city than a city itself. And there was the Schuylkill River, from this distance an inky trickle, and somewhere along its bank was my father's tiny farm and tiny garden. My new bird-sight awed me into silence, the men in the street, forgotten.

CHAPTER 5

The Morning Watch

Mr. *Faries switched another lever, and the hissing ceased. The* ship slowed her ascent and came to a stop, hanging in midair. My father released me.

"Thrilling," he said.

Mr. Faries looked around, nodded to himself, and said to me, "We never completely empty the air from the spheres."

"What would happen if you did?" I asked.

"We'd keep rising."

I looked up. Even though the distant earth below looked utterly changed, the moon and the stars appeared no closer, nor different. "How far would we rise?"

"I don't know," Mr. Faries said.

"Until our wings melted," Mr. Godfrey said. "So to speak."

"How high are we?" I asked.

Mr. Faries checked the barometer. "Based on air pressure, I estimate our elevation at two thousand feet."

I swallowed. What would it be like to fall from such a height? How long would it take to hit the ground? I looked down at the earth again, feeling sick to my stomach, and I noticed the geography had changed. It seemed Philadelphia had moved. Or . . .

"Is the *de Terzi* moving?" I asked.

"Yes," Mr. Faries said. "The spheres present a large surface area for the wind to push against. But once we raise the sails, we'll have control over the direction and speed."

"Speaking of which," Mr. Colden said. "Now that we're in the air, I believe it's time we get under way."

Mr. Faries nodded. "Phineas! Prepare for sail deployment!"

He triggered a switch and cranked a wheel. As he did so, sails to the fore and aft began to climb and stretch up their masts.

My father watched them. "Ingenious."

"Indeed. Our ship can be manned by a much smaller crew than would otherwise be needed." Mr. Colden took hold of the ship's wheel with both hands. "Mr. Faries has also shown me his designs for a water elevator and a carriage that moves under its own propulsion. Without a horse! I advised that he patent them with haste."

The sails had almost reached their full height, the wind whipping and billowing them as Phineas manned the lines and the *de Terzi* lurched forward.

"She also has a reserve sail, but we hope we won't ever need to use it. Heading, Mr. Faries?" Mr. Colden asked.

Mr. Faries looked at his compass. "Fifteen degrees to starboard."

"Fifteen degrees to starboard!" Mr. Colden called. He turned the wheel, and the *de Terzi* tipped and swung to the right. "Everything is controlled from this helm. Even the direction of the sails."

Mr. Faries, watching the compass, held up his hand. "Let go and haul."

"Let go and haul!" Mr. Colden called, righting the wheel.

Phineas trimmed the sails, and the aeroship steadied her course. Within moments we had picked up speed. And we continued to accelerate as the world rolled by beneath us. We were flying.

"You sound like a proper captain, Cadwallader," my father said. "With a proper crew."

Mr. Colden chortled. "I'm glad you find our little show convincing."

My father tapped my shoulder. "I want to show you something," he said, and led me upship along the starboard side.

I waited until we were out of earshot and then said, "Father, may I ask you a question?"

"You may."

"Why is Mr. Colden the one leading this expedition?"

"Who would you rather see in charge of it?"

I thought it was obvious. "Well. You."

He looked up at the spheres. "We all have our separate gifts, Billy. Sometimes it can be difficult to avoid envy and accept what is ours. Mr. Colden is a much more natural leader of men than I. As is Mr. Franklin. But I am content to support them, for I have my garden, and I am proud of its renown."

He then went to the rail. He pointed. "Speaking of my garden, though you can't see it, it's right down there. Your brothers and sisters will be asleep by now."

"And Mother," I said.

He was silent a moment. "I'm afraid she finds it difficult to sleep when I'm gone." He shook his head. "So that is the Schuylkill River, and that over there is the Wissahickon feeding into it."

Hearing the name Wissahickon reminded me of a story I'd once heard from my brother Moses.

I turned to my father. "Didn't someone throw a magic rock into the Schuylkill River somewhere?"

"You're thinking of Johannes Kelpius. And as the story goes, it was the philosopher's stone, which supposedly grants eternal life."

"Truly?"

"Kelpius was a monk, a magician, a madman, or perhaps all three, depending on who tells the story. He led a group of mystics up north near Germantown. It's said they dabbled in forbidden occult practices, and that as he was dying, Kelpius had one of his followers throw a box containing the philosopher's stone into the Schuylkill where it meets the Wissahickon Creek."

"Oh." I peered down at the black, secretive water, imagining a lost box resting somewhere at the bottom. But then something about the story started nagging at my wonder. "Wait. If he really had the philosopher's stone, then why was he dying? And why would he throw it away? Wouldn't it have made him live forever?"

My father chuckled. "You see the problem with such stories."

And then the river was just a river once again. I looked back out over the surface of the earth, at the rivers winding without appearing to move. At the mountainous horizon reclining to the west. From up here, the world looked ever at rest. My earlier unease began to fade, and in its place I felt a nameless and tranquil joy.

"This aeroship will change the world," my father said. "I think perhaps it already has."

Someone called to us. "John, Billy."

We turned to see Mr. Colden striding up the deck.

"It's nearly midnight," he said. "Mr. Faries and Mr. Godfrey will finish the first watch. Then, if it's agreeable, John, you and Phineas will have the middle watch. I thought Billy could join me for the morning watch."

"A fine plan," my father said. "But if I'm to be up in a matter of hours, I'd best get some sleep. You, too, Billy."

Sleep? How could they expect me to sleep?

But I followed my father below deck to our quarters,

where we found Mr. Kinnersley already snoring in his berth. My father rolled into his bunk, and I slouched into my hammock, put my hands behind my head, and stared up at the ceiling.

I closed my eyes and tried to feel the sky beyond the hull of the ship. I imagined myself at Mr. Faries's podium and I let the rest of the air out of the spheres. The ship rose higher, and kept rising until the earth disappeared from view, and I was floating in an infinite space. I felt that I could become lost in such vastness, and before long, all the work and exhilaration of the day caught up with me and pulled me down into sleep.

Mr. Colden woke me. "Billy, it is time."

I sat up in my hammock, feeling as though I'd just fallen into it. My father's bunk was empty, as was Phineas's, but Mr. Faries lay sleeping in his. Next to Mr. Kinnersley, Mr. Godfrey reclined serenely on his back nearby, eyes closed, his arms folded across his chest, and I hadn't noticed any of them coming or going.

I yawned. "Yes, sir."

I followed Mr. Colden up through the hatch onto the weather deck. The air was colder, and to the east the sky had lost its stars and bore a slightly lighter shade of blue. We had long ago left Philadelphia behind, and the earth below now looked completely foreign. I shivered a little as we crossed to the helm.

My father nodded to us as we approached.

"Good morning, John," Mr. Colden said, far too lively for the hour.

"It isn't morning yet," Phineas said. "I'm going to bed." And he trudged away, down the hatch.

"And I think I shall follow suit." My father rubbed his red-tinged eyes. "Good night. Or morning. Or whatever you call this evil hour." Then he, too, went below deck.

Another yawn stretched my ribs.

"You'll grow accustomed to the schedule," Mr. Colden said.

It felt as though my voice were still back in my hammock, so I simply nodded.

"I'm used to rising this early," he said. "If I don't beat the first cock to his crow, I feel as though I've missed half the day. My daughter is the same way. She rises with me and prepares my breakfast. She'll be up now, I should think."

I looked behind us to the east. My mother would be rising soon as well, and I could picture her going about her morning routine. She and the rest of my family suddenly felt very far away.

"We have some hours to pass," Mr. Colden said. "Let me show you around the deck."

We worked our way up the port side, and he showed me the different lines and how they worked to trim the sails, the way to tie and coil them, and how to avoid and secure the booms. He took me up to the bow and showed me instruments for measuring wind speed and air pressure and moisture and many other natural qualities of the air.

Soon after that, as the sky lightened and the first smudge of red appeared on the horizon, the sails began to flap in the changing wind.

"We need to adjust," he said. "You remember how I showed you?"

I didn't, but I nodded.

"We'll do it together," he said. And he guided me through the steps of loosening and hauling the ropes. We soon had both sails taut and full of wind.

We returned to the helm, and Mr. Colden checked the compass mounted on Mr. Faries's control podium to make sure we were still on course.

"What is the whirling speculum for?" I asked.

"It measures our degree of tilt. It's not as easy to tell if you aren't on the ground." He rechecked the compass and nodded. "You're curious. I admire that. It is well for you to take an interest in the world around you."

"Thank you, sir."

"My Jane is a curious one. She —" He stopped. "I hope you don't mind my talking about her."

"Not at all."

"She's a skilled artist, like you. Your drawings are nearly as good as hers."

I hesitated but decided that was a compliment. "Thank you."

He checked the compass for the third time. "She's my youngest. Dutiful and modest. Her mother would tell you she takes after me. We're cut from the same cloth, as they say."

After that, we sat watching the sunrise in silence. A true silence marked by what was absent, and which made me realize I didn't know what silence was. No cock's crow could reach us up here. No bird song. No lowing cows or bleating sheep. No insect chirp or buzz or thrum. Only the wind whispering and sighing and buffeting the sails.

The dawn was unlike any other I had seen. From our vantage, I was able to observe the sun's reach expanding across the earth from the east, a tide of light coming in. And before long, Mr. Kinnersley and Mr. Godfrey emerged from the hatch. Mr. Kinnersley winced as he walked, shaking and stretching his limbs.

"If all my sleep shall be as misshapen as last night's," he said, "I think I shall fall to pieces before the end of our expedition. Perhaps I am too old for this."

But Mr. Godfrey strode with a vigor that belied his age. "Come now, Ebenezer. Age is a state of mind as well as body. And of the two, one's mind holds preeminence."

"Then you, sir, may tell my joints to bend, for they refuse to listen to me."

"Have you gentlemen eaten?" Mr. Colden asked.

"We have," Mr. Godfrey said.

"Good. You have the helm. Are you hungry, Billy?"

"Yes, sir."

"Let's go have some breakfast."

We left the aged philosophers quibbling on the deck and went below to the galley. We sat at the narrow table and ate slices of dark rye bread with butter and some peaches. I tried to enjoy it, knowing we would have such fresh foods for only another week or so. Afterward, our meals would be confined to what had been dried, smoked, salted, or pickled.

As we ate, I looked at the door to Mr. Kinnersley's cabin. "What do you suppose he has in there?" I asked.

Mr. Colden wiped some peach juice from his chin. "It would take an electrician to recognize much of it. However, I did see some Leyden jars among his cargo."

I remembered the name, the thing Mr. Kinnersley wanted to show me.

"We all have our passions," Mr. Colden said. "Mr. Kinnersley. Phineas. Your father."

"If you don't mind my asking, what is your passion, sir?"

"As I mentioned, astronomy. The movement of celestial bodies and the cause of gravitation, on which I wrote a treatise some years ago. Perhaps one night you and I will observe the heavens together."

"I would enjoy that, sir."

CHAPTER 6

Mr. Kinnersley's Cabin

M y *father woke a short time later and joined us for breakfast.* Afterward, he and I went to our stations on the Science Deck, while Mr. Colden went above. At his station, my father sorted through a few last items and set up his microscope. My paper lay unused on my desk, waiting for subjects to fill them up with purpose.

"You should practice your drawing," my father said, pointing to where I was looking.

"We haven't collected any specimens yet."

"We will. For now, draw something else to keep your skill honed."

"I don't know what to draw."

"Anything at all. Find something of interest to you about the ship."

I didn't move fast enough.

"Do as I say, Billy."

"Yes, Father."

I gathered what I needed and took it up to the weather deck. The sun had fully risen, the sky was clear, and the vista of trees and hills below reached in every direction to a distant horizon. Even though I had seen the view many times since leaving Philadelphia, it still hunkered me down with an involuntary need to reassure my footing on the deck.

Mr. Colden stood at the helm with Mr. Godfrey. Mr. Kinnersley bent over the instruments at the prow, scratching in a small notebook, and Phineas stood beside him, the wind blowing his yellow hair.

I looked up at the sails and tried to rehearse the names of the lines Mr. Colden had taught me. The foremast halyard. The mainsail downhaul. The mainsail outhaul. Were those right? I couldn't remember. But I did know the ratlines, the rope ladders climbing precariously up to the spheres from the gunwales. A fall from one of those on this ship meant death at the end of a long, windswept plunge.

I shuddered and turned my attention to the spheres. Now, *they* were of interest to me, so I sat down cross-legged on the deck to make a drawing of them. But it was more difficult than I thought it would be.

Their shape was easy enough. What proved difficult to capture was the way they reflected things around them. Fragments of sky and sail and deck, and even the elongated forms of our crew all twisted and mingled across their round surfaces.

At one point a shadow fell across my drawing. I looked up, holding my flat hand above my eyes.

"That is very good," Mr. Godfrey said.

I wrinkled my nose. "Thank you, sir, but it could stand a great deal of improvement."

"In what way?"

"They should look more like real spheres."

"Real spheres? Plato would wonder if you're drawing the sphere, or the shadow of the sphere."

"Pardon me?"

"What you must do is draw how *you* see the sphere, which you have done, for therein lies the value of your art."

I blinked, trying to grasp what he had just said, and gave up. "I'll keep practicing."

He nodded. "You do that, young man. You do that." And he walked away.

I looked at my drawing. I wasn't satisfied with it, and I thought about starting over on a blank sheet of paper but, instead, decided to just find another subject.

I looked up at the clouds. I looked down at the landscape. I looked at the masts in their straight and fearless leap from the deck. And I noticed a metal spear atop the mainmast very similar to the lightning attractor Mr. Franklin had installed on his roof. But Mr. Franklin had said the rod was supposed to conduct the electrical fire safely into the ground. Up here in the air, if lightning struck the *de Terzi's* mainmast, where would the electrical fire go?

While the foremast's foundation stood in the center of the Science Deck, I hadn't seen the root of the mainmast. It would be somewhere aft, beyond the galley. Perhaps in Mr. Kinnersley's cabin? Was that where the electrical fire would go?

I looked at the prow. Mr. Kinnersley still appeared involved in his instruments. In fact, I saw every member of the Society on deck. I rose to my feet, went below, and deposited my drawing tools at my station. I then slipped downship through the galley, until I stood alone before the cabin door.

What I was doing was wrong. I knew that. But Mr. Kinnersley had told me he would show me his cabin once we were in the air. So apparently he didn't mind my knowing what he had in there.

I grasped the handle.

Locked.

I scowled in disappointment. Then I dropped to my knees to see if I could at least get a glimpse of the electrical equipment. Maybe those Leyden jars people had talked about. Something. I put my eye to the keyhole.

And I yelped and fell back.

There was an eye on the other side, staring back at me. Then it was gone.

"Hello?" I said.

Silence.

If everyone else was up on the weather deck, who was down here?

"I saw you," I said. "I know you're in there."

"You mustn't tell," came a muffled voice through the door.

"I won't," I said, but in that moment I felt more curiosity than conviction.

"Do you promise?" It was a girl's voice.

"I promise."

There was only one girl it could be. A moment passed, and I heard the jangle and click of a key in the lock, and the door creaked open.

"Come in," Jane said, peeking through. "Hurry."

I slipped through, and Jane shut the door behind me. She leaned her back against it and let out a long, slow breath through pursed lips. I was shocked to see that she wore trousers and a boy's coat, and her hair was all pulled back.

She looked at me "Your name is Billy, isn't it?"

"Yes. And you're Jane. You stowed away?"

"Talk quietly."

I lowered my voice. "You stowed away?"

"Yes. Until he caught me."

"Who?"

"Mr. Kinnersley. But he didn't say anything to anyone, and he let me hide in here with his electrical equipment."

I looked around the cabin I had wanted so badly to see. Bundles of wire, canisters, sheets of metal, and glassware thicketed the corners. The same materials covered a work-bench against the hull, while an empty horse trough lined the wall on the other side. I wondered what such a thing had to do with electrical fire. Several large, narrow-neck jugs circled the mainmast in the middle of the room. A skin of foil covered the outside of each jar, and a tangle of wires connected all the jars to the mast.

"Are those Leyden jars?" I asked.

She shrugged. "I think so. Why?"

"No reason. So your father doesn't know you're here?"

"What do you think?" she said. "He told me I couldn't come." She chewed on one of her fingernails, and I saw by their length it was something she did often. "I was only supposed to hide in here until after we'd departed. But I started to worry that my father might turn the aeroship around and take me back if I came out right away."

I thought back to all the things Mr. Colden had said, doting on his daughter. The Jane standing before me, the stowaway, did not seem quite like the Jane he had described. But I liked this Jane better.

"So how much longer are you going to stay in here?" I asked.

She rolled her eyes. "Just another day or two. Look, you're not going to tell, are you? You promised."

"I won't tell," I said.

Her eyes narrowed. "Good. Now leave."

"What?"

"They're going to miss you soon enough, and then

they'll come looking for you. And they'll find you here, which means they'll find me here. So you must leave."

"But —"

She had already put her ear to the door. "All clear." She opened the door and made a sharp gesture for me to exit. She mouthed the word *go*.

I didn't want to.

But I did as she ordered. There didn't seem to be anything else I *could* do. I stepped out into the galley where I'd eaten breakfast with Jane's father just that morning, knowing now she'd been on the other side of the door, listening. But that thought brought another with it.

"Are you hungry?" I asked. "I can —"

But the door shut in my face, close enough to bump my nose.

I stared at the wood grain for a moment. And then I ambled up onto the deck, a little befuddled. The others were mostly as I'd left them. Except for Mr. Kinnersley, who had now become someone I viewed with a mixture of suspicion and secret camaraderie.

"Are you well, Billy?" my father asked. "You seem somewhat lost."

"I'm fine," I said. I wasn't sure why, but Jane's presence on the ship, the thought of her down in Mr. Kinnersley's cabin, had changed the way I felt about the entire expedition. It felt as though I had a friend on board. Someone like me. I smiled to myself, glad that she had stowed away.

CHAPTER 7

Aughwick Old Town

The rest of that morning it was hard to concentrate and make any more drawings, and it was hard to resist the urge to go back to Mr. Kinnersley's cabin.

The *de Terzi* maintained an enthusiastic pace. We crossed rivers and low bald hills and dense forests. The occasional wisp of smoke clinging to the treetops marked the site of a frontier settlement or an Indian town. And nearby those, patchwork fields, some cleared, some prickly with bare trees notched to kill the leaves and let the sunlight down to the crops. Every time I looked over the side, the land below had changed — a new world by the moment.

"How far do you think we've traveled?" I asked Phineas.

"Close to one hundred miles, I'd say. We're above the Cumberland Valley, now. That's the Blue Ridge up ahead." He pointed west at a long, high mountain wall. It girdled the whole of the horizon, jutting up as far to the southwest as I could see, crossed in front of us, then flanked us to the north.

He continued. "We'll pass over several ridges and valleys of the Appalachians before arriving at Aughwick."

The name reminded me of what Mr. Franklin had told my father. "We're meeting someone at Aughwick?"

Phineas nodded. "George Croghan."

"Who is he?"

"He is the Trader King, and an Irishman." He frowned. "We're hoping he'll offer us his assistance."

"Why wouldn't he?"

"In the last few years, he has grossly undermined his former Pennsylvanian partners and begun advancing the interests of Virginia. And at times, he takes the side of the Indian. Mr. Croghan, you see, does whatever will promote his business and keep his trade routes open, and if he sees no advantage in aiding us, I doubt we can expect much from him." Phineas looked to the west. "But we'll discover his intentions soon enough. And now, I must go below. I've been wanting to read a new treatise on the medical uses of seawater. Perhaps I'll finally have the time to do so."

I nodded, and he left.

I spent the rest of the afternoon watching the Blue Ridge grow closer and rise higher. Before long, we sailed right over the long mountain at its peak, close enough, it seemed to me, to scrape clean our keel against the treetops. I was half tempted to reach out my hands to try to snatch a leaf or a branch. And then we were on the other side, and the slope fell away from us into a narrow valley choked with dense trees and thickets.

We crossed the vale quickly and crested another mountain ridge, followed by another valley and then another mountain ridge. They kept coming, ridge after valley after ridge, great waves of earth, and the *de Terzi* skimmed them like a gull at sea. I felt a little sorry for Jane, locked below deck in a cabin.

My father came up beside me, his eyes boring into the sky before us. He sighed. "There is something I would like to speak to you about, Billy."

"Yes, Father?"

"Mr. Croghan's outpost is near an Indian village. Till now, I have done my best to limit your familiarity with the Indian. But soon we must go among them. I would caution you to keep your guard up. On occasion you may find one among them blessed with wisdom and temperance, but as a race I have found them wanting. They are full of guile and jealousy, and though they are lazy, they are nevertheless quick to violence."

I was shocked and didn't know what to say to him. Neither he nor my mother had ever spoken this way before. There were many, many in Pennsylvania who despised the Indians, but I had always thought that my father was a tolerant and forward-thinking man. Like some of our fellow Quakers in the Darby Meeting, I'd assumed he was a friend of the Indians, one who promoted the cause of peace with them.

"Do you understand me, Billy?"

"I — I . . . think so, Father."

"There is much you are too young to understand. Your mother and I do not see eye to eye on this, and till now I have respected her wishes in not speaking of it. But in time, you will learn that I am right." He put his hand on my shoulder. We stood that way for a while, side by side. Then my father looked to the earth. "I wonder what plants and animals we might discover down there. What new species are under our feet at this very moment?"

I looked anew at the forest beneath us, the great passages of oak, chestnut, and hickory, punctuated here and there with tall spruce and fir. I wondered what might be lurking beneath their canopy, hidden from our view. And I realized that while we could not see what was down there, what was down there could certainly see us. Beast or man. Possibly even follow us. That reminded me of what I'd seen in the streets back in Philadelphia.

"Father, I should have told you something earlier."

"What is that, son?"

"As we launched the *de Terzi*, I saw two men running in the streets."

"Oh?"

"And before that, I felt as if we were being followed to the warehouse."

"I see." My father nodded to himself. "The French have been too aware of this expedition from the beginning. I shall speak with Mr. Colden about it."

We watched the landscape pass beneath us for another hour or more, until we entered a wide valley. Mr. Colden and Mr. Faries began to give orders from the helm. Phineas brought the sails down by their mechanical chains and pulleys, the aeroship slowed, and then Mr. Colden called for our descent. Air vibrated the deck boards beneath my feet as it rushed into the empty spheres, and we began to lose altitude.

I looked over the side, at the ground rising up to meet us. A creek flowed through the valley, and near its shore a small village hunkered down among several cultivated fields. I saw a few small cabins, and a few larger, longer buildings, from which tiny ant-people scurried. They all came out into the open and froze, no doubt looking up at us as we fell from the sky.

Mr. Faries steered us toward an opening in the middle of the village, and before long it was possible to make out the features and faces of the people waiting on the ground. There were Englishmen among them, but mostly they were Indian. Men, women, and children. I had never seen so many gathered in one place. Some of the men held weapons, wooden clubs and spears. A few had muskets and long rifles. I swallowed, remembering my father's warning.

We could hear their excited shouts, in a language foreign to my ear, and when it became clear where we would land, they all collected there, eyes wide and mouths agape. Mr. Faries took us down until we almost touched the ground, and then we dropped our anchor, against which the *de Terzi* bobbed and swayed in the breeze. Most of the Society, including my father, then went below deck.

I looked over the side at the Indians, feeling the weight of a great many eyes on me. I offered them all a vague and nervous smile and waved at no one in particular. A moment later, my father and the others came back up on deck, adjusting their coats and their wigs. Mr. Colden pulled out a rope ladder, tossed it over the side, and took a deep breath.

"We are expected, gentlemen, but nevertheless, let us hope we find the reception we seek." And he climbed over the side.

Phineas followed him, wigless, with a broad grin.

My father went next. "I'll be waiting for you at the bottom, Billy." That meant it was my turn.

My heart beat against the cage of my chest as I hoisted myself up and over the rail. The ground was a lot farther down than I thought it would be, and I gripped the rope ladder so tightly my hands hurt. It seemed to dodge and weave away from my feet, but I held my breath and wriggled my way down it until I touched a toe to solid earth, surprised that it already felt odd to stand upon a floor that wasn't in motion. Once I had recovered my bearings, I looked up at the crowd surrounding us.

The Indians stared at us and at the *de Terzi*. Some of the men wore leather leggings, and some went bare-chested. Others wore woolen trousers and cotton shirts, much like mine. The women wore skirts and cotton shirts ornamented with beads, their raven hair in braids. Some of the men, too, had braids, but others had shaved most of their hair, ornamenting what was left on top with porcupine quills and feathers. Some had gold rings in their ears and even their noses. I had to keep myself from staring back at them.

"Well, well!" came a loud bellow. The crowd parted, and a man with red hair and a red beard passed through it. He was very large, both tall and broad, but walked with an ease that belied his size. "Mr. Franklin warned us about the manner of your arrival!"

The captain of our expedition stepped forward. "I am Cadwallader Colden. Are you George Croghan?"

"The very same." Beneath his beard, he had ruddy, leathered skin.

Mr. Colden extended his hand. "It is a pleasure to finally meet you in person, Mr. Croghan."

Croghan eyed Mr. Colden's hand for a brief moment before clasping it. "Likewise."

I noticed a young man standing just behind and to the side of Croghan. He was older than me by several years and wore a brown coat over a scarlet waistcoat. His skin and features were those of an Englishman, but a broad sweep of Indian paint encircled his face, and pendants of brass and plaited wire hung from his pierced ears. And he wore what looked to be a woman's locket around his neck.

Mr. Colden gestured back toward us with an open palm. "With me are some of the other members of the Philosophical Society. May I present to you Mr. Kinnersley, Mr. Godfrey, Mr. Faries, and Dr. Bond." The Society members all nodded at the mention of their names. "Mr. Bartram and his son Billy."

"Bartram?"

"Yes," my father said.

"John Bartram?"

"Yes," my father said. "You know me?"

"I know of you," Croghan said. He smiled, a seismic act that lifted his beard and formed a corona of lines in the skin around his eyes. "John Bartram, Flower Hunter."

"And hunter of *incognitum* and bear-wolves," my father said. "But plants are indeed of special interest to me."

Croghan nodded. "Welcome to Aughwick, gentlemen. If you'll follow me, I'll take you to my trading post. Then you can tell me all about that" — he pointed at the *de Terzi* — "and why you've brought it here."

He ordered two of his men to stand guard at the aeroship. Then he turned and led us back the way he'd come, through the parted throng, a corridor of eyes and gazes I could not meet. I worried about leaving Jane alone on the ship, in the middle of an Indian town. But I told myself that Mr. Kinnersley's cabin was locked and that she would

74

be safe. We passed through the settlement, near the buildings I'd seen from the air. Croghan indicated them with a nod of his head.

"We call them the Six Nations, and the French call them the Iroquois. But to themselves, they are the *Kanonsionni*, the people of the longhouse. Those are longhouses."

The buildings he pointed to were large, perhaps twenty feet tall and wide, and more than fifty feet long. Wide strips of bark plated the roof and the walls, and smoke rose from several openings down its length.

"They house several families," Croghan continued. "A matriarch and the families of all her daughters."

"We are aware of the customs of the Six Nations," Mr. Colden said. "In fact, some years ago I wrote their history in two volumes. Of course, then they were the Five Nations."

Croghan chuckled. "You wrote their history, did you?"

"Yes."

"You did."

"You take issue with that?"

Croghan shrugged. "Would you read a history of England written by a Frenchman?"

Mr. Colden's face turned a little red. "That depends on the Frenchman."

Croghan chuckled again. "Maybe."

I noticed the young man with the painted face following us. We came to the edge of the town, and a short distance beyond we arrived at a group of cabins and large storehouses. Men armed with muskets milled around before them, standing a loose guard.

"If things keep on their present course," Croghan said, "I'm going to have to build a stockade or even a fort to protect my home from the French and their Indian allies."

"That touches the subject of our visit," Mr. Colden said.

"I suspected it might." Croghan led us to the door of the largest cabin and opened it. "Please, come into my home, gentlemen."

We entered a room with a long, rough table. Croghan had us all sit, and the young man with the painted face set out cups and poured beer for the Society members. When he had served everyone, he sat in a chair against the wall near the door.

Mr. Colden cleared his throat. "This matter is quite sensitive." He glanced toward the young man.

"Ah," Croghan said. "This is Andrew. He acts as my interpreter and is one of my closest associates. You may speak freely in front of him."

"Very well," Mr. Colden said. And he proceeded to explain the *de Terzi*'s origins and the purpose of our expedition to find the people of Prince Madoc. Croghan listened with a grave expression, rubbing his beard, exchanging glances now and then with Andrew. When Mr. Colden had finished, Croghan remained silent for several minutes before speaking.

"Let me deal plainly with you. You propose to use this flying machine to find the people of Madoc, make them allies to the English crown, and then use that alliance to either frighten or drive the French out of the Ohio Country."

"Those are the essentials, yes," Mr. Colden said.

"Do I really need to point out the problems with this plan?" Croghan said. "Or are you undeserving of your reputation as intelligent men?"

That seemed to ruffle the members of the Society. They all sat up, and Mr. Kinnersley grunted. Mr. Faries, normally mild, slammed his cup on the table.

Mr. Colden folded his arms. "There are risks, of course."

"Risks?" Croghan said. "I haven't been to the Ohio Country since last June, when the Frenchman de Langlade led the Ottawa in a massacre at Pickawillany. They killed Chief Memeskia, my friend, because he sided with the English. Do you know how many men I've lost to the French and their Indian allies? Not to mention the price on my head. And you're proposing to travel right through this same territory?"

"*Fly* right through this territory," my father said. "Well above the danger."

"How long did it take you to travel from Philadelphia to Aughwick?"

"A night and a day," Mr. Colden said.

"Remarkable." Croghan shook his head. "Instead of chasing some Welsh legend, you'd be better off letting me use that ship to secure my trade alliances with the Indians. That, gentlemen, is how we'll win the Ohio. And maybe turn a profit."

"I can see Mr. Franklin was wrong to place any faith in you," Mr. Colden said. "You are certainly deserving of *your* reputation."

That brought Croghan to his feet. "How dare you? You city men have no idea what it's like out here along the frontier. You sit there, comfortable in your homes and taverns and halls of government, and you think you know what needs to be done. For God's sake, you think you can actually write a history of the Six Nations!"

The room was quiet after that for several moments. And then my father leaned forward.

"I take this to mean you won't guide us?"

"Can't afford to," Croghan said. "And if you have any sense, you'll abandon this fool's errand and leave that ship in the hands of more capable men."

"You've read the reports," my father said. "You've *made* some of the reports. You know Madoc's people are out there."

"They may be," Croghan said. "But I don't know that finding them will bring any advantage. And I'm not yet desperate enough to put my faith in them."

"I know something of faith," my father said. "And I know much of loss. I am here because I put my faith in this New World. I am here to prevent even greater loss."

I didn't know what my father meant by that. What loss had he suffered? And why hadn't I heard of it before?

Croghan stared at him for a moment. And then he

smiled. "John Bartram, Flower Hunter. Among these philosophers, you alone may know of what you speak."

"Come with us," my father said.

"Nay, Flower Hunter. I'll not go."

At that point, Andrew rose from his chair, went to Croghan, and whispered something in his ear. Croghan leaned away and looked him in the eyes. "Are you sure?"

Andrew nodded.

Croghan rapped the table with his knuckle, scowling. "Very well. Go."

"Thank you," Andrew said. He left the room.

Croghan watched him go and then turned to us. "While I oppose this folly of an expedition, it seems that Andrew is willing to accompany you."

This took me aback. I turned to my father, who had turned to Mr. Colden.

"I'm certain he is an able interpreter," Mr. Colden said. "But —"

"But nothing," Croghan said. "He is one of the few men in the world I trust. He knows this land, he knows the customs and languages of her tribes, and he is a capable frontiersman. If you refuse him, you are even more incompetent than I gave you credit for."

Mr. Colden worked his lips as if he were about to say something, but nothing came out.

"You may trust him," my father said. "But we don't know him. Who is he?"

"He is the son of the renowned interpreter Madame Montour and Carondawanna, an Oneida war chief."

"He is part Indian?" my father asked.

"Yes," Croghan said.

My father leaned back. "I would advise against this, Cadwallader."

Croghan's voice sharpened. "Why?"

Mr. Colden said nothing.

"Cadwallader," my father said. "We discussed this. No Indian guides. It is too risky."

"You don't trust Indians, Flower Hunter?" Croghan asked.

"No, Mr. Croghan, I do not."

"Without a guide, I promise, you won't make it," Croghan said. "There's a reason Franklin sent you to persuade me."

"He's right, John," Mr. Colden finally said.

Next to me, I could feel a nervous bouncing in my father's leg beneath the table. "I strongly oppose this," he said. "What if we take this Indian into our confidence, and he betrays us to the French?"

Croghan's expression acquired a subtle menace. "You judge my friend harshly with very little knowledge of him."

"It is nothing personal," my father said. "It is all Indians. As a race, they are irredeemable."

"Is that so?" Croghan asked.

"I know what lies in their hearts," my father said. "Let me tell you about . . ."

His words fell off as an Indian woman entered the cabin. She was tall and she was beautiful. She carried an infant girl in her arms. Croghan rose from the table and met them by the door. He took the child into his own arms and kissed her forehead.

"My wife, Catherine Takarihoga," he said. "And my daughter, Catherine Adonwentishon." He held up the little girl with obvious pride.

My father's expression had fallen, his face red.

Croghan's wife nodded to us. "Sirs, we welcome you to Aughwick. I hope you will be staying with us."

"No —" Mr. Colden coughed to clear some hoarseness from his throat. "No, ma'am. Though your offer is most gracious."

Croghan whispered something to his wife and kissed her cheek before returning the baby to her arms. She bade us farewell and left the cabin, a wake of silent tension behind her.

Croghan resumed his chair. "I believe you were about to say something, Flower Hunter. Something about what lies in Indian hearts."

I was nervous. We were there at Croghan's mercy, with his armed men and a village of Indians between us and the *de Terzi*. And my father had clearly angered the Trader King and insulted his wife and daughter. I felt something for my father then that I never had before.

Shame.

"I have nothing to say," my father said.

"In that case, you will leave this place," Croghan said. "And I can assure you that Andrew will *not* be going with you, after all."

The other members of the Society had been silent until then but now spoke up, affirming that they did not hold to my father's views. They wanted Andrew to come and valued what he might contribute to the expedition. My father said nothing more, staring darkly at the table. After much pleading and assurances, Croghan finally held up his hands.

"Enough. It is Andrew's decision to make. Go to your vessel now and wait for one hour. If Andrew does not come before then, you will depart this place without him, for I will not have you linger here."

"Very well," Mr. Colden said. To the rest of us he ordered, "Come."

I left Croghan with my cheeks burning. We hurried from the trading post and through the village until we reached the aeroship. Croghan's guards watched us as one by one we climbed the rope ladder to the deck. For the next half hour, we all milled about silently. My father stood off by himself at the bow, and I had no desire to be with him, nor to appear aligned with him. As the end of the hour drew near, he turned around and spoke.

"I said nothing that you have not all said and thought yourselves, and you know that to be true."

No one responded, either to agree or deny.

"You assume much," Mr. Godfrey said.

"We all have our beliefs about the Indian, John," Mr. Colden said. "You must temper yours with charity and Christian love. They are as equally capable of nobility as they are savagery. In my books, I compare them to the heroes of ancient Rome, and in some respects find them superior to the —"

"Do not lecture me, Cadwallader," my father said. "I cannot abide such words coming from the mouth of a man who owns slaves."

"That is different," Mr. Colden said.

"Whatever our thoughts on the Indian may be," Mr. Kinnersley said, "we must restrain them now, for here he comes."

We all looked over the side and saw Andrew approaching us, a pack and a rifle over his shoulder, with Croghan at his side. At our distance, it seemed that they were arguing. Croghan gestured and pointed, while Andrew remained stoic and walked with a measured gait.

Mr. Colden looked at my father and then threw the rope ladder over the side. "Come up!" he called. "You are most welcome aboard!"

"Cadwallader," my father said. "He has a gun."

"So he has," Mr. Colden said.

"We agreed," my father said. "No guns."

"No guns for the Society members," Mr. Colden said. "But I do not oppose our guide arming himself."

When they reached the ladder, Andrew took hold of it, and Croghan's shoulders sagged in defeat. Then he pulled

Andrew into a tight hug before glaring up at us, turning, and walking away. He never looked back, but Andrew remained there until Croghan was gone from sight, and I saw myself in him, standing in the road watching my father. Andrew started climbing.

We waited for him in a semicircle and greeted him with smiles when his head peeked over the railing. He had scrubbed the paint from his face and looked even more like one of us, though he still wore his earrings and locket. Mr. Colden stepped forward and helped pull him onto the ship.

"Welcome, Andrew. Now, introductions."

"Thank you, but I remember everyone from before," he said. "Mr. Kinnersley, Mr. Godfrey, Mr. Faries, Dr. Bond." He looked at each of them as he said their names, but there was the slightest pause when he came to my father. "Mr. Bartram, Billy, and Mr. Colden."

"I'm impressed," Phineas said.

"As an interpreter, my duties require that I know who I am speaking to."

He made me anxious. He seemed like a good and honest man and had given me no cause to fear him. But I kept hearing my father's warning over and over in my head, and it felt to me as if I'd be betraying my father if I accepted him.

"We are pleased to have you with us, Andrew," Mr. Colden said. "If you'll follow me, I will show you below deck where you can stow your things."

"Thank you, sir," Andrew said.

"Mr. Faries," Mr. Colden said. "Weigh anchor and get her in the air."

Mr. Faries nodded. "Aye, sir."

Before long, the villagers had regathered to watch our departure, but as the air rushed out of the spheres beneath us, it blew a choking cloud of dust into their faces, forcing them back.

"Sorry!" I yelled, but I doubted they could hear me.

Within moments, we were aloft, first tree-height, then hill-height, then above even those. Andrew and Mr. Colden emerged from below, and as Andrew looked around, his eyes opened wide. He took one cautious step at a time toward the edge of the deck until he could look over the side.

"I knew we would be flying," he said, a quaver in his voice. "But I realize now that isn't something you can really know until you've done it."

Mr. Colden grinned. "Let's show you what she can do."

CHAPTER 8

Electrical Fire

I *wanted to see Jane again. I wanted to tell her about Croghan* and talk with her about Andrew. But I wasn't sure how to do that without drawing suspicion. The *de Terzi* was not that large, and the Society members were constantly moving from one deck to the other. They might have seen me knocking on Mr. Kinnersley's cabin or heard me whispering through the door. So I stayed up on the top deck, watching and waiting for the right opportunity.

Mr. Colden showed Andrew around the ship, just as he had done for me. I kept my distance from them. But I didn't seek out my father, either. The thought of talking with him felt just as uncomfortable. Instead, I moved toward Phineas, who was in conversation with Mr. Godfrey.

"You are interested in the Fountain of Youth?" Mr. Godfrey asked.

"I am," Phineas said.

"It is an interest of mine, as well," Mr. Godfrey said. "You've read Fontaneda's account of it, of course."

"Naturally." Phineas adjusted his coat. "Hello, Billy."

"Hello, sir," I said. "I didn't mean to intrude."

"Nonsense," Mr. Godfrey said. "Have you heard of the Fountain of Youth, young man?"

"I haven't."

"It is a legendary mineral spring," Mr. Godfrey said. "The Water of Life. Those who drink it are said to be restored to the prime of their youth. In other words, it grants eternal life."

"That is overstating the matter," Phineas said. "I suspect the legend is simply based on a natural spring with very potent healing and restorative effects."

"Perhaps," Mr. Godfrey said. "But where's the pleasure in that?"

"So you're hoping to find it on this expedition?" I asked. They both nodded.

"In addition to the primary purpose of the mission," Phineas said, "I think we all have our individual reasons for being here."

"Some more openly than others," Mr. Godfrey said.

As their discussion turned to the book on seawater that Phineas had started reading, I wandered away from them, watching Mr. Faries at the helm, until Mr. Kinnersley appeared from below deck and walked over to me.

"Billy, are you still interested in seeing my electrical equipment?" He winked.

"Um . . . yes, I am," I said, thinking of Jane.

We crossed the deck and went below, through the Science Deck and galley. Mr. Kinnersley pulled out his key and unlocked the cabin door. "Inside," he said.

I slipped through, and he followed me. When he had shut the door, Jane walked around from behind the mast where she'd been hiding. "Hello, Billy. I hope you don't mind, but I told Mr. Kinnersley that you'd found me."

"That's fine," I said. "I was hoping for a chance to come back."

"You were?"

"Well . . . yes." I felt awkward. "I mean, I wanted to come see Mr. Kinnersley's electrical equipment."

"Oh," Jane said.

"And so you shall," Mr. Kinnersley said. "Right this way. All of what you see relates in some way to my work with electrical fire."

"Even the horse trough?" I asked.

"Oh, yes," he said. "I use that to study how electrical fire burns through water. But I think I promised you a Leyden jar. Isn't that right?"

"Yes, sir." I pointed at the jugs clustered around the mast. "Are those Leyden jars?"

"They are, but they are unconventional, and I must ask

that you refrain from going near them. But here . . ." He led me to his workbench, where I saw a smaller version of the other jugs. "This one will do." Mr. Kinnersley positioned me before the jar and moved around to stand behind me. "Now, Billy, touch the outside of the jar there with your right hand."

"What will it do?"

"Nothing. Yet."

"But what is it?"

"It is trapped electrical fire," Mr. Kinnersley said. "Stored power. And, oh, Billy. When that power transfers to you, it makes *you* feel more powerful. Touch the jar."

I hesitated. My father and Mr. Franklin had given me enough reason to be cautious of Mr. Kinnersley.

"Don't be frightened," Mr. Kinnersley said.

Jane stood nearby, watching me.

I stood up straighter. "I'm not frightened."

"Good," Mr. Kinnersley said. "Touch it."

I reached out. But nothing happened. The metal foil felt cold beneath my fingertips.

"Now," Mr. Kinnersley said, "I want you to touch the wire sticking out of the cork."

I looked at Jane, and she smiled back at me. Then I lifted my finger toward the wire. I knew I shouldn't. I knew I should've just pulled away and said no. But I couldn't. In spite of the arguments gathering like a mob in my mind, I could not pull my finger away and instead found it getting closer to the wire.

Jane was watching. My hand was an inch away. Then less than an inch. Then —

My bones hummed. A cold fire burned through my flesh and my skin. A great bell clanged deep in my ears. And beneath that, I heard something. A voice . . .

". . . ake up, Billy."

. . . and a slapping on my cheek. I opened my eyes.

My father leaned over me. "Oh, thank heavens."

"That was unexpected." Mr. Kinnersley stood above my father, his fingers an agitated knot in front of his chest. "But there, no harm done."

"No harm?" my father shouted. "No harm!"

As my vision focused, I saw the others had crowded into the cabin and doorway. Mr. Colden, Andrew, the other Society members. And Jane peered at me, her hand over her mouth.

I found my voice. "I'm fine, Father."

My father looked at me, mouth partway open, his eyebrows jammed together. I sat up and looked at my hands, which tingled and quivered and did not feel like they belonged to me.

"There, you see?" Mr. Kinnersley dabbed his forehead with a handkerchief. "He's fine."

My father exploded. "You shocked my son unconscious!"

"I'm fine, Father." I tried to get to my feet and stalled on one knee. My father gripped my arms and helped me the rest of the way.

"You are not fine," he said.

I wasn't. But I wasn't hurt, either. I felt shaken, from the inside. At the edges of my body, I smoldered. The aftermath, I supposed, of the electrical fire that had blazed through me. And my hair felt like it stood up at attention.

Mr. Kinnersley tucked his handkerchief away. "It will take a few moments for his body to ful —"

"Ebenezer, this time you have gone too far!" My father let go of me and rose up to his full height over the shorter, older man.

"But it was not me!" Mr. Kinnersley said.

"It was *your* jar," my father said. "Is this what you intended?"

"No! This, this was an accident, John." Mr. Kinnersley bowed his head, eyes darting to all the corners of the room. "I don't . . . I don't understand. It should not have been so strong a shock. Something happened, something . . ."

I felt a little sorry for him. I knew how it felt to have my father's anger boiling over you.

"It happened because you are both incompetent and reckless," my father said. "And you endanger everyone around you with your fanatical zeal —"

"Calm down, John," Phineas said. "I understand you are angry, but we mustn't let this get out of hand."

"Phineas," my father said. "How can you say that with Jane standing right there? The situation would already seem to be well out of hand."

Everyone turned to look at Jane as if noticing her for the first time. She dropped her hands to her sides and lifted her chin. Her fingers touched and tugged at the boy's trousers she wore. She had been discovered. Or rather, my accident had forced her discovery. It wasn't really my fault, but I still felt guilty.

"Perhaps it hasn't occurred to anyone else," my father said, "that Jane must have been hiding in here since we left Philadelphia. Which means that Ebenezer knew she was on board."

Mr. Colden's eyes bulged, and he grabbed Mr. Kinnersley by the collar of his coat. "Is this true?"

Mr. Kinnersley squirmed. "Let me explain. I —"

"How dare you?" Mr. Colden threw him to the floor. Mr. Kinnersley hit with a loud thud and grimaced.

"Father, please," Jane said.

Mr. Colden pointed at her. "Do not speak! I'm going to instruct Mr. Faries to turn this ship around. We're going back to Philadelphia."

"Now, wait," my father said. "I think we should discuss that."

"Discuss what?" Mr. Colden pointed down at Mr. Kinnersley. "I'll not have this treacherous snake on this ship one minute beyond what is necessary. I'm tempted to throw him overboard right now."

"As am I," my father said. "But as furious as I am with Ebenezer, going back may not be an option."

"Why?"

My father turned to me. "Tell him what you saw before we left, Billy. In the street."

I remembered the men running, and I described them, as well as the feeling of being followed. After I'd finished, the mood and the silence in the small cabin tightened even further than it had already.

"Add that information to what was stolen during the break-in at my home," my father said, "and not only are the French aware of this ship, but they also likely observed us depart in her. We cannot turn back. It is too risky, and we cannot lose any more time."

Mr. Colden chewed on his cheek.

"You know I'm right, Cadwallader."

Mr. Colden stood over Mr. Kinnersley, who still sat on the ground, cradling his arm. "You'd best stay out of my way, Ebenezer."

Mr. Kinnersley nodded without looking up.

"Are you all right, Billy?" Mr. Colden asked me.

"Yes, sir."

"Good. Jane, come with me. You and I must talk."

I felt for her as she bowed her head and followed Mr. Colden out of the cabin. But then my father clamped a hand on my shoulder. "We must talk as well."

I sighed. "Yes, Father."

He led me out, past the Society members and Andrew, whom I imagined to be rethinking his choice to join us. We climbed up onto the weather deck, and I saw Mr. Colden speaking with Jane up at the bow.

"This way," my father said, and led me toward the stern.

We passed Mr. Faries at the helm. "Are you well, Billy?" he asked.

"Yes, sir."

"Good. It gave us all a terrible fright when Jane came running up from below. She said you were dead." He turned to my father. "How did she get on board, anyway?"

"It seems that Ebenezer helped her stow away," my father said.

Mr. Faries shook his head, and we went on by him, to the rear of the ship.

"So it was Jane who called for help?" I asked my father.

"Yes. And our surprise at seeing her was quickly replaced by concern for you." He turned his back to me and gripped the rail, facing the sky behind us. "What were you thinking?"

I didn't know what he meant. "I'm sorry, Father." I stepped up beside him. "It was foolish of me. But Mr. Kinnersley assured me it was safe."

"And did you know Jane was down there? You must have seen her in the cabin."

"I did."

"Why did you not say something to me?"

"I promised her I wouldn't."

"Likely the first of many foolish things you will do for the sake of a woman." He glanced at me and chuckled. "Your hair is standing up like a field of corn."

I reached up and tried to smooth it down with my palm.

My father laughed and put his arm around me. "I'm relieved you are not hurt. I don't know what I would have done if . . ." He trailed off. "Bah. Better not to think about it. You're safe. That's the important thing."

"I'm safe."

The world fled by, and I imagined that we left an invisible wake curling and roiling in the air behind us. We had long since left Croghan's valley behind, and the earth below us had smoothed from steep to rolling hills, puckered here and there like a blanket someone had clenched in their fist.

"I brought you up here to talk about something aside from Jane and Mr. Kinnersley," my father said.

I felt a cold snag in my gut. "What else did you want to talk about?" I asked, even though I thought I knew.

"Andrew," he said.

I was right. "What about him?"

"Just . . . be wary. That is all I will say for now."

"Yes, sir." The snag became a tangle. I didn't know what to say, or to think. My father had almost cost the expedition a guide. And yet, he was my father. But I didn't understand him anymore. "But you oppose slavery. You said to Mr. Colden —"

"I am *not* suggesting we enslave the Indian, Billy." He leaned away from me, as though I'd offended him. "How could you . . . ?" He sighed. "The truth is not always easily understood. I hope that I am wrong about Andrew. But in the interests of this expedition, and until he proves me so, I am compelled to mistrust him."

"The others seem to feel differently."

"They have not had the experiences I have had. They do not know what I know."

Neither did I. So I had to rely on him, wishing that I knew what had happened to my father.

After a few hours had passed, I sought out Jane. I found her below, on the Science Deck, reading.

"What is that book?" I asked.

"Linnaeus's *Genera Plantarum*," she said, without looking up. "Do you know it?"

"I've read from it before."

She turned the page.

I pulled a chair up next to her and sat down. "I'm sorry, Jane. I didn't mean for you to be found out."

"It isn't your fault. I had to come out eventually. I'm just sorry I got Mr. Kinnersley in trouble."

"I don't think you need to feel bad about that. I suspect he gets himself into trouble quite often without you."

"I suppose that's probably true."

"But I also wanted to thank you. You went for help. For me."

She looked up. "I thought you were dead. I thought I'd just watched Mr. Kinnersley kill you with that horrible jar."

"Not quite," I said.

She closed the book. "What was it like? When you touched it?"

I rubbed my fingers through my hair, hoping it wasn't

still standing up. "Have you ever hit your head really hard, and it stuns you for a moment?"

"Yes," she said. "One time on a shelf in my father's study."

"It's like that, but all over your whole body."

She winced. "Oh."

"It wasn't so bad."

"What do you suppose the big jars are for? The ones around the mast?"

"I don't know," I said. "But I would advise against touching them."

She laughed. "Thank you for the warning."

"Is your father angry with you?"

"He says he is. But I know he's secretly happy I'm here. Honestly, I think he's more upset that I only brought boys' clothes." She frowned. "It's my mother I'll have to worry about when I get home. She won't know where I am until my letter is delivered. She'll think I've been carried off."

"You wrote a letter?"

"Of course. But I made sure it wouldn't arrive until long after we'd gone. I didn't want to take any chances."

"You planned this very well."

"I always do."

"Well, it looks like your plan worked, in the end."

She smiled and gave a quick nod. "Yes, it looks that way."

"Why *did* you only bring boys' clothes?"

"Just how well do you think a dress would fare in the wilderness?"

I smiled back at her. "Welcome to the expedition, Jane."

CHAPTER 9

The Forks of the Ohio

Evening came on, and the sun set ahead of us, beating us to the horizon once again. We ate a supper of ham, boiled eggs, peaches, and buttered bread. And then we prepared for the first watch, which Mr. Colden assigned to Mr. Faries and me. Then it was time to work out new sleeping arrangements. Mr. Colden didn't want Jane anywhere near Mr. Kinnersley's cabin, so he hung a sheet and partitioned off the most forward bunk for her, creating a little space for her modesty.

We all then went up and sat on the weather deck to watch the stars bloom. But the earlier tensions of the day remained, and no one spoke much to one another. My father still lingered at the edge of the group. Mr. Kinnersley wasn't with us at all, choosing instead to perch himself at the bow, fixing a hawk's stare on Mr. Colden.

Andrew avoided looking at anyone and kept his gaze up at the sky as the last of its sunlight drained away.

Phineas broke the silence. "It is nice to have you with us, Jane."

Mr. Colden whipped his head in the doctor's direction.

"Thank you, sir," Jane said.

"It is not at all nice to have her with us," Mr. Colden said. "Make no mistake, she should not be here."

Phineas lifted his shoulders. "I merely meant that —"

"Don't bother, Phineas," my father said from several feet away.

And the silence returned.

A moment later, Andrew stood. I watched him go below, wondering what he was doing, only to see him return holding a fife. He took up a position a little way away from us and put the instrument to his lips. He began to play a quiet, gentle song that soon set us all to swaying. When that was over, he chose a more lively tune. Something to set our toes tapping.

When he started into a third, Phineas got to his feet. He went over and stood next to Andrew, watched him play a moment, and then started clapping along, his hands up by his head. Then he began stomping his foot on the deck boards with the sound of a loud, deep drum.

The rhythm of the music got some of the others to their feet, stomping, too. I looked at my father before joining them, but soon even he and Mr. Kinnersley had started in, and before long we were all jigging and filling the night sky with our laughter and the thunder from our feet. Even Mr. Colden, whose style of dance looked something like a fence post bobbing in a river. When that song was done, we all fell back to the deck laughing and applauding.

Andrew grinned around his fife. "Would you like another?"

Panting, Mr. Kinnersley waved both arms. "No! No, thank you. I don't think my heart could take it."

Andrew bowed, tucked his instrument beneath his arm, and sat down.

"But if all of you would indulge *me*," Mr. Godfrey said. "I would like to sing."

No one encouraged him, but no one objected, either, so he stood. And he sang. His voice surprised me. It wasn't good, and it wasn't bad. It sounded like the wind through a hollow log. He sang in what I thought was German, the melody both mournful and heavy, and by the end of it, the *de Terzi* felt as if it had descended several feet in the air under the weight. No one applauded, but Mr. Godfrey didn't seem to mind.

"What was that song?" Phineas asked.

"'Bittersweet Night Ode,'" Mr. Godfrey said. "A hymn by Johannes Kelpius." ·

I sat up at the name. "I know him. My father told me about him." My father nodded.

"And what did your father say?" Mr. Godfrey asked.

· "That he was a monk, a magician, and a madman."

Mr. Godfrey laughed. "Well, he might be right about one or two of those."

Everyone retired after that, leaving Mr. Faries and me alone on deck. Much about the small, sad man was still a mystery to me. He took up his position at the helm, and I went to stand next to him. Whether from the night air or the echo of Mr. Godfrey's song in my ear, I felt a chill. I pulled my coat in tight and folded my arms, watching the banks of icy white clouds slide over and around us. And then I gasped as we flew right into one.

The world became a gray void. The ground was lost, the sky was lost. Forward and backward were lost. We were suspended in a moonlit mist that wet my lips and bejeweled our wool coats. The air felt heavy in my chest.

"They appear so solid," Mr. Faries said. "From the ground." I nodded.

"And yet, when you get close to them, they're nothing more than a wisp of moisture in the air. So much in this world is like that. Things that seem real, things you believe in, turn out to be nothing more than a phantasm. A cloud in the wind."

I could only nod again.

"I'm sorry, Billy. I shouldn't trouble you with my grief. Let's talk about something else, eh?" He rapped the ship's wheel hard with his knuckle. "Would you like a turn at the helm?"

"Me, sir?"

"Certainly."

"Yes, sir!"

"Take hold, then."

He broke away and I slipped into his place. The wood felt warm where his hands had been, and the wheel turned easily.

"Hold her steady," he said.

"Yes, sir," I whispered. I stared ahead, as intently as I could, feeling powerful and almost overwhelmed by it. I was in control of the ship.

"Now, check the compass there," he said. "It looks like we're a few degrees off course, so you need to adjust your heading."

I tightened my grip on the wheel. "How do I do that?"

"Just turn the wheel and watch the needle. We need our heading to be two hundred and eighty degrees."

I breathed deep and turned the wheel, just a little. The mist around us gave no indication that we had changed course, but the needle on the compass flicked into place.

"Excellent," Mr. Faries said. "Hold her there."

I sighed a little but didn't loosen my grip. A few moments later, we broke out of the cloud, emerging on the solid world of mountains and rivers, the moon, and the clean sharp air. As time passed and the miles glided by, the wheel felt more comfortable, and I found myself relaxing into my role.

"May I ask you a question, sir?"

"Of course."

"Why did you come on this expedition?"

"What do you mean?"

"Well, aside from finding Madoc, my father came to study plants. Phineas is looking for the Fountain of Youth. And Mr. Godfrey said that everyone on this expedition has their own reasons for being here."

"I suppose I . . ." He paused and checked the compass. "I suppose I just wanted to fly."

As I stood there at the helm, the wheel in my hand and the ship at my will, that seemed reason enough to me.

At the end of our watch, Phineas and Andrew came up to relieve us. We went below, and I climbed right into my hammock. But I lay there for a while with my eyes open, kept awake by the fading exhilaration of flying.

"Billy."

Someone shook me.

"Billy, wake up. We've arrived."

I opened my eyes. My father stood over me.

"We'll be setting the ship down shortly." He squeezed my arm and left.

I rubbed my eyes and rolled out of the hammock. I put on my boots, grabbed my coat, and snatched a biscuit from the galley on my way up to the weather deck, where I found everyone else admiring the vista below us.

From the northeast came the Allegheny River, and from the southeast flowed the Monongahela, both mighty and a quarter mile wide. They met at the tip of a spit of land and merged to form the Ohio, which continued on to the west.

"So this is the Forks," Phineas said. "Equally coveted by England and France."

"The trading post is located there." Mr. Colden pointed. "Where the rivers come together."

"So much trouble for such a small piece of wilderness," Mr. Kinnersley said.

Mr. Colden scoffed. "That piece of wilderness down there has absolute command of all three rivers. It needs a fully garrisoned fort."

"Shall I take us down?" Mr. Faries asked.

"Yes," Mr. Colden said. "Close to the water's edge."

Mr. Faries returned to the helm and let air into the spheres with a familiar rushing sound. As we descended, the trading post appeared among the trees, where once again the sight of our vessel brought the inhabitants out into the open to gawk at us. Mr. Faries flew the *de Terzi* over the cluster of cabins and outbuildings and landed her on the opposite side, at the confluence of the rivers.

"Let go anchor!" Mr. Colden called, and with a little jerk the aeroship came to rest.

We gathered by the rope ladder. I could make out the trading post through the woods, but saw no one waiting for us below. Instead of climbing down, Mr. Colden said, "We're not expected here. Hopefully they've seen our English flag. But just in case . . ." He produced a white handkerchief and waved it over the side. "We hail from Philadelphia! We're coming down!" He looked sideways. "Jane, you will wait here."

"But, Father —"

"You dare defy me now?" he said.

Cowed, Jane backed away from the edge.

And with that, Mr. Colden descended the rope ladder, as did we all. On the ground, we were about to move toward the trading post when a dozen men erupted from the woods and surrounded us, guns aimed. I froze, and my father pushed me behind him. A tall, red-haired man in military uniform stood at the fore.

"Gentlemen," Mr. Colden said, still holding the handkerchief. "We are servants of the Crown. There is no need for such hostility. We are here to assess your situation and make recommendations to the government as to your needs."

"Which government?" the military man asked.

"Pennsylvania," Mr. Colden said.

"Who are you?"

"I am Cadwallader Colden, and with me are several members of the Philosophical Society, sent by Benjamin Franklin. You may have heard of him."

"I've heard his name," the man said. He looked to his side. "Lower your weapons."

The barrels came down, and I let out a long, deep breath.

"I am Major George Washington," the man said. "I, too, was sent to survey this location."

"On whose authority?" Mr. Colden asked.

"Governor Dinwiddie of Virginia," he said. "These men are all with the Ohio Company. What business does Pennsylvania have here?"

"What else but the common interest of our opposition to the French," Mr. Colden said.

Major Washington looked back and forth between us and the *de Terzi*, shifting a little on his feet. "Proceed to the trading post," he said.

His men parted, and with a glance back at the *de Terzi*, Mr. Colden led the way through them. The Society members followed, and my father set me on the path in front of him, bringing up the rear. Major Washington fell in behind us with the rest of the Ohio Company traders, their guns at the ready. We took a well-trod trail some distance through maple and black locust trees, until we entered a clearing lined with log buildings and sheds. A massive *incognitum* skull leaned up against a wall, a hunting trophy, perhaps, and away to the side, livestock filled a small paddock. The men of the post, more fur traders and a few Indians, had all stopped in the middle of what they were doing to stare at us.

"This way," Washington said, continuing past us. With the exception of a few who went with him, our armed escort broke apart and gathered with the others, whispering.

Washington marched us to a smoldering fire pit encircled with stumps and rocks for sitting. "Please," he said, and motioned for us to take them.

"I must admit," Mr. Colden said. "This is not exactly the welcome we'd hoped for."

Washington propped a boot up on a stump and rested an elbow on his knee. "Mr. Colden, any offense I've given you is unfortunate, but I won't apologize for taking precautions. You send no word of your coming, and then you arrive here in a ship that sails the air like a bird? Under the circumstances, I hope you'll forgive these men for not showing you the manners to which you are accustomed."

Mr. Colden nodded. "Of course."

"The mind leaps to witchcraft and dark arts when you see a schooner in the sky," Major Washington said. "But let's leave the topic of your ship a moment and return to your reason for being here. The king granted Virginia and the Ohio Company rights to this land six years ago. Pennsylvania has no claim —"

"We are not here in that capacity," Mr. Colden said. "Nor do we dispute Virginia's rights."

"Then why?"

"The French incursion into the Ohio Country must be stopped. We were simply tasked with assessing the strength of this position and those stationed here."

"Is that so?" Washington said, his eyes narrowed in suspicion.

"How many men do you have here, Major?" Mr. Colden asked.

After a moment's hesitation, he said, "The post has thirty-six men. It needs a fort constructed, manned by a company of regulars, and twice that in militiamen."

Mr. Colden looked around. "I agree with that assessment."

"Good," Washington said. "When you report back to Philadelphia, you may assure them that Virginia will see it done."

"Oh, for pity's sake," my father said. "If the French take this territory, do you think it will be Virginia alone that suffers? And if England and France go to war, will Virginia alone be called upon to fight?"

Major Washington scowled. "Do not presume to lecture me about war, sir."

"How old are you?" my father asked. "Twenty? Twenty-one? Have you ever seen war, Major Washington?"

The major said nothing.

"The French are building forts in the Ohio Country," Mr. Colden said. "Are you aware that Captain Paul Marin is leading an army of fifteen hundred men south as we speak?"

I noticed the other Society members exchanging glances, and I remembered that Mr. Franklin had intended for that information to be withheld from them. Mr. Kinnersley and Mr. Godfrey began to whisper, while Mr. Faries shook his head. Only Phineas appeared undisturbed by the news. Perhaps Mr. Colden or my father had already told him.

"I am aware of that," Washington said. "My orders are to deliver a letter to the French commanders demanding that they withdraw from the territory."

"A letter," Mr. Colden said. "The French send soldiers, and Dinwiddie sends a letter? And not only that, but he entrusts this letter to a boy? If you are not careful, Major Washington, you could end up starting a war rather than preventing one."

Major Washington brought his boot down hard and stood up tall. "I was entrusted because I am more than capable. If your motives truly are to secure this territory for England, then let me take your flying ship north to deliver our demands. Can you imagine what the French would think? Have you considered its tactical and military potential?"

"The *de Terzi* is a vessel of philosophy," my father said. "It is *not* a ship of war. We have no weapons on board."

Washington turned to my father. "And what would you do with it, then?"

"We are searching for allies," Mr. Colden said.

"What allies?" Washington asked. "Indians?"

"No," Mr. Colden said. "The Welsh."

Washington cocked his head for a moment. "Madoc?"

Mr. Colden nodded.

"The governor is very interested in Madoc," Washington said. "I've heard the reports, of course. And out here on the frontier there are rumors."

"What kind of rumors?" my father asked.

"Hearsay, mostly. Men who've talked to men who've talked to men who've talked to men who claim to have seen them. They are supposed to live somewhere beyond the place where the Mississippi and Missouri Rivers meet."

"Then that is where we will search," Mr. Colden said.

Washington snorted. "You're mad, the lot of you. Chasing a frontier legend."

Mr. Godfrey spoke up. "Legends often trace their roots to fact, young man."

"Perhaps so," Washington said. "Regardless, I wish you luck in your —"

"Major Washington!" someone shouted. A man came running from the woods, skidded to a halt, and bowed.

"What is it, Corporal?"

"The French, sir!" He looked pale. "They're here."

CHAPTER 10

Marin

T he Society members all stood up at once.

"Report," Major Washington said.

The scout swallowed. "A large company approaches by water."

"How far?"

"We spotted them a mile upriver."

"How many?"

"I counted eight boats, perhaps twenty men to a boat."

"Colonials or regulars?"

"Marines, sir."

Washington nodded. He turned to Mr. Colden. "We must consider surrender."

"Surrender?"

"We are outnumbered four to one," Washington said. "And we have fur traders for soldiers. Theirs are experts at wilderness maneuver and combat, almost as dangerous as the Indian."

"They must not be allowed to take the *de Terzi*," Mr. Colden said. "We must depart at once."

"I can't allow that yet," Washington said. "We may have need of your ship."

"You have no authority to — !"

A cry went up at the edge of the trading post, and a few of the traders emerged from the trees with two men between them. They wore light-colored military coats with leather leggings, and one of them carried a white flag. Major Washington moved to meet them, and I edged closer to listen.

"Major." One of the strangers bowed and presented a letter. "I speak on behalf of Captain Paul Marin de la Malgue" — he gestured to his companion, a grizzled and hardened burl of a man — "whose reputation, I am certain, precedes him, and who brings terms for your surrender."

Major Washington eyed Marin and took the letter. "Perhaps your captain needs to be reminded that this land belongs to England, secured by treaty. Why would we surrender what is ours?" He cracked the wax seal.

The messenger smiled and nodded. "At present, Captain Marin is content to leave this" — he looked around — "trading post in English hands. If you comply with his terms."

"And what might those be?" Washington asked, reading the letter.

The messenger looked past Washington and scanned the

faces of the Society members. "Captain Marin demands the flying ship."

I gasped, but recovered myself. They'd known about the *de Terzi* since at least the break-in at our farm. But how had they known we would be here at the Forks?

"With due respect," Washington said, "such a request might call a man's sanity into question. A ship that flies, you say? What else does the captain demand? A carriage that swims?"

The messenger's smile remained, but his eyes held none of it. "We know it exists and it is here somewhere, Major."

I resisted looking over my shoulder, but apparently the *de Terzi* wasn't visible over the trees.

"And we will take it by force if necessary," the messenger said.

"You may convey to Captain Marin that I have received his terms." Washington folded the letter. "And I will do my utmost to provide him with a fictional flying ship."

The Frenchman lost all traces of his smile. "You would be wise to do so."

"Where is the ship?" Marin asked, his accent thick, his voice menacing.

It surprised me to hear him speak, and even Washington seemed caught off guard. "It isn't here, Captain."

"You are lying," Marin said. "But it does not matter." His gaze battered each of us as he turned his back and stormed away, his interpreter close behind him, off into the trees the way they had come.

Washington nodded to the traders who had escorted the Frenchmen. "Follow them. Make sure they head back up the river. I don't want them scouting around."

"Yes, sir." The men left.

"Corporal," Washington said. "Take some men and watch the banks. I want to know the minute they've landed."

The scout saluted. "Yes, sir."

Washington turned to Colden. "Marin seems to want your ship even more than he wants the Forks, which I find hard to believe. That fact alone makes it imperative that he not get his hands on it."

"We'll leave at once," Mr. Colden said.

Washington held up a hand. "No. Wait until we receive word that their boats have landed. That will purchase you the most time. But you should return to your ship and be ready for my signal."

Mr. Colden extended his hand. "Thank you, Major."

Washington shook it. "I still think you're all mad, but I'll do what I can to make certain your escape. Go, now."

Mr. Colden led us back down through the trees to the shore, and one at a time we climbed the rope ladder. The process seemed interminable. Mr. Kinnersley and Mr. Godfrey both labored up slowly, while each passing moment brought the French closer. I paced around, waiting, listening, and watching for any signs of Marin's men. When at last it was my turn, I scurried up as fast as I could, grateful when my feet hit the deck.

My father landed behind me, and then he turned to

face the river and the trees. "Now we wait for Major Washington's signal."

No one spoke. We listened. We watched.

"Where is Jane?" Mr. Colden asked.

I looked around. She wasn't on deck. "I'll go look below," I said.

"Hurry, Billy," Mr. Colden said.

Only she wasn't below. Not in her bunk, not on the Science Deck, not in the galley, and not in Mr. Kinnersley's cabin. I ran back up. "She's gone!"

"Mr. Faries!" Mr. Colden shouted. "Get the ship ready to fly." He headed for the rope ladder. "She must have followed us to the trading post. I'll hurry, but if we're not back before the signal, you must leave without us."

"I'll come with you," Andrew said.

"No," my father said. "I'll go."

I swallowed. What if the signal came before my father returned? What if he was captured? I stepped forward. "I'm coming with you."

"No," my father said, already climbing down. "Stay here."

But I ignored him and started down the ladder.

"Billy! Get back up there!"

"I'm coming with you!" I said, and kept climbing.

My father looked down, then up at me, then down again, and seemed to decide he couldn't stop to argue. When we reached the ground, he grabbed my neck. "Stay close to me."

We ran into the trees, following Mr. Colden.

"Jane!" he shouted. "Jane!"

My father and I did the same.

Several minutes later, we reached the post. The traders had all taken up strategic positions behind the buildings and trees. They all held guns. Major Washington stood in the middle, giving orders. When he saw us, he marched our way, pointing toward the river.

"What are you fools doing? Get aboard that ship!"

"My daughter!" Mr. Colden shouted. "Has anyone seen her?"

"You brought your daughter?" Washington said.

"No! Of course I — !" Mr. Colden sputtered. "There isn't time to explain. Has anyone seen her?"

Dozens of blank faces met Mr. Colden's question.

"Jane!" Mr. Colden spun around, his gaze scrambling around the trading post. "Jane!"

"She's not here," my father said. "She must be in the woods."

"Major!" The corporal sprinted into view from the east. "They've landed."

"You have to leave," Major Washington said. "Now."

Mr. Colden's voice broke. "She's my daughter."

Washington regarded him for a moment, then cursed. "Corporal, take five men and find the girl. The rest of you, with me. We'll harry them and hold them off as long as we can."

"Thank you," Mr. Colden said. "Bless you."

But Major Washington hadn't waited to hear it. He and his men were already racing into the trees. The corporal and his men took up the call for Jane, fanning out in different directions. Mr. Colden raced off to the north.

"Let's stop and think," my father said. "Where could she have gone?" He looked in all directions, seeming to consider each one. Then he stopped and looked at me.

"What is it?" I asked.

"She may be east of here. She knew she wasn't supposed to leave the boat. I wonder if she tried to sneak around and reach the trading post through the trees, overshot it, and ended up lost on the other side."

My stomach was starting to hurt. "But that's where Marin is."

"Go back to the ship, Billy." My father ran off in the direction Washington had gone. "Go now!"

It was like the moment on the stairs during the break-in at our farm. I stood there, frozen, wanting to obey and get myself to safety, but also wanting to follow him. Wanting to find Jane.

And then I heard the first gunshot, a loud crack in the trees, and I jumped. I sprinted after my father.

"Jane!" I shouted. "Jane!"

For several yards I could still see my father ahead of me, barely. But then I lost sight of him.

"Father! Jane!"

Another gunshot. I realized that my shouting might draw the enemy. I fell silent, dropped to a crouch, and pressed forward. The trees and the brush thickened, and I pushed through, fending off branches and listening. Before long, I worried that I, too, could become lost. But I checked my bearing and made sure I knew the direction I'd come.

The sound of gunfire multiplied, getting closer.

"Jane!" I hissed, as loudly and as quietly as I could. "Jane!"

And then I heard voices up ahead yelling in French. Something grabbed the shoulder of my coat from behind and pulled me to the ground. I yelped.

Jane slapped her hand over my mouth and held a finger to her lips.

"Where is the ship?" she mouthed.

I pointed the way I had come.

She nodded, released my mouth, and started off in that direction. But my father was still out there somewhere. Jane glanced back at me, and made an urgent motion for me to follow. I shook my head. The shouting was getting closer, the gunfire was loud enough to leave a ringing, and I could smell the tang of gun smoke.

Jane hurried back to me and leaned in. "What is it?" she whispered, her lips touching my ear.

I got in close to her. "My father," I whispered.

She started scanning the trees, and I did the same. That was when I noticed the figures darting through the woods in the distance. They were Washington's men, which meant the French would be upon us in moments. There was no time. I decided to take a risk.

"Father!" I shouted.

Nothing.

"Father!"

"Billy!" came a distant reply.

"Father!" I smiled at Jane. "I found her!"

A short pause.

"Go back! I'll meet you there!"

That was enough for me. "Come," I said to Jane. Together we ran back toward the trading post. Once there, we continued through it, feet pounding the ground, down the path to the river. I gave her a gentle push toward the rope ladder.

"You first."

After she had started up, I put my weight on the lower rungs to pull the rope tight and ease her climb. She reached the top, disappeared over the rail, and then looked back down at me.

"Billy, come!"

"My father," I said. But just then he burst out of the woods.

"Up, Billy!" he shouted, and then, "Faries, weigh anchor!".

Something whipped and whizzed through the leaves above my father's head, shredding them. A bullet. And then another, and another.

I started to climb. As I did, the ladder lurched and lifted off the ground. The rising anchor had freed the *de Terzi* of her mooring, and the movement made the ladder more difficult to scale. I looked down as my father reached the bottom and latched on, his feet dangling. And then I heard a rushing sound and a blast of wind hit me and set the ladder twisting and spinning. Mr. Faries was venting the spheres to get us higher. The ground fell away, ten, twenty, thirty, fifty feet, and we slid out over the river.

"Climb, Billy!" my father shouted.

I wanted to, but I couldn't get my fingers to let go of the rope. I couldn't move. I could only watch as French soldiers rushed the shore below us, shouting, and pointing their rifles at us. A bullet struck the *de Terzi*'s hull an instant before I heard the report and saw the smoke.

And then the ladder jerked upward, lifting me. They were raising it from the deck. I closed my eyes, trying to ignore the wind and the swinging of the rope, the sound of the guns, and before long, I heard someone say, "Hurry, Billy."

I opened my eyes as Andrew grabbed my arms and dragged me onto the deck. A moment later, I turned and helped him do the same for my father. We all kept our heads down, bullets striking the ship and her instruments all around us, splintering wood, breaking glass, sparking on metal.

Through it all, Mr. Faries stood bravely at the helm and finally announced that we were out of the French weapons' range. Even so, I only allowed myself a peek over the rail. We were sliding down the Ohio, the jut of land at the Forks growing distant. The French soldiers had stopped shooting. I felt like collapsing.

We had made it. We were safe. I started laughing, I don't know why. I couldn't help it. But when I looked at the others, all I saw were somber faces.

"Where is Cadwallader?" my father asked, recovering his breath.

I scanned the deck. He wasn't there.

"Where is my father?" Jane asked.

"He did not return in time," Phineas said.

"You left him?" Jane cried.

Phineas looked away. "We had no choice."

Jane raced to the helm. "Mr. Faries, take us back. You have to take us back!"

"I'm sorry, Jane," he said.

"No!" She tried to wrest the ship's wheel from his hands, sobbing, but my father hurried over and gathered her into his arms. She hit him, and scratched, and fought him, but he lifted her away from the helm and led her below deck.

"It looks like they might be following us," Mr. Kinnersley said from the stern, a spyglass to his eye. "They're getting back into their boats."

"We'll outrace them," Mr. Faries said. "Phineas, hoist sails."

Phineas just stood there.

"Phineas!" Mr. Faries shouted.

"Yes?"

"Hoist sails!"

"Aye," he murmured.

Mr. Faries worked the levers from the helm, and Phineas hauled the lines. Moments later, the sails billowed and snapped taut, and before long, the *de Terzi* had put several miles between us and Marin.

Between us and Mr. Colden.

CHAPTER 11

Damage

"**G**entlemen, *we must reexamine our situation*," *my father said.* We were gathered on the Science Deck, some seated at their desks, others standing, forming a circle around the central mast where my father stood. Jane sat in a chair by the bookcase, hunched and red-eyed. Phineas stood behind her with a hand on her shoulder.

"Mr. Faries, have you been able to assess the damage?"

Mr. Faries nodded. "We lost several instruments, but nothing that can't be replaced from the spares we brought. Injury to the ship's hull was superficial. But . . . we aren't maintaining altitude."

"What does that mean?" my father asked.

"It would appear that at least one bullet struck either a sphere or a pipe, allowing a small amount of air to leak in. We're losing vacuum in one of the spheres."

"Meaning?" Mr. Kinnersley asked.

"Meaning we won't be able to achieve higher altitudes. Mountains could be problematic going forward."

"Can you repair it?" my father asked.

"If I can find the leak, yes."

"Good. That will be your first priority once we're finished here." My father rubbed his chin. "For our next order of business, we must attend to the matter of leadership." He looked in Jane's direction. "The expedition needs a new commander. Are any of you willing to take on such duties?"

No one spoke, at first.

"I nominate you, John," Mr. Faries said.

"I second that," Mr. Kinnersley said.

"I would be willing to lead," Phineas said.

My father sighed. "Then according to the procedure of our Society, we must vote. William?"

Mr. Faries frowned and stood. "Very well. We'll do this election by raised hand. All for John Bartram, show by that sign."

Every hand but Phineas's went up, and for the first time since we'd landed in Aughwick, I felt proud of my father again.

"All for Phineas Bond?"

Phineas raised his hand.

"The matter is settled. This election has named John Bartram the interim leader of the Madoc expedition." Mr. Faries took his seat. Phineas bore a measured scowl on his face but tipped his head in acknowledgment.

"I thank you for this honor," my father said. "I shall strive to my utmost to lead you with wisdom, prudence, and temperance. Now, while we knew the French were aware of the existence of this ship, what we do *not* know is how they determined our location. I have a theory, but I would like to hear yours first."

"The most likely explanation," Mr. Godfrey said, "is that someone back in Philadelphia disclosed our plan. Did anyone here, however innocently, share our objective with someone outside the Society?"

"No one here would do such a thing," Phineas said. "But Ben had several conversations with those in government, to which none of us were privy. Perhaps someone higher up is a spy for the French."

"Both are plausible," my father said. "But I would suggest that our betrayal occurred more recently. But days ago."

"Who?" Mr. Godfrey asked. "You suspect Croghan?"

My father turned to Andrew, who sat silently nearby. "Or one of his associates. Your mother was French, was she not, Andrew?"

Andrew faltered as he spoke. "She was of mixed birth, sir. Her past is something of a mystery, even to me."

"Why did you want to come on this expedition?" my father asked. "Why did you volunteer to go with Mr. Colden in search of Jane?"

"I . . ." Andrew blinked. "I wanted to help."

He appeared sincere to me, and I started to believe him.

But my father would not be suspicious of him without cause.

"You wanted to help?" My father began to circle the room. "Or did you simply see an opportunity to join up with your French allies?"

"Sir, I —"

"Admit it," my father said. "You volunteered because you and Croghan are working for the French."

"*Lex parsimoniae*, John," Mr. Godfrey said. "This theory of yours calls for too many new assumptions."

"Such as?" my father asked.

"We left Aughwick scarcely more than a day ago, and we are traveling by air. You therefore assume Croghan had enough time to send word to the French. You assume him to be in league with the very men who have ruined his trade. And you assume the French then had time to reach the Forks of the Ohio."

My father folded his arms. "The French may have already been near the Forks."

"And further," Mr. Godfrey said, "how would Andrew have made contact with these hypothetical French allies? He has been on this ship the entire time. I think your biases are blinding you to the impossibilities in your theory. They are so obvious that I — Well, to be perfectly frank, I am embarrassed for you."

My father glowered. I was embarrassed for him, too, but also angry at Mr. Godfrey for shaming him. But I also knew Mr. Godfrey was right. Andrew bore no blame in this. But that did not mean I should now trust him.

My father spoke slowly. "You are right, Francis. The other two theories offer simpler solutions."

"Where is my father?" Jane asked from the corner.

Everyone turned to look at her.

"You philosophers have your elections," she said. "You have your theories, and you even have theories about what's wrong with your theories! But none of you are talking about my father. Where is he? What is happening to him?"

The only sound in the room was the creaking of the aeroship.

"Well, my dear, there are several possibilities." Mr. Godfrey held up a finger as if he were about to report the hour and the date. "First —"

"Francis!" my father said. "That's enough." He walked over and knelt in front of Jane. "Your father is fine, Jane. Major Washington will see that he gets safely back to Philadelphia."

"Are you sure?" she asked.

"Quite certain." He took her hands in his. "And until you are reunited with him back home, I want you to know that I will do everything I can to see to your needs as he would have done were he here. You have nothing to fear."

Jane sniffed and nodded. "Thank you, Mr. Bartram."

"You're welcome," my father said. "Gentlemen, let's set the matter of our betrayal aside, for the time being. Mr. Faries, please begin your repairs to the air system."

"Yes, sir."

"Billy," my father said. "I want you to assist Mr. Faries."

I hadn't taken my eyes off Jane. "Yes, sir." I wished there was something I could do for her.

Mr. Faries led me up to the weather deck. I followed him as he went to the starboard rail and turned to face the ship.

"The bullets came from this direction," he said, leaning back, arms outward. "They would have hit the pipes and spheres on this side. Come." We crossed to the foremast. "Start looking here."

I did as I was asked, tracing each of the pipes from the deck, up the mast, to the spheres. Mr. Faries climbed a ladder up the mast, inspecting as he went, until he reached the base of the spheres. My stomach lurched at the thought of having to do that myself.

"I don't see anything," he said. "You?"

"No," I said.

He climbed back down most of the way and then leaped to the deck.

"It must be on one of those two starboard spheres. I don't mind admitting, I'm not looking forward to inspecting them." He let out a sharp breath. "But there's nothing else for it."

He retrieved a coil of rope and tied one end around his waist, then he hopped up onto the rail and climbed out onto the ratlines. I barely breathed as he carefully made his way up to the spheres, inspected their underside, and then climbed past them onto a platform. From there, he tossed down a short, knotted rope that clanged against the metal. He took hold of the rope and used it to walk out onto the spheres. He crossed one, scanning its surface, and then the other, before pulling himself back up, hand over hand, to the platform.

"I found it," he yelled down to me. "It's not big."

He returned to the ratlines, scrambled down to the deck, and untied the rope from his waist. "It should be a simple metal patch."

"How will you secure it?" I asked.

"The vacuum in the sphere will suck it tight, but I'll solder it to seal the edges." He shook his head. "Which means we're going to have to land the *de Terzi*."

"Why?"

"The fire I need to heat the solder isn't safe on the ship. If anything catches fire, we could all burn up before we hit the ground. I'll go below and tell your father."

He trudged away, and I coiled the rope he had just used and hung it over a belaying pin. Jane came up on deck then, and I decided to go talk with her, even though I wasn't sure what to say. But when she saw me, she waved, and before I could greet her she spoke.

"Billy, I was just looking for you."

"You were?"

"I wanted to thank you for coming to find me. I was lost in the woods." She stepped closer. "But I heard you calling my name, and that was how I found you."

I remembered the way her breath felt when she whispered in my ear. And I remembered the smell of lavender in her hair when I whispered in hers. Was I just imagining that now?

"It was brave of you to come for me." Her lip started quivering. "I'm so sorry I put you and your father at risk."

"Please, don't apologize —"

"No, I must. It was my fault. It's all my fault."

I still didn't know what to say to her.

She turned and walked away with tears in her eyes.

"We need to land the ship to make repairs," my father said, addressing us all that night. "But we can't land until we've put a safe distance between us and Marin."

"What kind of distance?" Mr. Kinnersley asked.

"They're paddling with the river," my father said. "Which means they'll make good time. But they can't match our speed. If we stay aloft for two or three more days, we should have enough time on the ground for Mr. Faries to complete his work."

"They're confined to the river," Mr. Godfrey said. "But we are not. Why not simply strike out overland?"

"We need to follow the river for the time being," my father said. "It is the surest way to reach the Mississippi, which will then lead us to the Missouri. From there, we will strike west in search of Madoc's people. Perhaps by then, Marin will have given up his pursuit. Are we agreed?"

"Agreed," came the reply, in unison.

"We must rely on Andrew," my father said, "our . . . guide. To help us find a suitable place to land."

Andrew accepted this with a nod.

My father then outlined the watches for the night, and after a solemn supper, everyone retired. I tried to get a few hours of sleep, but was unable to. I heard, or at least imagined that I heard, Jane's muffled sobbing on the other side of the curtain, and it kept me awake.

Midnight found me with Mr. Godfrey, yawning, facing the next four hours of the middle watch. Since we were supposed to follow the river, rather than the compass, we had to keep a sharper lookout than previously, and make adjustments as the river changed its mind. Mr. Godfrey took the helm, and I positioned myself at the bow, so I could alert him as needed to alter course.

That left me alone for long stretches, facing the horizon with nothing but my thoughts. Earlier, my father had tried to reassure Jane with the promise that Mr. Colden was on his way back to Philadelphia. But I think everyone in that room had known the truth. Mr. Colden might be dead. Or captured.

"How does the river look, Billy?" Mr. Godfrey called.

I snapped my attention back to the ground. The river had already bent to the northeast. I scanned to see if it would right itself and double back, but in the darkness I couldn't tell. I grunted and stalked down the deck.

"We need to turn, sir," I said, pointing.

"Aye!" Mr. Godfrey said, taking obvious delight in both the word and the action of turning the wheel.

I trimmed the sails the way Mr. Colden had shown me, and I was about to resume my post, but Mr. Godfrey called to me again.

"Why so dour, Billy?"

Why was he in such high spirits? "Mr. Colden, sir. And Jane." The smile dropped away. "Of course. His is a tremendous loss to this expedition. And to Jane. But I suspect he is alive and well back at the Forks. The French were after this ship, and the moment we took to the air they took to the water in pursuit."

That offered me a measure of reassurance. "I hope you are right, sir."

"I am right," he said. "And now I have a question for you. Why does your father think ill of the Indian?"

An uncomfortable shrug seized my shoulders. "I don't know."

"There is something personal in his hatred."

"Nothing that I know of, sir."

"You came on this expedition to be with him, didn't you?"

"Yes, sir." Though as I thought about his question, and about how I felt toward my father now, my answer felt less true than it had when we started. "I wish to be a botanist."

"I have no sons to take after me. Nor daughters to dote on me in my old age."

"I'm sorry, sir. You never married?"

He sighed. "No. For much of my life, I gave little thought to such earthly matters. A wasted youth spent chasing dead Greeks. I suppose that is why I came on this expedition."

"How so, Mr. Godfrey?"

He gripped the ship's wheel, his earlier glee returning. "I wanted to feel young again."

CHAPTER 12

Incognitum

Over the next two days, the more I thought about it, the more I believed Mr. Godfrey had to be right. Mr. Colden was safe.

The Ohio River meandered south and west below us. The country to either side of the river alternated between lowland meadows and densely forested hills, the peaks of which appeared to dangerously approach our keel. I was adjusting to the rhythms of manning the ship, and some of the tasks had started to become routine. Boring, even. Between my watches and those times when I had chores to do, there wasn't much to occupy me.

So I made drawings. And it felt good to have the quill back in my hand and to feel the paper beneath my fingertips. Mostly, I drew whatever I saw below us. Like the Indians fishing from their canoes, traveling up and down the river. Or the occasional village near its banks. I can't imagine what they must have thought of our ship. I don't know what I would have thought, other than to doubt my own senses. But one thing I was sure of: Marin would only need to follow the trail of wide eyes and shocked expressions to find us.

On the morning of the third day since leaving the Forks, my father proposed landing the *de Terzi* for repairs.

"I advise against landing in this country," Andrew said. We had all gathered in a circle on deck.

"Why?" my father asked.

"There's a large salt lick down there that is well-known to the people of this region. And we are very near the old migration routes of the *incognitum*. We are more likely to encounter armed hunting parties, here."

My father turned to Mr. Faries. "What are your thoughts?"

Mr. Faries looked up at the spheres. "I'm reluctant to travel much farther. To maintain our elevation, I've had to take more air out of the three good spheres to compensate for the damaged one. I'm afraid of what that strain will do to them if we don't land soon."

Phineas tucked his blond hair back behind his ears. "Andrew, you mentioned a salt lick down there. Are there mineral springs?"

Andrew nodded. "There are."

Phineas turned to my father. "I would like to land here, John."

"What do you think, Francis?" my father asked.

Mr. Godfrey stood against the rail, looking over the side. "I have always wanted to see an *incognitum*. I vote we land." Andrew shook his head. I hadn't let myself start to trust him, yet, but I did wonder why the Society had wanted to bring a guide along if they were simply going to ignore him.

"I believe the matter is settled," my father said. "Mr. Faries, look for —"

"Does my opinion no longer matter?" Mr. Kinnersley spoke with a defiant chin held high.

"No, Ebenezer," my father said. "For your previous lapses in judgment, I do not wish for your counsel."

Mr. Kinnersley stamped his foot on the deck, like a child, and stormed below.

My father sighed. "As I was saying, Mr. Faries, look for a suitable place to set the *de Terzi* down."

"Yes, John."

The landing was much rougher than previously at Aughwick and the Forks. With one sphere not working, the ship lurched and swung, off-balance, until Mr. Faries was able to plop her down just a few feet off the ground. We had landed near the river, facing a dense and shadowed woodland. The sight of it set my skin tingling with the thought of men and beasts lurking beyond our sight, ready to strike when we turned our backs. We disembarked, gathered some dry driftwood, and made a fire.

Mr. Faries lowered his equipment down by pulley from the deck. As he began assembling it, my father called to everyone.

"I'd like to remain for as short a time as possible. Mr. Faries assures me he can have the repair made within a few hours. You have that time to do with as you please."

"Andrew," Phineas said, "would you be able to guide me to the mineral springs in this area?"

Andrew didn't answer at first. "I believe so, yes."

"Good." Phineas swung a small pack over his back that chimed with the sound of empty glass bottles. "Lead the way."

"My gun is on the ship," Andrew said, though I saw his powder horn at his side.

"Let us venture without it," Phineas said. "Unencumbered by emblems of fear."

He and Andrew stepped into the forest, and within a few paces it had swallowed them.

"Come, Billy." My father put on his wide-brimmed hat and thumped his walking stick. "You and I shall gather some specimens."

"Yes, sir," I said, and fell in behind him.

We entered the woods and came under its canopy of endless dusk. It felt oppressive and even sinister, but the sight of my father's back proceeding through the brush and trees ahead reassured me. I was doing what I had always wanted to do, following him into the wild places.

His gaze swung from side to side. "These are common trees." He pointed with his walking stick. "*Liriodendron tulipifera. Gleditsia triacanthos. Magnolia acuminata.*" In those few words, he wove a spell. "Do you recognize them?"

I studied the trees he indicated. They did look familiar, especially the one with the jagged and evil-looking three-inch thorns. "They're all in your garden."

"They are," he said. "I have them all."

Apparently, even when my father wasn't finding something new, coming across a plant he already possessed brought its own satisfaction.

"But keep your eyes open, son. You must let yourself be guided by evidence and fact. As Linnaeus wrote, 'All that truly can be known by us depends on a clear method by which we distinguish the similar from the dissimilar.' You must learn to see the world that way. The blossom with six petals instead of five. The leaf with serrated edges, rather than smooth. Once you start to see them, those differences sound a clarion call and are all you notice."

Was that how he looked at Andrew, too?

I followed him for some time, up hills, through glades. He stopped often to study a flower or a bush or a weed or the bark of a tree. But to each he eventually said, "Ah," as if recognizing an old acquaintance.

It went on that way for an hour. An hour that settled into monotony.

Before, when I used to imagine exploring with him, I never thought about this part. The countless specimens he had to sift through to find just one undiscovered and unclassified jewel. And I was beginning to grow bored.

But then, without any warning or preamble, he bent over a flower and whooped. "Look at this!"

I examined it, and even though I didn't know enough for it to appear remarkable to me, I grinned with him, catching his excitement and joy.

"Beautiful," he said. He took out a small trowel from his bag and dug up the plant by its roots. He then wrapped it and put it gently into his bag. "You'll draw it back on the ship."

"Yes, sir."

After that, we began finding new plants with greater frequency. Two new trees, whose leaves and seeds my father pressed in a book. A new shrub, from which he took a cutting. And two more flowers, which also ended up in his bag.

We eventually emerged from the forest onto a large, sodden meadow that held a spring. The ground around it had turned to mud and marsh in places, and the grass and reeds grew tall. Mosquitoes and flies clogged the air with their swarms.

"This is part of the lick," my father said. "Animals gather here to lick the salt and other minerals that come from the spring."

I looked around and noticed dozens of animal tracks in the mud. Deer, raccoon, and even little bird scratches. But then I saw a round, deep indentation. It was large, the size of a platter. And then I saw another. And another. My perspective widened, and I realized they were everywhere, layer upon layer, all around us. Beneath our feet. My own boot print fit easily inside them.

"Are these . . . tracks?" I asked.

My father studied them. "Yes. *Incognitum* tracks."

I suddenly felt very small standing there, imagining the marshy meadow filled with a herd of the towering animals, their tusks and trunks swinging low.

"This was a large herd," my father said. "It is rare to see so many together. They must have come for the salt lick and then moved on. By the looks of it, they're heading west."

"Like us," I said.

"Yes, like us. Perhaps, if we're lucky, we'll see them. But judging by the state of these tracks, they were here some time ago."

I hadn't taken my eyes from the ground. What would they sound like on the move, all those beasts? I crouched down to put my hand inside one of the footprints, and noticed another track. It was almost as large as the *incognitum* print, but it had toes. And dagger points in front of those.

Claws.

But there was only one animal I knew of with paws that size.

"Father?" I pointed at it. "What kind of animal made that?"

My father looked at it, and then jerked upright, scanning the forest. "We should get back to the ship."

His reaction confirmed what I feared. But I needed him to say it. "What is it?"

"Come, son." He pushed me forward.

"Father."

"It is a bear-wolf, Billy. Now, hurry."

On the way back to the ship, I jumped at the snap of every twig, and every rustled leaf sounded like the breath of a bear-wolf lurking in the trees. I had never seen one before, but I had seen their eight-inch claws, and I could imagine the rest. Seven feet tall on all four paws, twelve feet when standing on its hind legs. It was said they could run as fast as a horse, and their jaws could crush *incognitum* bones.

"Father —"

"No talking," my father whispered.

He led us swiftly back the way we'd come, and before long we reached the river. Mr. Faries dangled in front of the spheres, suspended in a leather harness. Mr. Kinnersley stood on deck, passing up equipment to him by rope and pulley. Mr. Godfrey sat on a log by the fire as Jane cooked something in an iron kettle over the coals.

My father called to Mr. Faries. "How close are you to being finished, William?"

"Ten minutes!" he said.

My father nodded. "Jane, you need to pack up whatever it is you're doing there. Quickly, now."

"Beg your pardon, Mr. Bartram," Jane said. "But the stew isn't ready yet."

"You'll have to leave it," my father said.

"What's the matter, John?" Mr. Godfrey asked.

"Billy spotted a bear-wolf track," my father said. "It appeared fresh."

Mr. Godfrey stood. "How fresh?"

"Fresh enough. Even five miles away, it will still be able to smell us, and especially the food on that cook-fire. It could be upon us in no time at all."

Jane looked at the kettle. "I'm sorry."

My father ignored her. "Is Phineas back yet?"

"He and Andrew haven't returned," Mr. Godfrey said.

My father looked up and down the line of trees. "Let's get everything else loaded. We need to be ready to pull up the ladder as soon as they're on board. With any luck, the beast will be on the trail of the *incognitum*, but we should take no chances. We are in no position to fight off a bear-wolf."

He and Mr. Godfrey went to Mr. Faries's equipment and began to break it down, while Mr. Kinnersley helped lift it up to the deck. Jane was looking at her stew.

"Sorry," I said.

"I think I'll dump it in the river for the fish," she said.

"Jane," my father said. "Please board the ship now. It will be safer there. You, too, Billy."

So I was supposed to go with the girl now.

"I suppose we should do as he says." Jane hoisted the kettle down to the river and tipped its steaming contents into the water. Then she lugged the empty pot to my father to be lifted up with the other gear.

"Coming?" She took hold of the rope ladder.

"Coming," I said, though I begrudged each step I took toward her.

By the time I had reached the base of the ladder, she was almost to the top. And then someone yelled behind me.

"Bear-wolf!"

I spun. Phineas came sprinting out of the forest down the river from us, followed by Andrew. And behind them charged the behemoth. A surging mass of brown fur and power. When it hit the riverbank, it saw all of us. It saw the ship. And it stopped. Then its broad jaws opened in a roar, exposing its fangs. But it didn't come at us. Instead, it stood up on its hind legs, towering twice as tall as the tallest man I'd ever seen, and roared again.

"Everyone on the ship," my father hissed. "Quickly."

"What about the equipment?" Mr. Godfrey said. A pile of Mr. Faries's gear remained to be loaded.

"Leave it," my father said. "Billy, go now."

I struggled up the ladder, one eye over my shoulder.

The bear-wolf dropped to all fours. It sniffed the air, its huge nostrils lifting and flaring. It paced back and forth, inching closer.

I reached the deck and scrambled over the rail. Below me, Phineas started climbing.

The bear-wolf seemed to be overcoming whatever apprehension had kept it at bay. It approached directly now, pausing and sniffing along the way.

Phineas reached the top, and my father pushed Andrew toward the ladder.

"Up you go," he said.

The bear-wolf roared again, a different sound this time. An angry sound. It charged right at my father.

"Look out!" I yelled.

But Andrew pushed my father aside and flung something into the fire just as the bear-wolf reached it. A bright flash, an explosion of flame and smoke, and the bear-wolf backed away. *Gunpowder.* The animal's roar sounded of pain and confusion.

"Go, Mr. Bartram!" Andrew shouted. He threw another handful of powder into the fire, and a second explosion sent the bear-wolf back another few feet.

My father shot up the ladder, and once he'd reached the top, Andrew threw a third handful into the flames before making his own climb.

When he reached the top, we pulled him over.

"Mighty clever trick, young man," Mr. Godfrey said, panting.

By that time, the bear-wolf had skirted the fire and now circled the bottom of the rope ladder. As my father tried to pull it up, the bear-wolf snagged it with one of its paws and yanked it easily from its anchor on the ship. The whole length of it fell to the ground. The bear-wolf sniffed it and then approached the hull of our vessel.

"Mr. Faries!" my father shouted.

Mr. Faries still hung up in the rigging, working furiously on the spheres.

"How soon?" my father asked.

"Two minutes!" Mr. Faries shouted back.

The bear-wolf stood on its hind legs, looked up at us, and slammed both of its front paws against the ship's hull with its full weight. The *de Terzi* jolted, and I felt the reverberation through my boots.

"We don't have two minutes!" my father shouted. "That thing is strong enough to crack the hull!"

The bear-wolf heaved itself against the ship a second time, and I heard the sound of wood splintering.

"I'm working as fast as I can!" Mr. Faries shouted. "Someone take the helm!"

Mr. Kinnersley raced to the controls. "I'll do it!"

"Wait for my mark!" Mr. Faries said.

The ship thundered with a third blow from the bear-wolf. The animal roared, and something in it sounded triumphant. Almost as if it had realized it was breaking through.

"Mr. Faries?" my father said.

"Now!" Mr. Faries said, letting a rope loose in his harness. I shouted in alarm as he plummeted toward the deck, but he pulled the rope tight just as he was about to hit and stopped his fall.

Mr. Kinnersley threw a lever, and the *de Terzi* eased upward out of the bear-wolf's reach. We all looked over the edge, watching the animal grow smaller as our ship moved slowly down the river, and I began to feel safe enough to relax a little. But the bear-wolf pursued us, never taking its eyes from us as it stalked down the riverbank, parallel with the ship. The beast wasn't giving up any more than the French had.

"Mr. Faries," my father said, "deploy the sails."

"Aye," Mr. Faries said, staring at the bear-wolf. He went to the controls, raised the sails, and we jumped forward on the wind.

But still the bear-wolf came. It galloped after us, matching our speed, and it was fast. As fast as a horse. I stared at it in disbelief, but as we increased our own speed, the animal fell farther and farther behind. I eventually lost sight of it in the trees, but even then, in that last moment, it was still running.

Still hunting us.

CHAPTER 13

Repaired

"It would seem," Mr. Godfrey said, "that we are now being pursued by both the French and a bear-wolf."

"It would seem that way," my father said. "We can only hope the two parties meet one day. For now, all we can do is continue to put distance between us and them. The French are still far behind us, and the bear-wolf will have a difficult time not only tracking our scent but also traversing the terrain below."

"Your escape was narrow, John," Phineas said.

I looked at Andrew. Were it not for his quick action, it was likely my father would have been killed. I felt a sickening weight in my chest at the thought of it.

"Yes," my father said.

Phineas clapped Andrew on the back. "A brilliant tactic, that gunpowder, wouldn't you say?"

"Yes," my father said, but with little enthusiasm. It seemed the others waited for my father to say more, but he didn't.

Why could he not admit that Andrew had done an astounding thing and saved his life?

My father turned to Mr. Faries. "I take it the repair is complete?"

"It is." Mr. Faries squinted up at the spheres. "But I was rushed at the end and pray I made no mistakes." He looked back at us. "We left my equipment behind in the attack. Further repairs of this nature will be impossible."

"Understood," my father said. "We're safe now. I suggest we resume normal activity, and continue to follow the river."

Everyone agreed and went their separate ways, that is, as separate as they could be aboard the ship. I caught up with my father as he went below to the Science Deck. He set his bag on his desk and began to unpack his specimens, the ones we had found together. Even after what had just happened, he hadn't forgotten about his plants.

"Father," I said.

"Hm," he said.

"I . . ." I lost the words.

"Yes, Billy?"

"I'm — I'm just relieved you're unhurt."

One corner of his mouth smiled. "As am I."

There was something else I had to say to feel honest and right with myself. "I'm grateful to Andrew," I said. Then I winced inside and waited for his response.

"Yes," he said. "I am grateful as well." But his voice did not sound grateful.

I pressed him further. "He saved you."

"And he saved himself. Do not forget that." My father went back to his specimens. "I have to see to these. When I am finished, you will draw them. Understood?"

He may have saved himself, but Andrew sent you up the ladder first. "Yes, sir."

"I will summon you when they are ready for you."

I was being dismissed. "Yes, sir."

My father remained working at his desk, while I went up on the weather deck. I felt the need for air and openness. I couldn't understand why he treated Andrew so poorly, but I had to believe he had cause for his actions. There was no other way to reconcile the father I knew from this father I didn't recognize. Perhaps one day he would explain his reasons to me.

But having watched the bear-wolf charge at him, and having feared he was about to die, I felt even worse for Jane in her ordeal with her own father. So I sought her out.

I found her sitting at the stern of the ship, staring at the countryside behind us. I sat down next to her, but didn't dare disturb her thoughts. Several long moments passed.

"I didn't think it would be like this," she finally said. "I wanted to come mostly because I heard you were coming."

What did she mean by that? "Oh?"

"Yes. I didn't think it was fair."

Oh.

"And now my father is missing. Yours was almost killed by a bear-wolf." She closed her eyes. "What a fool I am."

"You're not a fool," I said. "Your father certainly doesn't think so." I thought back to all the things he had said about her that night we shared a watch, and I remembered something that gave me an idea. "My father asked me to draw some specimens we collected. I could use some help."

Her eyes opened. "It feels like weeks since I've made a drawing."

"Would you like to make one now?"

She chewed on one of her fingernails. "Yes. I think so."

"Good."

She stood slowly, and we went below. My father was just finishing, so I took out some paper and sharpened two quills. After he left, we each took one of the flowers and began to draw.

It was hard for me to concentrate on mine. I kept sneaking glances at Jane and her drawing. She seemed to be completely engrossed in the petals and the stem and the leaves. Her drawing was very, very good. Much better than mine, I had to admit.

I leaned over to her. "That's very good."

"Thank you."

"Your father said you were more talented than me, and I think he may have been right."

She looked down. Tears gathered in her eyes, and I panicked. What had I said wrong?

"It's a very nice drawing," I said again.

She covered her face with her hands and cried. "It's all my fault, Billy."

"Don't say that."

"But it is. If I hadn't disobeyed and left the ship, none of this would have happened. My father would still be here."

She sat there, sobbing, hugging herself. This was a time a sister or a brother or a parent might put his or her arm around her and comfort her. But I didn't know how to do that, or even if I should. So I lifted my arm up in an offer I only half meant, and seeing that, Jane leaned into me. I gave her a hug and patted her on the back, and tried not to hold her too tight.

"It's not your fault," I said. "You couldn't have known the French would be there. *They're* the enemy."

She nodded against my shoulder, and a moment later, she pulled away. Her nose was running. She realized it, looked around, shrugged, and then smeared it on her sleeve.

She laughed. "First I dress like a boy, and now I wipe my nose like one."

"Next you'll be spitting off the side of the ship and singing bawdy ballads."

She smacked my arm. "Don't be crude."

"Ow." I chuckled. "Sorry."

She lifted an eyebrow at me, but a moment later it came down. "I just hope he's safe."

"I'm sure he is."

She returned to her drawing, and I returned to mine. I found it easier to focus and had soon finished it to my satisfaction. I still didn't think it quite as nice as Jane's, but it was good. After we had both finished, we moved on to the next plants, and the next, until we had drawn all the new specimens.

I sat back, satisfied. "Thank you for your help."

"You are welcome," she said. "It was a pleasant distraction."

Up on the weather deck, I discovered the sun had dropped almost to the horizon. Our work with the specimens had taken up the rest of the afternoon and the beginnings of the evening. I found my father and told him the drawings were finished.

"You drew them all?" he asked.

"Jane helped me," I said.

"I see. Good. It was right that you asked her. I think Mr. Colden would appreciate that."

I nodded. "Do you really believe he's safe? Like you told Jane?"

"Well . . ." My father looked from side to side and lowered his voice. "I don't know, Billy. I told her what I pray to be true. And I do not make it habit to pray for things that appear completely out of reach." He clasped my shoulder. "Try not to worry."

"Yes, sir."

He left, and I remained there. I was assigned the first watch, which began before the sun had set, so I was able to watch its decline. The stars appeared, and I wondered if Jane would be able to acquaint me with them the way her father had promised to do.

Andrew appeared beside me. "It seems it's you and me for the first watch."

A slight panic seized me. Andrew and I had never shared a watch, something I suspected my father had engineered when he arranged the schedule. "I thought it was Phineas's turn."

"He asked if I'd swap with him. He prefers the middle watch."

"He does?" I tried to keep my discomfort from showing. "I hate the middle watch."

"Me, too. I have to wake up when it feels like I've just fallen asleep, and by the end of it, I have to prop my eyes open. But afterward, when I finally hit my hammock, I can't seem to get any rest."

I knew exactly what he meant. "Did you tell my father about the switch?"

"No. Should I?"

I knew my father would change the watch if he knew. But I didn't want him to. Andrew made me nervous, but I felt somehow guilty about that. I wanted it to be acceptable that I shared a watch with him, to me most of all. So I resolved to do it and forced a stiff shrug. "I wouldn't worry about it."

Andrew accepted this with a nod. "All right, then."

"All right," I said.

But I didn't know what to say after that.

"This is a —" he started, but stopped.

"What's that?" I asked.

He shook his head.

"Please, speak," I said.

"Well. This is a very . . . peculiar group of men."

I found myself chuckling. "You are right about that."

"Electrical fire, a flying ship, bottles and bottles of spring water." He scratched his forehead. "When I was out there in the woods with Phineas, going from pool to pool, I kept wondering if he was playing a prank at my expense."

I chuckled again. "I don't think most of these men know what a prank is, and I can tell you with certainty that electrical fire is not a joke."

"Oh, I've kept my distance from Mr. Kinnersley ever since he shocked you."

"A wise decision," I said, already feeling much more at ease than I had a few moments ago.

"Have you ever seen a bear-wolf before today?" Andrew asked.

"No." I thought back to its size, its ferocity, its awful strength. "And if it hadn't almost killed my father, I think I would admire it."

He looked away in thought. "I admire it."

"But it almost killed you, too."

"That's true. But what if it's starving right now and needed to eat us to live?"

"It looked plenty healthy to me."

"I suppose it did. And if I hadn't left my gun behind, I would have tried to shoot it, for the little good it would have done me and your father. Bear-wolves don't go down easy." He turned to me. "Why are there no guns on the ship?"

"The *de Terzi* is a vessel of philosophy. Not a ship of war. That's what my father says."

"That is a good point. If Major Washington had wanted to conscript this ship, and I think he did, guns or cannons on board would have justified him. Perhaps I shouldn't have brought my rifle."

"I'm glad you have it." Without it, he would not have had his gunpowder. I cleared my throat. "I need to thank you for saving my father. I owe you a debt of gratitude."

"You owe me nothing," he said.

But that wasn't true. I also owed him an apology, though he didn't know it. I had doubted him without evidence and thought ill of him without cause. I still didn't know whether I could fully trust him, but until he gave me reason not to, I decided that I would. Hadn't my father said that I must be guided by evidence and fact? Well, it was a fact that he had saved my father's life, and I wanted my father to be wrong about him.

"I do owe you," I said. I wanted to say more, but I wasn't brave enough to find the words.

"Your gratitude is payment enough. And what I said before, I didn't mean to speak ill of the philosophers. They have been gracious and accepting of me. Which is more than I can say for many other white men."

Men like my father.

"But you are half-French, aren't you?" I asked.

"I have no country," he said. "The Indian looks at me and sees a white man. The white man looks at me and sees an Indian. They're both right and they're both wrong."

And I saw that for myself. His clothing bespoke a Pennsylvania farmer, while the pendants and wire in his ears glinted in the cold moonlight. When looking at Andrew, you could see what you wanted to see. What you were prepared to see.

But his appearance made me wonder something else. How would it be to not belong anywhere? To always feel like an outsider?

"Living on the border of two nations has made me a good interpreter," he said. "My mother was an interpreter, and she raised me to be one."

"Croghan said your mother was Madame Montour."

He nodded.

"She was French?"

His smile was one-sided and mischievous. "That depends on who you ask. She never told the same version of her story twice. Even to me. But yes, I believe her father was French, though she was raised among the Six Nations."

"Why would she tell different stories?"

"She did not want others to know where she came from."

"Why?"

"I don't know." He paused. "But she was a good woman. A stern woman, but loving, and a respected interpreter. I only hope to meet her expectations of me."

Upon hearing him, I realized that I might easily say something very similar about my father. Andrew and I were both walking in the paths laid down by our parents before us.

"Tomorrow we'll fly over a ridge," Andrew said. "It has high stone walls around it. No one knows who built them. Perhaps it was your Madoc?"

Stone walls? A fortress? "Perhaps," I said. "Tomorrow, we should tell my father."

CHAPTER 14

Mist and Stone

When I came up onto the deck the next morning, yawning, I noticed the storm brooding ahead. We all did. It crouched on the horizon, black and baleful, waiting for us to get close enough before it pounced.

"Our first storm," my father said. "It's too big to fly around. But this was expected. Prepare the ship as we planned."

"We may not be able to do as we planned," Mr. Faries said.

My father turned to him. "Why not?"

"Our strategy in dealing with storms would have been to fly above them, rather than through or below them. With the damage the ship sustained, I'm not certain it will be safe to attempt the necessary elevation. My repair may not hold."

"I see." My father cupped his elbow with one hand and cradled his chin with the other. He glanced around at the assembled group. "Suggestions?"

"We fly through it," Mr. Kinnersley said with what I took to be excitement. "Right into its heart."

"I would recommend we fly beneath it," Mr. Faries said. "Low to the ground. I believe the ship can handle it if I'm at the helm."

My father nodded.

Andrew stepped forward. "May I make a suggestion?"

My father didn't look at him, but he said, "Of course."

"We could land and wait it out."

My father's hands fell to his sides. "What?"

Andrew pointed westward. "That is a powerful storm. It might be safest to avoid it altogether."

"Are you mad?" my father asked. "The French are coming down the river after us, we have a bear-wolf on our trail, and you think it prudent to land and wait? For what? For them to catch us?"

"Just until the storm passes," Andrew said. "There is a place. I spoke with Billy about it last night during our watch, and he thought you should know of it."

My father turned to me. "You shared a watch with Andrew?"

I gave him a firm, defiant nod. "I did. You should hear him out, Father."

My father leaned away from me. "Is that so?" His voice held no anger. No judgment. Only disappointment.

My resolve faltered, but I said, "Yes, Father."

He paused. Then he turned to Andrew. "What is it that I should know?"

Andrew's gaze roamed among the gathering. "Ahead of us, there is a ridge surrounded by a high stone wall. Rumor and legend suggest it was once the site of a fortress, but no one knows who built it. Perhaps it was made by your Madoc. It might be wise to examine it while we wait out the storm."

A jolt ran through the Society members, as though they'd been shocked by Mr. Kinnersley's electrical fire.

"Describe these walls you mentioned," Mr. Godfrey said.

"I have not seen them myself," Andrew said. "But they are said to be made of tightly stacked stones, without mortar."

"That manner of construction would be consistent with a Welsh origin," Mr. Godfrey said.

"You think we should land?" my father asked.

Mr. Godfrey nodded. "I do."

"I'm inclined to agree," Phineas said. "If we gain some intelligence on the subject of Madoc while also avoiding the danger of the storm, would that not be worth the risk of landing?"

"I would rather stay in the air." Mr. Kinnersley shot his pointed hand straight forward. "Fly through the storm."

My father turned to Mr. Faries. "William?"

"It's your decision, John. Though I do have concerns for the ship. And our mission is to find Madoc, after all."

During the discussion, the storm clouds had reared up, even darker.

"Where is this ridge?" my father asked.

Andrew looked over the side. "We should reach it within the hour."

"I will make my decision when we arrive," my father said. "Until then, prepare the ship for the storm."

We all set to work stowing, tying, and covering. Jane and I helped Phineas wrap sheets of oilcloth around the instruments to protect them from the rain. When we had finished, we stood at the bow watching the land ahead. Mr. Faries brought us down low, and we swept along a bluff, perhaps two hundred feet high, that buttressed the eastern shore. Black forest smothered every inch of ground and filled every crevice.

"There." Andrew pointed.

Ahead of us, a smaller creek joined up with the Ohio River, running a tight parallel to it in such a way that it almost pinched off a section of the ridge, forming a tear-shaped peninsula of high ground.

"That is the place," Andrew said.

My father squinted down at it. He turned to us. "Bear-wolf and the French notwithstanding, our mission is to find Madoc. If something can be learned of his people down there, we are obliged to risk the pursuit of it."

Mr. Kinnersley scowled, but everyone else appeared to be in agreement.

Mr. Faries brought the *de Terzi* around the tip of the peninsula and set her down in one of the few open patches of ground near the river. By the time he had let go the anchor and brought us to a halt, thick woolen clouds had moved in and covered the sky. Distant thunder rumbled.

"I will not have the same mistakes repeated," my father said. "There will be no independent excursions. Those who leave the ship must remain in company. Mr. Faries, if you'll pardon me, I wish for you to remain on board so as to keep the ship ready for immediate flight."

Mr. Faries accepted this with a nod.

"At any sign of danger," my father continued, "storm or not, I want you to leave us behind and take her up. Understood?"

Mr. Faries hesitated. "Yes, John."

"Jane," my father said. "It is my duty to keep you safe. You will remain on board as well."

Jane accepted this with a curt nod, and given what had happened at the Forks, I didn't think she would disobey such an order again.

"Andrew." My father clenched his jaw. "Bring your rifle."

"Yes, sir," Andrew said, and left to retrieve it from below.

I waited for my father to order me to stay on the ship as well, ready to argue with him, but he never did. Perhaps I had demonstrated the value of having me along. Or perhaps he simply wanted me close by him in the event of another attack.

Mr. Kinnersley decided to remain with Jane and Mr. Faries, which left Phineas, Mr. Godfrey, Andrew, and myself in my father's party. We descended a new rope ladder, a spare that had replaced the one ripped down by the bear-wolf. On the ground, by the river's shore, we peered into a gray mist that had crept in ahead of the storm and made the dense woodland of yew, hickory, and giant hemlock even more impenetrable.

"Stay close together," my father said. "Andrew, lead the way."

Andrew held his rifle at the ready and stepped into the trees. The rest of us advanced in a column behind him. The mist grew thicker among the trees, a shroud that seemed to muffle every sound. Tree trunks and branches loomed out of it with little warning, and the uneven ground of roots and rocks tried to trip me at every step. My eyelashes gathered droplets of moisture. I breathed the heavy air and focused on the shape of my father ahead of me, resisting the childish urge to grab hold of his coattails.

We marched and stumbled down into a ravine, followed the bed of a trickling stream, then climbed upward, grunting and whispering. Within a short distance I felt very far from the *de Terzi*, and from Jane. The fear that quickened my heartbeat was not the nervousness I felt at the Forks prior to the French attack, nor the panic that followed, but something nameless and more menacing. The deeper we pressed into the forest, and the higher we climbed, the tighter it gripped me.

"Where are the animals?" Phineas whispered behind me. "I haven't even heard a bird."

"Quiet," my father hissed.

But Phineas was right. Something about this place felt wrong.

We continued upward, well past what I guessed would have been the highest point of the *de Terzi's* tallest mast. Were it not for the mist, we might have been able to look back down on her from above.

"Halt," Andrew said.

I nearly ran into my father, who had stopped in front of me.

"It is here, Mr. Bartram," Andrew said.

I strained to see through the mist and took a step forward.

And the wall emerged.

The seemingly endless expanse of stone faded into the fog above us and to either side. It beckoned me to follow it, to chase its edges into the gray void. It had been made as Andrew described. A fortification of flat, tightly packed stones, without mortar. But the wall had fallen into a state of disrepair, collapsed in places, sprouting trees and weeds. A ghostly quality hung about it, ruined, ancient, and somehow untouchable. So I reached out my hand to make sure it was real. The stone felt very cold beneath my fingers.

The others had done the same. My father, Phineas, and Andrew, their arm's-length contact with the wall appeared tentative, while Mr. Godfrey's seemed almost reverent. He eyed it up and down the way my father admired a beautiful plant.

"What do you make of it, Francis?" my father asked.

"Difficult to say." Mr. Godfrey's mouth hung open as he studied the stone. "It could be Welsh. Or it could be of Indian origin."

"Truly?" My father turned to Andrew. "Do you think your people could have built this?"

I winced, but Andrew appeared unbothered. Perhaps he was simply accustomed to it.

"I do not know who built it," Andrew said.

"What do you think, Phineas?" My father asked.

"Phineas?"

I looked to where Phineas had been standing, but he was no longer there.

"Phineas!" My father called.

We waited.

"I'm here!" came a reply. "I . . . wanted to follow the wall. Come see this, John."

"Wait here," my father said. He walked away in the direction from which we had heard Phineas's voice.

"What do you suppose is on the other side?" Mr. Godfrey asked, looking upward.

I shivered. The mist had slinked in through my clothes and reached my skin. I didn't want to know what was on the other side of the wall. Such things were built to keep things out, but also to keep things in.

Time passed, and my father and Phineas hadn't returned.

"Where do you think they are?" Andrew asked.

"I don't know," Mr. Godfrey said.

"Father!" I called.

No response came.

"Perhaps we should go after them," Andrew said.

"You go that way," Mr. Godfrey said. He started in the opposite direction, tracing the wall with his hand. "I'll go this way."

Andrew called to him. "I think perhaps we should —"

But Mr. Godfrey was already gone, dissolved in the mist.

"Stay with me, Billy." Andrew renewed his grasp on his rifle and started forward in the direction my father had gone.

I followed behind him, though not as close as I had followed my father before. I studied the wall as I walked, the irregular precision in the placement of its individual stones, no two alike. Gradually, the way they fit together into a whole assumed a kind of pattern. And then I thought I heard something. A low murmuring.

I stopped. "What is that?"

Andrew looked back at me. "What is what?"

"That. It sounds like voices."

Andrew tipped his head up and held it still. A moment later he said, "I hear nothing. Let's go."

The sound was coming from my right. From the wall. I leaned toward it, and it grew louder. Were they voices? They seemed to be shouting. Screaming. But heard at a great distance. I leaned in closer, until my ear was almost touching the stone. I thought I heard the clang of metal, grunts and groans, as though a battle were being fought on the other side of the wall. I leaned away, and the sound faded.

Ahead of me, I could still see Andrew creeping forward through the fog.

I put my ear against the stone and closed my eyes.

The sounds I had heard before returned, and the voices assaulted me. I gasped. I did not know the language in which they spoke, or even if they spoke in words, but I understood them. Pain, rage, and grief require no translation. It was as though the echo of a great war had become trapped in the stone, the rock itself crying out in anguish and blood. Was I imagining it?

"Andrew," I whispered. "Come listen to this." I opened my eyes.

Andrew was gone.

I leaped away from the wall.

"Andrew?"

I was alone. I set off at a trot along the wall, thinking I would catch up with him.

But I didn't.

"Andrew!" I shouted. And then, "Father!"

More wall. And more wall. And no one else.

I stopped. Would it be better to keep going? Or should I wait here? Andrew would realize he had left me behind, wouldn't he?

A peal of thunder exploded overhead. It took the world by the throat and shook it, announcing the oncoming storm. I found it hard to breathe through my growing fear. The wall ran straight. If I followed it, I would have to reach someone eventually, Andrew or my father.

And then I heard a different sound. Not from the wall, but from the forest. A deep, rumbling breath, almost a growl. Leaves and branches cracked and crunched under something very heavy as it moved through the trees. *It couldn't be.* And then I smelled the pungent musk of damp fur. *How could it have found us?*

I backed up tight against the wall and held my body still, staring into the blank mist, my eyes suggesting movement where there was none. The haze seemed to writhe around the smudged black tree trunks. And then a larger shadow lumbered into view.

I held my breath. A quivering seized my legs.

The shadow came closer. And then it stopped. It turned sideways and moved along the wall in the direction Mr. Godfrey had gone. I was just out of its view, and it out of mine, but I could make out the shifting silhouette of its head, the massive bulk of its body, and its long, long limbs. The bear-wolf had found us, and it was stalking through the woods but feet from where I stood. Could it not smell me?

It disappeared into the mist, and I waited, terrified, until I couldn't hear it anymore. And then I crept in the opposite direction, careful of each footstep, avoiding twigs and leaves. I hurried along the wall as quickly as I could, pausing with almost every step to listen, expecting to hear the roar of the beast and the crashing of its charge toward me.

But it never came. And eventually, I heard someone talking. Not the voices from the wall, but someone real. It was Phineas. And then I heard Andrew. And my father. They were speaking out loud, for anything to hear them. I hurried forward, and they materialized out of the mist, standing next to the wall.

They turned at my approach. My father smiled, and then I guessed he saw the expression on my face. "What is it, son?"

I formed my lips into words without speaking. *Bear-wolf.*

Their eyes all widened, scanning the fog.

"Are you sure?" my father whispered.

I nodded.

"Back to the ship," he said, and indicated the direction with the chop of his hand through the air.

"What about Mr. Godfrey?" Andrew asked. "He went off exploring in the other direction."

"That's the way the bear-wolf went," I said.

My father closed his eyes and dropped his chin to his chest. "We'll fire Andrew's rifle once we've reached the *de Terzi*. Hopefully Mr. Godfrey will interpret the signal, and the sound will drive the bear-wolf away, out of his path. Andrew, lead on."

Andrew nodded and skulked away into the trees. Phineas followed him, and then it was my turn. My father came after me. We traveled several hundred yards without any sign of pursuit, and I felt relief with every step closer to the ship.

A few moments later, Andrew yelped up ahead, and then so did Phineas as he appeared to vanish right into the ground.

"Father!" I called.

He rushed up beside me, and we pressed forward until we reached the spot where Phineas had gone down. It was the blunt edge of a fog-choked ravine.

"Phineas!" my father called down, a whisper-shout. "Andrew!"

"We're here," Phineas called from somewhere below.

"I'm sorry," Andrew said. "I couldn't see the ravine in the fog."

"Are either of you injured?" my father asked.

"Yes, but not badly," Phineas said.

"Good." My father looked to the left and right. "Billy and I will find a way down. You two continue on to the ship."

"Are you sure, John?" Phineas asked.

"Yes. Go, Phineas." My father marched up and down the ravine's edge, neck craning outward, studying the terrain. He stopped at one point and tapped his foot. "I think this is a good place. Are you ready, son?"

CHAPTER 15

A Message

I took a deep breath before stepping over the side. The ground fell away, steep and slippery, thick with undergrowth. I scrabbled down through it sideways, right foot first, my left hand gripping branches and roots.

"Easy now," my father said ahead of me. "Take it slowly."

I tested each placement of my foot before putting my weight on it, and then I waited until the last second to release my grip on whatever anchor I had before grasping for the next.

"I don't remember the ravine being so deep," I said.

"We crossed it farther east," he said. "But we should almost be to the bottom."

I stretched my foot downward, felt a rock beneath my boot, and trusted it. But it teetered and shifted. I lost my balance and fell, dropping past my father.

"Billy!"

"Help!" I yelled, sliding and toppling down the hill.

Branches whipped me, rocks bruised me. I managed to get my feet under me, but had too much momentum and fell forward on my face, smacking hard, getting a mouthful of dirt and leaves. But my body had stopped. I heard the gurgle of the stream and looked up. I had reached the bottom.

"Billy!" my father shouted.

"I'm down here!" I shouted back.

"Wait there," he said. "I'm coming."

I spat, rinsed my mouth with the stream water, but still chewed grit. The noise of my father's descent filled the ravine. A few moments later, he stumbled into view and rushed to me.

"Are you hurt?" He looked me over, feeling my arms, my shoulders.

"I don't think so."

And then we heard the bear-wolf roar. I could not tell where it came from, but the beast sounded close, somewhere above us.

"We must run," my father said. "Follow me closely."

He charged up the other side of the ravine, which wasn't as steep. We made the climb with our hands as much as our feet, and the muscles in my legs burned hot before we'd reached the top. As soon as we hit level ground, another deafening wave of thunder broke over our heads. We set off in the direction of the river, and within a few paces, the rain started.

I didn't feel it at first, but I heard it pattering against the leaves all around me. And then the first cold drops found my cheek and my neck. The rain had also begun to thin the fog, and we could see farther in front of us as we careened through the trees.

Before long, we broke from the woods onto the shore and into the open. Downriver, the *de Terzi* waited for us, a ghost-ship rising up through the falling mist.

A gunshot cracked the air, loud enough for anyone nearby to hear.

"Andrew," my father said.

We hurtled down the riverbank, slipping in the mud. We had almost reached the ship when I spotted something bobbing in the water against a piece of driftwood. I veered a little and snatched it up. It was a glass bottle. What was a bottle doing here?

"Are you with me?" my father asked.

"Yes, Father."

We skidded up to the rope ladder and made our ascent. I struggled, trying to hold on to the bottle, exhausted from the climb up the ravine and our sprint to safety. Phineas and Andrew waited at the top, both of them scratched and battered. My father followed behind me, and from the deck, we all looked out over the woodland, rain-soaked, listening.

Jane came up next to me, the wet curls of her hair stuck to her forehead and cheeks. "Where is Mr. Godfrey?"

I nodded toward the forest. "And the bear-wolf's out there, too."

"The bear-wolf?" Mr. Faries said.

"Be ready to fly, William," my father said.

The storm continued to gather, and the rain fell in earnest, hammering the copper spheres above us and slicking the deck wood. Every so often, we heard the bear-wolf roar, each time from a slightly different location. It was still on the move. Still hunting.

"Francis!" my father shouted through both cupped hands.

The forest remained still.

"What's that, Billy?" Phineas asked. He looked at the bottle still tucked in my arm.

"Oh." I had forgotten about it. "I found it in the water."

"May I see it?" he asked.

I was about to hand it to him when I heard a shout from the trees.

"I'm here!" Mr. Godfrey called. "I'm coming!"

"Francis, hurry!" my father yelled.

A moment later, Mr. Godfrey shuffled from the trees. He lurched toward the rope ladder, shaking his head. "I don't think I can climb it!"

"Take hold," Andrew shouted. "We'll pull you up!"

Mr. Godfrey locked a knee and an elbow around the rungs of the ladder, and Phineas and Andrew heaved him up. My father helped pull him over the rail, and he fell to the deck gasping and clutching his chest, his eyes closed.

The *de Terzi* shifted beneath my feet and rose, Mr. Faries at the helm, until we pressed up through the rain into the low-lying clouds, leaving the mist on the ground for the mist in the air. Water droplets seemed to permeate the air we breathed.

"Are you all right, Francis?" my father asked, kneeling down beside him.

"Yes." Mr. Godfrey wheezed. "Yes, I'm . . . I just need a moment."

Somewhere below us, the bear-wolf roared again, sounding more distant.

My father looked up at me. He gestured to the bottle. "Is that what you picked up from the river?"

"Yes." I handed it to him.

He rotated it in his hand. "It's corked. And there's something inside it." He bit down on the cork with his back teeth and pulled it out with a hollow squeak. Then he tipped the bottle into his hand, and something long and thin as a reed slipped out.

"What is it?" I asked.

My father set the bottle on the deck and gently examined the reed. "It's a piece of rolled paper." He worked it open, stared at it, and jumped to his feet. "Andrew, give me your rifle."

"What?" Andrew clutched his gun. "Why, Mr. Bartram?"

My father took a step toward him. "I think you know why." Then he reached out and took hold of the rifle. "Let go."

Andrew swallowed and released the weapon. My father passed it to Phineas. "Keep hold of that. The rest of you listen to me." He held up the slip of paper. "I have been proven right. We were wrong to bring this half-breed onto our ship."

"What are you saying, John?" Mr. Kinnersley asked.

"I'm saying that this man is a spy for the French."

Andrew's face paled. He shook his head. "I'm not, sir! I —"

My father cut him off. "You deny that you intended for us to land here so you could leave this sign behind?" He read from the paper. "*Captain Marin. We are following the Ohio River south and will keep to it until we reach the meeting of the Mississippi, at which junction we will turn west and travel overland.*"

Several of the Society members gasped. So did I. Someone on the ship had left that bottle for the French to find. But was it Andrew? Why would he do such a thing?

"Dear me," whispered Mr. Kinnersley.

"*I will delay us if I am able,*" my father continued. "*But you must make haste.*" He crumpled the letter in his fist and shook it at Andrew. "Is this why you wanted us to land here? To delay us?"

Andrew stood up taller, defiant. "No, sir. I did not write that."

"You lie," my father said.

"What shall we do with him?" Mr. Kinnersley asked.

"I say we drop him over the side," Phineas said. "Or set him back down on the ground to face the bear-wolf."

My father looked down at his fist. "It is true that I don't see how he can remain on this ship."

No. That wasn't right or just. "Father," I said. "He saved your life."

"Be quiet, Billy," my father said. "Stay out of matters that do not concern you. In fact, I want you and Jane to go below."

"But, Father —" I started.

"Now!" His shout drove me a step backward.

I turned to Jane, and she motioned for me to come with her. So I followed her, boiling inside, down the hatch onto the Science Deck, where I kicked one of the chairs. It clattered across the floor with a satisfying violence, and I was about to kick another one, but Jane stopped me.

"Are you a child?" she asked.

I folded my arms. "No."

"Then stop this fit and retrieve that chair."

I didn't stop to think about her order. I simply followed it, replacing the chair at its work station.

"Thank you," she said. "Now, why are you so cross?"

"Because!" I couldn't believe she was even asking me that question. "It's because . . ." Only I didn't know the answer. Why was I angry?

"Do you think Andrew is innocent?" she asked.

I wanted to say yes. I wanted him to be innocent. But when I thought about it, I had to admit I didn't know if he was or not. I'd spent only a single watch with him the previous night, and I barely knew him. But I knew the other members of the Society would never have done such a thing. And it had been Andrew's idea to land in this place.

"My father was right about him," I said. And as I said it I realized that was the reason I was angry. I had wanted my father to be wrong.

"That isn't certain," Jane said. "In my opinion, nothing has been proven. I still believe Andrew may be innocent."

"How?" I asked. "Who else could it be?"

Heavy footsteps on the stairs announced my father, who came down onto the Science Deck with slumped shoulders. "I cannot bring myself to do what needs to be done," he said. "You were right, Billy. I owe him my life. But until I decide on the next course of action, Andrew is to be tied to the mainmast. I want you both to avoid him. Do not converse with him. Do not even glance in his direction. Do you understand?"

I nodded. So did Jane.

"Good." He sighed. "I suggest you stay below where it's dry. We don't want either of you catching a chill."

"Yes, Mr. Bartram," Jane said.

"Yes, Father."

He trudged back up to the weather deck, and Jane and I looked at each other. When he closed the hatch, the room dimmed. I sat there in the gloom, feeling relieved but still angry. Outside, thunder pounded the hull and reverberated throughout the ship. The deck moved beneath our feet.

"I think we're under way," Jane said.

I simply grunted.

"What did you see down there?" she asked. "Did you find the wall?"

"Yes."

"How did it seem to you?"

"Mr. Godfrey thinks it might be Welsh."

"So Andrew was right?"

I looked at her, her green eyes the color of a raindrop resting on a leaf. "He was right," I said. But what did that mean? Had he simply been trying to delay us, why not land us anywhere along the river? Why choose a spot with an ancient fortress? Did that mean he was innocent, trying to further the expedition? Or was he simply trying to convince us of his allegiance?

"What did it look like?" Jane asked.

I thought about how to describe it and gave up. "I'll draw it for you," I said.

The storm abated a short while later, and strong winds buffeted the ship. It took more hands on deck to keep the sails trimmed, so I did what I could to help, shivering in my damp clothes. I worked alongside Phineas, his blond hair blown across his face.

"Sharp eyes," he said. "Spotting that bottle in the river."

"Thank you."

"Good thing you found it. Hopefully we've caught and dealt with Andrew before he was able to do any real damage."

"Hopefully," I said. "Was that one of your bottles?"

"Yes, it was."

I looked over at Andrew, seated on the deck, tied to the mast with his hands behind his back. His head hung forward, the brass pendants and coils in his ears dangling toward his lap. He looked as defeated as a person could.

Phineas shook his head. "He must have taken it while we were out gathering samples of mineral water from the springs. I should have noticed its absence, but I didn't."

While the wind brought extra work, it also propelled us at a faster clip. Toward evening, having put many miles between us and the fog-bound wall, my father called a meeting of the crew. He gathered us below, away from where Andrew could hear us.

"In spite of Andrew's betrayal," my father said. "The recent excursion did give me hope that we may yet find Madoc's people. The wall was obviously built by the Welsh."

"What provides you with such certainty?" Mr. Godfrey asked.

"The method of construction," my father said. "It was far too advanced to be of savage origin."

"Your argument is based upon a false premise, John," Mr. Godfrey said. "The Indians are quite capable of that and more."

Mr. Kinnersley spoke up. "Francis, are you saying the wall is unconnected with Madoc?"

"No," Mr. Godfrey said. "I believe it is directly connected

to Madoc. But I arrived at that conclusion by way of different evidence."

"What evidence?" my father asked.

"An inscription," Mr. Godfrey said. He then sat back, a slight smirk on his face as we all waited for him to continue. "You may remember, I followed the wall in a different direction, and I found the one thing that all walls must have."

Phineas rolled his eyes. "And what is that, pray tell?"

"A gate," Mr. Godfrey said. "And above that gate I found an inscription, of which I made a charcoal rubbing." He smirked again and pulled a rumpled piece of paper from inside his coat. He unfolded it and smoothed it over his knee before passing it to my father. "My Welsh is not perfect," he said. "But I believe the inscription could be translated as 'Aberffraw built anew in Unity and Justice.'" He paused. "Aberffraw being the seat of the Kingdom of Gwynedd in Wales. Madoc's father's kingdom, in fact."

The rumors were true. We weren't searching for a fiction, but something tangible. Something I had touched.

"It exists," Phineas said. "The Kingdom of Madoc exists."

"Or existed," my father said, studying the rubbing. "I agree with Mr. Godfrey's translation. But we must not forget that the wall we found, and the settlement it may have once enclosed, are long since abandoned. We must consider the possibility that Madoc's people are vanished."

"But, John," Mr. Faries said quietly. "The reports we've heard from the traders are recent and place Madoc's people farther west, beyond the Mississippi. Perhaps this wall you found simply belongs to an earlier, abandoned settlement."

My father folded up the piece of paper. "That is also a possibility." He handed Mr. Godfrey's rubbing to me. "Billy, will you make a drawing of these markings?"

I accepted it from him. "Yes, sir."

"Gentlemen," my father said. "We will continue in our purpose and pursue Madoc westward in the hopes that, as you say, William, what we found today was simply an older settlement. Are we agreed?"

"Agreed," came a dissonant chorus.

"There is another matter." My father rubbed both his thighs. "Andrew's betrayal has forced a decision. We have no way of knowing whether he has already left similar traces and messages behind us for Marin. It may therefore be prudent to change our course."

"In what way?" Phineas asked.

My father unrolled a map across one of the desks. "I propose we leave the river and strike west, traveling overland. We will eventually reach the Mississippi, at which time we can follow it south to its confluence with the Ohio. We'll have to wait and do it here." He jabbed a finger at a point on the map farther down the river. "That way, we'll avoid the French at Kaskaskia and Saint Louis, though we may have to contend with voyageurs traveling the river. We will arrive at the intended location, but by a different path. It may not stop Marin, but at the very least he will find no more sign of us along the Ohio. If Providence smiles upon us, he may even believe he has lost us and give up the chase." My father looked around at the assembly. "Are we agreed?"

This time, the chorus came staggered. "Agreed."

"Excellent," my father said. "On the morrow, we turn west." He grinned. "I confess that today's discovery has left me feeling emboldened in our quest."

It had done the same for me. We had found evidence of Madoc. His people were out there, somewhere. But the crumbling wall had also left me unsettled. Why had the place been abandoned?

The distant sounds of battle echoed in my ears.

CHAPTER 16

A Second Message

I drew the markings from Mr. Godfrey's rubbing, just as my father had asked. By the time I finished with that, it was evening. With supper, we ate the last of the peaches. The fresh bread was gone as well, which meant that from now on we'd be eating preserved food rations.

My father allotted the watches, assigning me the middle watch with Mr. Godfrey. I kept my groan inside.

"I'll take the middle watch for Billy," Phineas said. "If he would prefer, he can take my place at the first watch."

I did prefer it. I turned to my father. "May I?"

"I don't have an objection," my father said.

"Thank you, sir," I said to my father. I turned to Phineas. "Thank you, sir."

"Think nothing of it, Billy," Phineas said. "I prefer the

middle watch. It's the only hour upon which the day has no claim, and is entirely the property of the night."

"I think sleep is the property of the night," I said.

He laughed.

So I went up on the weather deck and prepared for the first watch with Mr. Faries, trying to ignore Andrew. The night was cold, even though I was wearing my coat and moving about the ship, but the hours passed without incident. A strong wind propelled us down the river.

I felt nervous when I thought about leaving the Ohio behind. It had been our only road through the wilderness, a reassurance of the way back home. I looked west, across a vast indiscernible landscape, and I could not help but think that until we reached the Mississippi, we would be lost in it.

Mr. Faries rang the watch bell, and a few moments later, Mr. Godfrey and Phineas came up on deck. They trudged toward us, and Mr. Faries bade them good night as he went below. I followed him, walking past Andrew at the mainmast.

His whole body shivered in the cold. But he looked up at me, trembling, and nodded, as though we were just two travelers passing each other on the road. I nodded back and continued on.

Down below, in my hammock, I could not rid my eye of that nod. The honesty in it. And I could not forget the cold. Traitor or not, he needed something to keep warm. I tried to push those thoughts away for an hour or more before finally surrendering to them. I eased out of my hammock, pulling my own blanket down after me. And then I crept from our sleeping quarters, through the Science Deck, and up the stairs.

Phineas stood up at the bow, his back to me, but I couldn't see Mr. Godfrey. I turned downship and hurried to Andrew.

"Here," I whispered, spreading the blanket between my raised arms.

"Th-th-thank you," he said.

I wrapped it around him, tucking the edges over his shoulders, between his body and the mast. It took only a moment for his shivering to subside.

"Much better," he said. "Thank you, Billy."

I rose to leave.

As I turned, I spotted Mr. Godfrey standing nearby in the shadow of the mainmast. It seemed he had been there the whole time, watching me. I hesitated, waiting for him to scold me or take the blanket away. But he just nodded his head.

Confused, I nodded back and scurried upship. Phineas was still at the bow, facing away from me. I took the first few steps down the hatch but noticed he was working on something. What could he be doing in the dark? The instruments were still wrapped in oilcloth from the storm. I paused in the stairwell, mostly hidden, watching him.

He hunched over something for a few moments, and then stood up straight, holding that something tight in his hand. He looked over both shoulders, didn't appear to notice me, and picked up a bottle from the deck. He slipped the something inside it, corked it, and tossed it over the bow.

I swallowed, shocked. It wasn't Andrew. *It was Phineas.*

At our elevation, I doubt the splash could be heard, but I imagined it landing in the river and bobbing along until it caught somewhere along the shore, only to be picked up by one of Marin's men.

I wasn't sure what to do. But as Phineas turned around, I fled down the stairs, back into our sleeping quarters. I leaped into my hammock and closed my eyes, pretending to be asleep. But my heart pounded and it was difficult to keep my breathing slow and even.

Phineas was a traitor, not just to us, but to the colonies, to England and King George.

I had to tell my father. I had to tell him now. Andrew was up there, tied to the mainmast unjustly. But I was afraid, and I lay there for a long while, eyes shut tight, wishing I had not just seen what I had seen.

I slipped out of my hammock.

"Father," I whispered, and jostled his arm. "Father."

He jolted awake. "What are they — ?" He blinked. "Billy? What . . . ?"

"There's something I need to tell you." I looked around at the sleeping men. "Will you come to the Science Deck?"

"Right now?" he asked.

"Yes, sir. It's very important."

He dragged a hand down the length of his face. "What is the hour?"

"We've not yet passed the middle watch."

He sat up and nodded. "I'm coming."

I led the way onto the Science Deck and looked up the stairs through the hatch to make sure Phineas wasn't nearby. My father slouched into the chair at his work station.

"Now what is this all about?" he asked.

"Andrew is innocent," I said.

"Billy." He sounded exasperated. "You woke me for this? We've talked about this."

"But I saw —"

"I don't care what you think you saw. The evidence —"

"It was Phineas," I said.

He closed his mouth and cocked his head. "What was?"

"Phineas left that message, not Andrew."

He sat up straight in the chair. "That is a grave accusation."

I stared into his eyes. "I know, Father."

"Tell me what you saw."

And so I explained to him what I had observed from the hatch. How Phineas had inserted a message into a bottle and dropped it over the side. "It was just like the one I found," I said.

After I'd finished, he nodded. "You were right to wake me. I will deal with this right now."

"What will you do?"

"I am going to speak with Phineas about it and hear what he has to say."

"You're going to speak with him about it?" He hadn't offered Andrew that privilege.

"Yes. Phineas is a trusted member of our Society, and as such, he is deserving of the respect that accords." He took the first few steps up to the weather deck. "Wait here for me." And he was gone.

My stomach felt ill. I paced around the mast in the center of the room, passing by each station. Mine with its paper and ink. Mr. Faries's with his tools. Phineas's, laden with his bottles.

"I knew he was innocent," Jane said from the doorway, and I startled.

"Oh, Jane, you . . ."

"I'm sorry I frightened you."

"Not frightened. Just surprised. Were you listening?"

"When you woke your father, you woke me, too." She folded her arms, wearing her boys' clothes. "And, yes, I eavesdropped. And I was right about Andrew."

"It seems you were."

"You don't seem pleased."

"I don't know what I am." Phineas had been kind to me since I had first met him, and I didn't like to think he was a spy. But I hadn't wanted to believe that of Andrew, either. "Nothing about this pleases me."

"What do you think your father will do?" she asked.

"I don't know," I said.

Moments later, he came back down the stairs with Phineas in tow. My whole body tensed up at the sight of them.

"Billy," my father said. "Phineas has something he would like to say to you."

Phineas pushed back his blond hair. "Yes, Billy. I am truly sorry for what you saw. I have failed in my duties. The drinking of alcohol while on watch is a danger to the ship and a disgrace to my better judgment." He looked me right in my eyes. "You were right to report it to your father."

"Alcohol?" Jane said.

"Jane?" my father said. "What are you doing up and about?"

"I'm sorry, your conversation woke me, Mr. Bartram."

"That's quite all right." He turned to me. "So you see, Billy. What you saw was not a man engaged in an act of treachery but a man discarding the evidence of his dereliction. An easy mistake to make in the dark of night."

That was not what I had witnessed. I had witnessed Phineas place something in a bottle, seal it up, and throw it overboard, all deliberately. Hadn't I? *Was* I mistaken? Right or wrong, my father had chosen to believe Phineas's accounting over mine and over Andrew's proclamation of innocence.

"Phineas has been reprimanded," my father said. "And I have his assurance that he will not drink alcohol while on watch again."

Confusion rendered me speechless. A reprimand? "That's all you plan to do?"

My father raised his voice. "Mind yourself."

"Allow me to beg your pardon once more, Billy," Phineas said.

I did not want to grant him my pardon. I wanted to protest and challenge his testimony. But I possessed just enough doubt over what I had seen to hold me back. A flat, "Thank you, sir," was all I could bring myself to say to him. But I did muster the courage to turn to my father. "I gave Andrew one of my blankets."

My father nodded. "I noticed that."

I waited with my chin in the air for *my* reprimand.

"I would never fault your compassion, Billy," he said. "You are like your mother in that way, and I admire it."

That was not the response for which I was prepared.

"And now I think it is time for you and Jane to return to your beds." He spread his hands and pressed them forward against the air. "Off you go now."

Jane and I looked at each other. We left the Science Deck, she to her little room behind the curtain, and I to my hammock. Only I didn't sleep. Confusion and doubt prodded me and kept my thoughts in constant motion. But the more I considered it and reconsidered it, the more I trusted what I had seen, and if Phineas had thrown a message overboard, as I believed he had, what had he written on it?

I felt certain that the French would soon learn of my father's new plan, and I worried that thought over until the sun came up.

*   *   *

After we had breakfasted, Phineas made an admission to the rest of the crew similar to the one he had made to me. My father stood at his side, looking severe and disappointed, but ultimately forgiving.

I seethed at the sight of it. Andrew remained confined to the mast, although they had briefly untied him so he could eat and relieve himself at the head. The clarity of morning had brought me a firm belief in his innocence. I believed it but could not prove it. Beyond my own word, I wasn't sure what evidence I would need to convince my father of something he did not want to see. Until I had such evidence, I felt I could do little to change his mind, and it hurt that my word was not enough to do so.

After Phineas completed his confession, the rest of the Society members expressed their indignation at his supposed misconduct but moved on quickly from it and went back to the business of the expedition. When we reached a place where the Ohio wrapped around a long meander and flowed away to the south, we left the river behind and took our journey overland to the west.

The ground we covered was flat and unremarkable. We flew over stretches of forest for twenty-five miles or so until we crossed the Wabash River.

"We're deep in French territory now," Mr. Kinnersley said. "The Illinois Country, as they call it."

"And Madoc lies beyond it," my father said. He ordered Mr. Faries to take the ship to a higher elevation to minimize the chances of our being noticed from the ground.

At the mention of the French, I imagined Phineas's bottle still floating in the river. How long until it was found? We had penetrated the enemy's land, and they would soon be in possession of our strategy.

Throughout the day, I did what I could to make Andrew more comfortable. I brought him food and water, and I left my blanket with him to sit upon or rest his head against. That my father allowed all of this suggested to me that perhaps the smallest root of doubt had weakened the mortar of his stone-walled will.

The ground below remained flat and densely forested, but from our distance I could not discern what types of wood they might be. Mile after mile, hour after hour, a thick rug of deep green stretched from one corner of the horizon to the other.

Jane appeared beside me at the rail, and together we watched the changeless terrain. "Do you believe Phineas?"

"No," I said.

"Then I don't believe him, either. I believe you."

Her words helped me feel more certain of myself. "Thank you." I turned to look at her. After the rain yesterday, much of her hair had escaped from its braid, forming a tangled blond corona around her head, and she had a little smudge of dirt on her cheek. "I have to do something about it."

"What?"

"I'm not sure."

CHAPTER 17

The Mississippi

The rest of that day passed, and then the night. Around noon the next day, we spotted a fracture in the unending foliage ahead of us. We had reached the great Mississippi River, and we had done it in just over one week. Such a journey would have taken months by land and many weeks by river. Hopefully that meant Marin and his men were far, far behind us. The bear-wolf, however, still frightened me. It seemed the beast could be anywhere.

My father stood at the bow, peering through one of the telescopes mounted there. He had it aimed to the northwest.

"I see the smoke from Kaskaskia," he said. "But I would estimate them to be seven or eight miles away. I doubt they can spot us from here." He checked a compass and called back to the helm. "Change heading, Mr. Faries! Follow the river southeast, one hundred forty degrees!"

"Aye, sir!" Mr. Faries called back.

The *de Terzi* slowed and turned as Mr. Faries set her sails from the helm and the rest of us trimmed them. She cut a broad, graceful arc through the air, high over the Mississippi, eight hundred miles from Philadelphia, and I was struck once again by the marvel of her existence.

"If we follow the reports we have received," my father said, "when we reach the confluence with the Ohio, we turn west again. We are approaching the edge of the Madoc legend and must soon sail over it."

The countryside below remained as it had been the day before. Dense woodland, giving way only occasionally to small patches of open prairie. But its topography began to show greater variation, with rounded hills and shallow valleys and ravines, and the river followed a winding horseshoe course back and forth along their contours.

"The soil will be rich down there," my father said. "When the river floods, it renews the earth with fresh deposits. One day, this land will realize its potential, and this will all be cleared for farming as far as your eye can see."

"What about the trees and plants?" I asked. "Doesn't it bother you that they'll be lost?"

"The resources of this earth are for our use, Billy, through wise and judicious stewardship. Until this land is tamed, it cannot reach its full potential. Much like the savage nations that now inhabit and neglect it."

As I listened, I realized that I didn't feel the same way as my father. I truly disagreed with him. When I thought about the trees below all cut down, I mourned them. I understood the necessity to clear ground for crops, and cut lumber for heating and building, but that did not mean I took pride in such destruction the way my father did. Was it not also wise and judicious to leave the management of nature to itself?

And it wasn't just this that we disagreed about. There was also Andrew and the Indians. I remembered what my mother had said to me before we left our farm. *You are like him in so many ways, but unlike him in others.*

Now I understood what she meant. And she was right.

After taking Andrew some food, I went to find Jane. She was on the Science Deck, reading from Linnaeus again. I approached her, and she looked up at me, briefly, before returning to her book. She had cleaned her face and restored her hair to its braid.

"What are you studying?" I asked.

She showed me a page with drawings of the stamens and other structures by which plants are discerned. "I've made drawings of some of these for my father," she said. "I draw them, and then I look here to identify them." She shook her head and shut the book. "I'm tired of reading. Let's go above."

We went up on deck, and found the horizon to the west had grown ominous and dark.

"Another storm," Mr. Kinnersley said. "And I trust we won't be landing to wait this one out?"

"No," my father said. "We will ride this one out in the air."

But as we sailed onward, it became apparent that this was a very different kind of storm from the last. Where the previous clouds had been heavy and low, these towered over us, taller than any mountain, far too high for us to fly over. A gale whipped past the ship, and lightning flared in the advancing, churning storm column.

I helped rewrap the instruments in oilcloth, and the canvas thrashed in the wind and tried to escape my hands. We stowed as much as we could below and secured every loose article. After we had prepared the ship, we waited and watched the storm draw nearer. But at a certain point before reaching us, it seemed to change its mind and altered its course to one parallel with ours, moving south down the river.

"Providence smiles upon us," Phineas said.

"Nature smiles upon us," my father said.

I spent the rest of the afternoon and evening uneasy and had little appetite when it came time to eat supper. My father assigned me the middle watch with Mr. Kinnersley, at which I groaned.

With the high winds, I worried about Andrew being cold and brought him an extra blanket.

"Thank you," he said. "That is a bad storm."

I glanced at it sideways.

"A bad storm," he said. "If it —" He stopped. He shook his head. I looked in his eyes, and they appeared fearful.

"If it reaches us," I said. "I will try to persuade my father to bring you below."

His whole body relaxed. "Thank you, Billy."

"You are welcome."

I left him and descended from the weather deck, hoping to get at least a few hours of sleep before my watch. As I passed through the Science Deck, I glanced into the galley. Beyond it, I saw light spilling out from behind the door to Mr. Kinnersley's cabin. He was in there, working on his devices. I rubbed my head and went to my hammock. But my unease at the storm kept me awake. I lay there with my eyes open in the darkness, counting the passing hours, and when the ship's bell rang at half past midnight, I sighed and got up.

Mr. Kinnersley was already on deck.

"Hello, Billy," he said, his eyes red, his voice loud and energetic. "Did you get any sleep?"

"No," I said.

"Neither did I," he said.

That was obvious, and I wondered what had him so agitated.

I looked to the west, and found the storm still lurking there, a black mass that blotted out the stars in its hemisphere. Lightning flashed deep within the furnace at its heart, illuminating the countryside, turning the black vein of the Mississippi River to silver.

"The storm seems to be keeping to a southerly course," Mr. Kinnersley said.

"Good," I said.

But I knew we would have to turn west, eventually, once we reached the confluence with the Ohio. I hoped by that time the storm would have weakened or broken up. At least for now, the high winds had abated, for which I was grateful.

I settled into the routine of the watch. The changing of direction to follow the river, the adjusting and trimming of the sails. Before long, I felt exhaustion creeping in. My joints felt loose and weak, my eyelids rode low, and I found myself longing for the hammock in which I had just been tossing.

"I hate the middle watch," I said.

"Are you fatigued?" Mr. Kinnersley asked.

"I am."

"Take a rest. The river runs straight on for some distance. I should be able to manage."

His offer tempted me. "We're not supposed to sleep on the watch."

"It won't be for long. And I can wake you if I need you."

"Are you certain?" I asked. The lure of sleep beckoned to my whole body.

"Quite certain."

I nodded. "Just for a few moments, then."

I went to Andrew and borrowed one of the blankets I

had earlier lent him. Without ceremony or apology, I lay down on the deck near him and closed my eyes.

Something splashed on my face, and I opened my eyes to rain. The storm clouds loomed above and around us, as though the ship were about to be swallowed. I sat up, gave the blanket back to Andrew, and hurried to the helm.

The wind had returned and I had to shout over it to be heard. "The storm changed course?"

He ignored me.

I looked over the side of the ship, buffeted by rain, and couldn't see the river. And we were higher. Much, much higher. I returned to the helm. "Mr. Kinnersley, where are we?"

"I turned west!" he said.

He had turned us into the storm. "Why?"

"To hunt lightning!" His eyes bulged. He gripped the ship's wheel, his knuckles white, and stared up into the rain.

Hunting lightning? How had he planned to trap it? I ran below. I had to wake my father. But as my feet hit the Science Deck, the first peal of thunder shook the ship, louder than anything I had ever heard. Loud enough to fill my whole body. The sound of it tumbled the Society members from their hammocks and berths.

My father charged from the sleeping quarters toward me. "All hands!" he shouted. "Billy, the storm?"

"I was coming to wake you," I said. "It's Mr. Kinnersley."

"What about him?"

"He steered us into it."

"What?" My father shot up the stairs toward the weather deck, and I raced after him.

"Ebenezer!" he shouted, racing toward the helm. "What are you —"

A blinding streak of lightning shot through the sky off the starboard side, searing my eyes, and the thunder knocked me off my feet. My father staggered to Mr. Kinnersley and wrested the ship's wheel from his hands. The rest of the crew had come up behind me, including Jane, who helped me up.

Mr. Kinnersley tried to take the wheel back from my father, but Phineas rushed up behind him and dragged him away.

"No!" Mr. Kinnersley shouted over the deafening sound of the wind and rain. "Just a few minutes more!"

"Mr. Faries!" my father shouted. "Take us down!"

Mr. Faries scowled over the controls, his jaw set. "I can't! He's closed a valve somewhere!"

"Find it!" my father ordered, and Mr. Faries began a hurried search through the tangle of pipes below the spheres.

My father gave the wheel to Phineas and shook Mr. Kinnersley by the shoulders. "What have you done?"

The ship started lurching in the wind, and we all struggled to keep on our feet. Lightning flashed again, overhead this time, lighting up the deck in a burst to rival the sun.

Through the sheets of rain, I caught sight of Andrew still tied to the mainmast.

The mast.

I followed its ascent with my eyes to its pinnacle, where the lightning attractor stabbed the sky. I remembered the Leyden jars arranged below in Mr. Kinnersley's cabin. That was how he planned to do it. Lightning would strike the attractor and be conducted down to the waiting jars. But Andrew was tied to the mast, right in the path of the electrical fire.

"Father!" I shouted. "You must release Andrew!"

He ignored me. "Ebenezer, tell me which valve!"

Mr. Kinnersley shook his head. "A few seconds more, John! That's all I ask."

"Father!" I shouted.

"Not now, Billy!"

I gave up and sprinted to Andrew. The knots in the rope were swollen and tight from the rain. I pulled and wrenched at them, but couldn't get them loose.

"Hurry, Billy," Andrew said.

"I'm trying!"

Another bolt of lightning flared, casting fell shadows against the storm clouds, and the thunder rattled my gut.

"I can't untie it!" I shouted.

But just then Jane appeared at my side with a knife. She sawed at the rope, and a moment later it snapped loose and fell to the deck. Andrew leaped away from the mast, rubbing his wrists.

"Why don't they land the ship?" he asked.

"Mr. Kinnersley did something," I said.

He nodded and looked up at the spheres, then ran for the hatch and disappeared below.

"Where's he going?" Jane asked.

I didn't know.

Mr. Faries had given up his search among the pipes around the foremast. "It must be one of the valves below!" he said, and followed Andrew down the hatch.

My father laid a hand on my shoulder. "Billy! Take Jane and get below!" And he gave me a push. But just then Andrew emerged. He had his rifle. What was he doing?

"Sir!" he shouted. "Mr. Bartram! We must shoot the spheres!"

I felt a tingling rising through my legs, up my back, to my scalp. The image of the Leyden jar came into my mind.

"Are you mad?" my father shouted.

Andrew took aim. "It's the only way to —"

But in that moment, the sky above us ripped apart.

CHAPTER 18

Icarus

When I opened my eyes, I was lying on my back. I saw fire. I heard nothing. My ears had ceased working. I rolled onto my side, and I saw Jane lying next to me on her stomach.

"Jane!" I tried shouting, but didn't know if anything had come out.

Her eyelids fluttered, and a moment later she opened them. I forced myself into a sitting position and helped her do the same. The other men around me looked just as stunned, lying on the deck, sitting up, staggering to their feet.

Mr. Faries rushed back and forth between them. He came to me and said something very close to my face. I saw his lips move. I nodded, even though I couldn't hear him, and he moved on. Would my hearing return?

Jane and I wobbled to our feet and we both looked up.

The sails burned, stretching a sheet of fire over the ship. The mast burned. And the storm raged on around us, the rain insufficient to extinguish the flames.

Muffled sounds began to find their way into my ears. Indistinguishable noise. I looked around for my father and saw him talking with Mr. Faries, pointing at the fire and the spheres. Mr. Faries gestured toward the deck, shaking his head. He had gone below to find the valve to land the *de Terzi*. It did not appear he had succeeded.

My father scooped up Andrew's rifle, and Mr. Faries went to the helm. My father aimed the gun upward and looked at Mr. Faries. Mr. Faries leaned against the helm and nodded. My father sighted along the barrel. He fired.

I heard the shot, just a little pop, and the ship tipped, spilling us all sideways. Another pop, this one louder than the last, and the *de Terzi* righted herself. And she started to fall.

A section of flaming sail tore loose, and the wind tumbled it over our heads, off into the clouds. I watched it flutter until it burned out.

"Billy!"

I heard someone calling my name as though from the kitchen door, while I worked in the orchard or fished by the river back home.

"Billy!"

Louder this time. Closer. I was in the lower garden, and they in the upper.

"*BILLY!*" my father shouted. I snapped my head in his direction. "Lash yourself and Jane to the ship!"

I cast about and spotted the rope that had bound Andrew. I took Jane by the arm and pulled her to the foremast, where I snaked the rope among the pipes. I reached one end around Jane's waist and then wrapped it around my own, binding us to the mast. I could see my father watching me, making sure I did as he asked. The others around us were doing the same thing, attaching themselves to various fixtures around the ship.

Our descent gained in speed. The bottom fell out of the storm clouds, and we hurtled through into open sky. Our fall was not straight downward but at an incline, the ground both sliding past and rushing toward us.

"Hold tight!" I shouted to Jane. She released her grip on the pipes and took my hand, her nails digging into my skin. But I didn't pull away.

The wind soon put out the fires on the sail and the mainmast, but we were still going to crash. My father had punctured two of the spheres. That left two remaining, but I didn't think they would be enough to stop our fall. Perhaps they could slow it.

"Deploy the reserve sail!" My father shouted to the helm.

The reserve sail! Mr. Colden had mentioned it as we'd left Philadelphia, hoping we wouldn't ever need it.

Mr. Faries shook his head. "Too soon!"

The ground drew nearer, all mountains and valleys.

Soon, we dipped below some of the topmost peaks. I was able to tell apart individual trees.

"Now?" my father asked.

"Now!" Mr. Faries shouted.

Behind the *de Terzi*, a hidden square sail opened wide, tied at its four corners to the ship. The wind strained it tight, violently wrenching the ship and throwing Jane and me forward hard against the mast. I banged my nose on a pipe, and my eyes started watering.

"It's working!" my father shouted. And it was. We had slowed.

I felt something hot and wet on my upper lip, and when I licked it I realized my nose was bleeding. I wiped at it with my sleeve, which sent a sharp pain shooting up right between my eyes. I blinked it back as the ship approached a hill, barely scraping its peak, and sailed into a valley.

"John, look!" someone shouted.

Then I heard a tearing sound behind us and glanced back, horrified, as one side of the reserve sail ripped free. The whole thing flapped and trailed uselessly behind us, and our fall quickened.

"Hold fast!" my father shouted.

I heard the sound of wood splintering before I felt it as the hull snapped the first few treetops. But then the splintering became a loud cracking as the ship broke branches on her way down. We jerked and shook, ramming tree trunks to either side. I lost Jane's hand, or she lost mine. The cracking became a pained roar as the ship heaved and struck ground, throwing Jane and me forward again. But this time we were better prepared for it.

The ship groaned and continued to slide along the ground, dragging the mast and spheres through the trees above us, branches and leaves raining down onto the deck. I closed my eyes tight, felt us slow and come to rest. When I opened them, the ship was leaning to one side.

I looked at Jane. Her lip was bleeding, but she didn't seem to be otherwise injured. "Are you hurt?"

She shook her head.

"Billy!" my father shouted. "Jane!"

"We're here, Father!" I shouted.

"I want verbal confirmation from everyone!" my father said. "William!"

"Here!" Mr. Faries replied.

"Francis!"

"Here!"

"Phineas!"

"Here!"

"Ebenezer!"

"Here!"

"Andrew!"

Silence.

"Andrew!" my father shouted again.

No reply. What had happened to Andrew? I worked on the knots tying Jane and me to the mast. We had to find him.

"Can everyone move to the helm?" my father asked, and we all affirmed that we could.

Jane and I got free of our binding and made our way there across a deck that had buckled and lifted in places. My father was waiting, and when he saw us he gathered us both into his arms, one on each side, and kissed the tops of our heads. He embraced each of the men, too, as they reached us, though not Mr. Kinnersley.

Almost everyone had sustained injury. Mostly cuts and bruises, but Mr. Faries had broken an arm. Only Mr. Godfrey seemed to have escaped any kind of wound.

"Phineas," my father said. "Would you please see to William's arm?"

"Yes, John."

"The rest of you," my father said. "We need to find Andrew. Search in pairs. Billy, Jane, you will come with me."

"Yes, John," came the reply from the others.

"Yes, sir," I said.

We traversed the battered deck, saw no sign of him aboard, and climbed down the rope ladder. The storm had moved on, and the forest was silent save the drippings left behind, the ragged swath cut by the *de Terzi* as it fell, an open wound through the trees behind us. The stars shone through it, weak against the first pale light of dawn. This was the path my father had us follow in search of Andrew.

"Spread out," he said. "The sun will be up soon, but take care in the darkness."

We called to Andrew. We searched through the underbrush and the trees. Half an hour later, we reached the place where the *de Terzi*'s crash through the trees had begun, and we had found no trace of him. I began to panic. Had he fallen from the ship while we were still inside the storm? Perhaps when the lightning struck? He could not have survived a plummet from such a height.

"Let's return to the ship," my father said. "We must survey the damage and determine our next course of action. I fear that Andrew is lost."

I refused to admit that. I could not admit that. But I obeyed the order, and we turned toward the *de Terzi*. Along the way, I noticed some of the sounds of the forest had returned. Morning birdsongs filled the trees, their melodies different than any I had ever heard, and the rain had released the smells of soil and vegetation into the air.

As we drew near the ship, we approached the tangled trail of the useless reserve sail. In frustration, I kicked it on my way past. The sail groaned.

"Wait!" I dropped to my knees and tugged at its folds.

"What is it?" my father asked.

I pulled away an edge and saw Andrew. He had a large gash on his head that had covered him in blood. But the wound appeared to have stopped bleeding.

"Let's get him to Phineas," my father said. "Quickly."

Together we carried Andrew the rest of the way to the ship. We had no way of lifting him to the deck, so Phineas came down with some blankets and made his examination on the ground. He found a second injury on Andrew's leg, a very deep puncture wound. He cleaned both, closing the cut on Andrew's head with sutures, and bandaged them. Through it all, Andrew moaned but never opened his eyes, even as the first rays of sunlight fell upon them.

"Will he live?" my father asked.

I leaned in close, anxious for the answer.

"The leg should heal," Phineas said. "And the skull is not fractured. But his head suffered a blow, the results of which are always unpredictable."

"Keep me apprised of his condition." My father turned around and looked up at the *de Terzi*, and for the first time since we had landed, so did I.

Her hull had collapsed in places and been torn away in others, exposing her ribs. Her sail hung in charred tatters, the mainmast a blackened spar. The abuse delivered to the spheres by our fall had deformed them with dents and cavities. She was a ruin, wrecked upon the mountainside as surely as a ship against a reef. The sight of it filled me with a terrible grief.

"Good Lord," my father whispered. "Come with me, Billy."

He climbed the rope ladder, and with one last glance at Andrew, I followed him. We found Mr. Faries on the weather deck, his arm in a splint and sling, standing at the helm. A branch three inches thick had fallen across it, bending the levers and controls into uselessness.

"How is your arm?" my father asked.

"It will heal," he said, staring at the damaged helm.

My father shook his head. "How is she below?"

Mr. Faries looked up, his tears glistening in the dawn light. "She's dead, John. The vacuum system is beyond repair. Her back's broken." His voice faltered and fell. "She'll never fly again."

I felt a squeezing in my throat for him.

"I'm so sorry, William," my father said. "The world had never seen her like."

"And never will again," Mr. Faries said.

My father cocked his head in an unspoken question.

"I just don't have it in me, John." Mr. Faries laid the palm of his good hand against the helm. "She was all there will ever be. At least, from my hands."

"Fair enough." My father looked around. "Where is Ebenezer?"

"Where else?" Mr. Faries said. "Below in his cabin."

"Of course." My father's voice descended into a growl. "It is time for a reckoning."

"Be merciful with him, John. He did not mean for this to happen."

"He has benefited far too long from the mercy of others. Billy, come with me. I will need your account of the events leading up to the storm."

"Yes, sir."

We descended the staircase onto the Science Deck, which we found in complete disarray. The contents of each desk had been strewn about. Shattered glass, books, and equipment littered the floor.

"We'll deal with this later," my father said, striding through it all into the galley.

I followed him and found the door to Mr. Kinnersley's cabin off its hinges, hanging across the opening. My father and I ducked past it, and inside we found Mr. Kinnersley circling the mainmast. He stooped to check the wires and seal on each of the large Leyden jars, nodding and smiling to himself. After all that had happened, he was *smiling*. Did he even care about Andrew or any of us? Several moments passed before he even noticed us, and when he did, he clapped his hands.

"John! Billy! I succeeded!"

My father's glare, his entire comportment, was the hardest and coldest I had ever seen in him.

"I trapped lightning!" Mr. Kinnersley said. "It is here, contained in these very jars!"

Still my father said nothing.

"Don't you see?" Mr. Kinnersley scurried over to us. "Our fall was not in vain. Look what we have achieved!"

"What we have achieved?" My father's eye twitched.

He looked around the cabin, calmly walked over to a corner, and pulled a length of wood from a pile of debris. It was the size and thickness of a large ax handle, and he gripped it with both hands, testing its weight. What was he going to do with it?

"John?" Mr. Kinnersley asked.

My father strode to the mast and looked at the Leyden jars. Then he lifted the length of wood over his head like a club and brought it down hard. The first jar exploded in a shower of water and crockery.

"John!" screamed Mr. Kinnersley. "What are you doing?"

My father smashed another jar. "You want to talk about what you've achieved, Ebenezer?" And he destroyed a third.

Mr. Kinnersley ran at my father, screeching, and tried to wrest the club from his hands.

"Get off me!" They struggled for a moment, but my father easily cast Mr. Kinnersley aside, menacing him with the club.

The older man cowered, shielding his head with his arms, and my father turned back to the jars. He broke another, and another. With each, Mr. Kinnersley sank lower to the ground, whimpering, then sobbing.

I pitied him. And watching him, I felt his loss and his pain, until I couldn't bear it any longer. As my father, out of breath and soaked to the waist, raised his arm to break the last of the jars, I rushed at him and threw myself between them.

"Stop, Father!"

He lowered the club. "Get out of the way."

"No, Father. Be merciful."

He wiped his forehead with his sleeve. "Merciful?"

"Yes. Remember what Mr. Faries said. He didn't mean for this to happen."

"All right." He tossed the club aside. "Then tell me, son, how *did* this happen? You were there."

"We —" I began. "We were flying south, following the river, and then . . ."

"Then what?"

"I — I went to sleep."

"You what?" He swung his anger from Mr. Kinnersley to me. "You slept on your watch?"

"Yes, but, Father —"

"No," he whispered, and that one word carried such shock, such weariness and dismay, that I folded under it. I could not carry the weight of his disappointment in me.

I bowed my head. "I'm sorry."

"Do not be angry with him, John." Mr. Kinnersley staggered to his feet. "I tricked him, you see. He would not have slept but for me."

My father nodded. Then he left the cabin. His footsteps were heavy, never lifting far off the ground, and I could not bring myself to call to him or to follow him.

When he was gone, Mr. Kinnersley got up and rushed to the last remaining jar, poring over it and caressing it.

"Thank you, Billy," he said. "At least you saved one of them."

In that moment, I resisted the temptation to pick up the club and finish my father's work.

CHAPTER 19

A Choice

I lingered in Mr. Kinnersley's cabin a few minutes more and then forced myself to leave the room and plod up the stairs to the deck. The sun had fully risen, and the forest around the ship gleamed emerald in that way only seen after a rain. A cool breeze sent waves through the undergrowth of fern, fluttered the oak and hickory leaves, and set the pine boughs breathing like bellows. Light and shadow played across the *de Terzi's* deck, while a bird of brilliant scarlet perched at the bow and chirped. It was almost as though the forest were welcoming the wooden ship back home, and I could think of no better burial for her than here among the trees.

I smelled smoke from a fire, and heard voices from below on the ground. I peered over the side. Other than Mr. Kinnersley, everyone was down there.

"Billy," Jane called. "Are you coming?"

"Yes."

At the bottom of the rope ladder, I saw my father murmuring with Mr. Godfrey and Phineas over Andrew. Jane sat by the fire with Mr. Faries.

"How is he?" I asked.

"He woke up briefly," Jane said. "But he didn't remember anything. Mr. Godfrey's theory is that he was probably knocked overboard by a branch when the ship first landed and then became tangled in the sail. He just went back to sleep."

At least he is alive.

I turned to Jane. "Have they figured out where we are?" I asked.

Mr. Faries leaned forward, wincing at the movement of his arm. "We're not as far off course as we might have feared. Apparently Mr. Kinnersley turned west just north of the confluence with the Ohio. And before your father shot the spheres, I was able to direct our fall westward as well. It seems we are in a fine location to begin a search for Madoc's kingdom by foot."

"Why did Mr. Bartram have to shoot the spheres?" Jane asked.

"With more time," Mr. Faries said, "I may have been able to find the valve Mr. Kinnersley had closed. But after lightning struck the mast and set it afire, we had to descend rapidly or risk burning up in the air."

"I still find it hard to believe that Mr. Kinnersley did what he did," Jane said.

"I suspect it is the very reason he came on this expedition," Mr. Faries said. "But each of us is devoted to a subject of philosophy that obsesses the mind, myself included. Mr. Kinnersley is hardly alone in that, and I find it difficult to condemn him for it."

"You are too kind, sir," Jane said.

"Perhaps," Mr. Faries said. "But while we're on the subject of obsession, I think I shall take a walk around my ship." He stood. "I will be forced to part with her soon."

We nodded, and he left us.

"I feel so bad for him," Jane said, watching him go.

So did I.

Later that evening, we sat in a circle around the fire as the sun went down and the wall of night closed in. Andrew had awakened a short while ago. He sat up, staring into the fire. A somber mood hung about all of us.

"We will remain here one more day," my father said. "Tomorrow will be spent preparing for a journey by foot. I am accustomed to traveling this way and feel confident we will be adequately provisioned. The following morning, we will depart."

No one responded to him.

"Are we in agreement, gentlemen?"

"What other choice do we have?" Mr. Godfrey asked. "It would seem our agreement is irrelevant."

"And yet," Phineas said, "I am still unsure how we will actually go about finding the people of Madoc. This land is vast, John."

"But we are in the correct region," my father said. "My strategy for finding the people of Madoc is to do as we have done until now. We follow the rumors. We seek out the Indians of this land and ask them."

"But the Indians here are allied with the French," Phineas said.

"I doubt their allegiance is so strong they cannot be swayed by trade." My father pointed at his open palm. "We came prepared with cloth, ax heads, knives, kettles, and other common goods. But instead of trading for furs, we will trade for information."

Phineas turned to Andrew. "Do you know the Indians of these parts?"

Andrew nodded, slowly, as if he were afraid his head might roll off his neck. "I know of them. The French . . ." He squeezed his eyes shut and then opened them very wide. "They call them the Osage, and these are their hunting grounds. They are . . . mighty warriors, very tall and strong. But if there are no French with them, they may trade with you."

"And what of the bear-wolf, John?" Phineas asked.

"The beast could not possibly have tracked our scent

through the storm," my father said. "The bear-wolf is behind us now."

His conviction comforted me.

But Phineas appeared unconvinced. "Your plan seems fraught with unknown risk."

I narrowed my eyes at the Chemist. I knew he was a spy and an enemy, with nefarious motives. If he objected to my father's plan, that meant my father's plan was the very course we should follow.

"I have heard you, Phineas." My father then spoke to the group. "I welcome any and all strategies. But in the meantime, let us rest for the night. I believe the sleeping quarters below deck are still serviceable. And we will maintain a two-man watch throughout the night, as before, with the exception of Andrew, due to his wounds. And Ebenezer, for obvious reasons."

And me? Would I be given a watch?

We let the fire burn low and boarded the ship. Andrew leaned against Phineas and hobbled to the rope ladder, which he was able to hold on to as several of us lifted him to the deck. Down below, we found the sleeping quarters usable, as my father had said, but my hammock did hang a little off-kilter with the cant of the ship.

"Which watch would you like me to take, Father?" I asked.

"I don't think we have need of you, Billy." His voice was flat. "Get some rest."

I threw myself into my hammock and closed my eyes. He no longer trusted me.

Within a short time, the room warmed to an uncomfortable degree, and I realized that up in the sky, the wind and the movement of the ship through it had kept the lower deck well ventilated. But here on the forest floor, our cabin became an oven.

I rolled in my hammock, trying to escape my own sweat, while my discomfort and my exhaustion sent me strange and fractured dreams. I woke repeatedly, disoriented, only to fall back into a sleep that brought no rest.

In the morning, we did what my father ordered, and packed for an overland journey. Food, bedrolls, tools, rope, and other supplies, as well as goods to trade with the Indians we might encounter. My father spread it all out on the ground, measuring and taking inventory, ticking things off a list he had made.

"We'll have to leave a few of the instruments behind," Phineas said, assisting him.

"Brass is heavy." My father didn't look up from his paper. "We will likely leave them all behind. Except for a telescope or two."

Phineas frowned. "You don't even seem perturbed by that, John."

"I do what must be done, Phineas."

Phineas spoke to me from the side of his mouth. "But will he leave his plants behind? That's what I'd like to know."

I ignored him.

"Yes, I will even leave my plants," my father said.

"Hmph," Phineas said, and a moment later, "Well I'm not leaving my books. Excuse me."

I wanted to go, too. I didn't want to be alone with my father. But before I could think of a reason to leave, he pointed at a pile of blankets on the ground.

"Count and roll those, Billy."

I did as I was asked. The wool picked up fragments of leaf from the ground, and I shook them off before rolling and tying the blankets.

"There are eight of them," I said. "Just enough."

He nodded. "Hm, yes."

"How will we move Andrew? With his leg."

He didn't answer me.

"Father, how will we move Andrew?"

"We will not be moving Andrew."

"What?"

"We're leaving him behind."

My voice rose with panic. "How can you do that?"

He lowered the paper. "He is a spy for the French. Why would we slow ourselves down by bringing him with us?"

"He's not a spy!" I shouted.

My father waved me off. "This has already been decided, Billy."

"It's Phineas! He's the one —"

"That is enough!" He stalked over to me. "This expedition is a breath away from utter chaos and dissolution. A feather could tip the scale. And I will not have you sowing discord. Do you hear me?"

I burned inside with a heat to match Mr. Kinnersley's electrical fire. He was choosing to stay blind to the truth. Choosing to silence me, his son. But I would not be silenced. Not anymore.

"He will die if you leave him!" I yelled.

"Then so be it!"

"So be it?"

"He is only an Indian!"

His words rang through the trees and in my ears. They horrified me. Andrew was a man, and I believed him to be a good one. But my father would rather leave him to die than see him as anything more than a savage. But I would not leave him. My actions had almost killed Andrew once, and I refused to allow that to happen again.

"If you leave him, you leave me," I said.

My father rolled his eyes. "Don't be ridiculous."

"I am not being ridiculous! If you leave Andrew behind, I will not follow you. I will stay here with him until he is healed."

"You would choose an Indian over the will of your father?" His eyes narrowed. "Such disobedience. I can see now I was wrong to bring you with me."

His words should have hurt me. But they didn't. "I don't need your approval anymore. To have it now would feel like a stain." I folded my arms and met his gaze with my own narrowed eyes. "I see now that I was wrong to want to come with you. I was wrong to want to be like you."

I thought he would strike me. His whole body tensed in a way that said he meant to. But instead, he turned his back and stormed away, leaving me alone among the carefully ordered supplies.

The second night around the fire was even darker in spirit than the previous night had been. We sat in utter silence. Jane clutched her knees to her chest next to me, orange firelight in her eyes. Andrew reclined against a pile of gear. Who was he, really? I had broken with my father for him. Something about the way he now rubbed his leg and tipped his head to one side made me angry.

When everyone got up to go aboard, I stayed where I was. "I'll just wait for the fire to burn out," I said.

"I'll stay, too," Andrew said.

I could see the anger threatening to erupt from my father. But he said nothing and left, and soon Andrew and I were alone, save for Mr. Godfrey and Phineas, who had the first watch and paced the broken deck of the ship above us.

Andrew looked at me across the fire. "They say you found me. In the sail."

I nodded.

"Thank you. For everything. I think I would have been burned alive if you hadn't cut me free of the mast. That's twice you've saved my life."

"You're welcome. How is your leg?"

"Healing. It is painful. I think perhaps your father might leave me behind."

"He won't," I said.

"Perhaps he should. The journey will be difficult for me."

"We'll help you."

He looked into the fire. So did I.

I was tired. Time passed, and the flames diminished to a pulsing glow. The coals smoldered with tiny slithering snakes of fire. I watched their movements, and my eyelids drooped. The forest blurred, and the firelight sparked and stabbed across my vision in multiple directions. And then it went out.

CHAPTER 20

A Hunting Party

*T*he next morning, my father announced that we needed to create a sled on which we could take Andrew with us.

"We will treat him better than his people treat us." He never looked at me, and he kept his voice calm and even. "We will show him what it means to be civilized men, even out here, far from civilization."

Phineas and Mr. Godfrey cut a length of canvas from a sail and sewed it around two wooden poles salvaged from the ship. As we prepared to leave, they strapped Andrew to it so that he could be carried. He protested, insisted we leave him behind, but no one listened to him.

Each of us carried a pack. Even Jane, though my father made hers lighter than the rest, and with his arm, Mr. Faries could bear only so much. But even with his injury, he had salvaged the large glass lenses used for lighting the cabins below deck and wrapped them carefully in a separate leather bag. He said they were one of the most expensive and painstaking parts of the ship to make, and he couldn't leave them behind.

We gathered one last time before the wreck of the *de Terzi*, and my father asked Mr. Faries if there were any words he would like to say.

The Mechanician kissed his fingertips and laid them against the hull. "First and last, farewell. You flew us true and did whatever we bade, even when it meant your ruin."

I glanced at Mr. Kinnersley. His bowed head seemed less out of reverence and more to avoid meeting anyone's eyes.

"Be with the trees, now," Mr. Faries said. "Speak with the birds and woodland creatures. And many years hence, some trader or Indian or settler will find you here, overgrown and fallen down, and the tales will spread. 'Have you seen the ship on the mountainside?' they'll ask. They'll wonder how you landed here, but to that question, there can be but one answer. They won't know how, but they will know that once you flew." He pulled his hand away and turned to us. "I'm ready."

My father nodded. "Very well. Let's be off."

He picked up one handle of Andrew's sled. I picked up the handle opposite him, aware of a vast distance between us, though we stood but a foot or two apart. Mr. Godfrey and Phineas picked up the two rear poles, and we set off westward into the trees.

Between the four of us, Andrew's weight did not feel heavy at first. But as we made our way down a gradual hill and then up another, stumbling and picking through dense forest and underbrush, the burden grew. Sweat soaked my scalp and my clothes, and before long we all took off our coats. The muscles in my arm ached, then burned, then lost feeling.

We took to switching sides periodically to give our limbs a respite, and I felt a wave of relief when we stumbled upon a path through the thicket.

Andrew craned his neck to see. "It's a hunting trail. This is definitely Osage territory."

The path quickened our pace, and we covered more ground than I would have expected before we stopped for the night. The exhaustion from the day stole any conversation, and after a quick and silent meal, we fell wordlessly onto our bedrolls.

I closed my eyes and listened to the wind through the trees overhead. A stream trickled somewhere nearby. The sounds flowed into my ears and gave me something to focus on, something other than the pain lancing from my shoulders to the tips of my fingers, and I fell asleep.

The next day passed in much the same way as the previous. We marched, following game and hunting trails on a winding course westward through hilly country. The trees grew denser, and the air more heavy, and again we collapsed after many miles into the deepest of sleeps. The sun rose and set on a third day that looked no different.

"At least we've had no more storms," Mr. Faries said on the morning of our fourth day in the wilderness. "And if the skies hold the way they are now, none today."

"Let us hope." My father laid out Andrew's sled. "We should be moving on."

Andrew leaned against a tree, testing his weight on his wounded leg. "I think I'd like to try walking on it."

My father turned to Phineas. "Can he?"

Phineas shrugged. "Possibly. If he can bear the pain. I don't expect it to break open or bleed."

My father turned back to Andrew. "We'll bring the sled with us. In the event that you need it."

Andrew nodded, stepped forward, and winced.

My father looked at his leg. "Are you certain about this?"

Andrew stood up straight. "Yes, Mr. Bartram."

"All right, then. Let's move out."

We formed a column and set off down the trail. Andrew hobbled along, slowing our progress, but it seemed we made better time than had we been carrying him, and my shoulders and arms were grateful.

Around midday, we came down into a valley where the path we followed intersected a vast tract of trampled earth and grass. It filled the bottom of the valley, curving away from us in both directions. At first, the openness of it suggested a country lane, like the Darby Road, which ran by my father's home and garden, only much broader. But the air about it felt off somehow, foreign and forbidding in a way that accused us of trespassing.

Phineas pulled his lank and sweaty hair back from his face. "It looks like a road."

My father knelt and touched the earth. "It is an *incognitum* road. As a species, they seem to have a kind of communal memory or instinct. They reuse the same paths for their migrations generation after generation, and century after century."

"What drives them?" Phineas asked.

My father stood. "Food. They devastate the flora whenever they stop to graze and must then move on."

Andrew panted harder than the rest of us. "If we ... follow their road, we might be more likely to meet a hunting party. ... If that is what you want."

"That is what we want." My father looked down at his compass.

How could he not see that Andrew was trying to help? How could he simultaneously accuse Andrew of treason but continue to use him as a guide? It did not make sense to me, and it led me to believe, or hope, that perhaps my father harbored some doubt of Andrew's guilt.

"This *incognitum* road runs northwest." My father snapped his compass shut. "We will follow it in that direction."

So we crept along the edge of the ancient path, in the footsteps of giants laid down through the eons. They had been traveling this road in their herds long before we colonists came. Perhaps longer than the Indians had been hunting in these woods. The true depth of the impression their feet had left on this land would be hard to measure.

I listened for them as we walked. I hoped, in spite of my fear, that I would hear them coming, either in front or behind us, and have a chance to see their terrible march. But nothing in the forest noise changed. Insects and birds. We stopped with the setting of the sun, and made camp just off the road in the trees.

Spirits seemed higher around the fire. Andrew had made the day's journey with little trouble, or at least with little complaint. But I noticed he was already sleeping as the rest of us prepared for bed. That night, I ended up lying near Jane, with my father on her other side. It felt odd to sleep so close to a girl who wasn't one of my sisters. I lay on my back, and at first, I wasn't aware of anything else around me. Just her.

But then I looked up.

I saw a broad span of crisp sky. The spray of stars stretched from one hemisphere to the other, along the *incognitum* road, and I realized it had been days since I had seen the heavens. I had grown used to camping beneath a shroud of trees.

"That is Ursa Major," Jane whispered.

I turned my head toward her.

She pointed up at the sky. "There, you see it?"

"No. Where is it?"

"Look."

She nudged closer, and I stretched slightly toward her to sight along her arm.

"Do you see the Plough?" she asked.

That I knew. It pointed to the North Star. "Yes, I see that."

"The Plough is Ursa Major's shoulder and foreleg." She traced the shape with her finger. "See, there is her nose, and those are her hind legs. She's the Great Bear."

A bear. I had not thought of the bear-wolf for several days, and the sight of the constellation now chilled me. "You say it's a her?"

"Yes. She used to be a beautiful nymph named Callisto, until the jealous goddess Hera turned her into a bear. Callisto's son, a mighty hunter, saw her and didn't recognize her, so to save her from being hunted, Zeus put her in the heavens."

With her story, the bear-wolf faded from my mind's eye. "Did your father tell you that story?"

"He did. We gaze at the stars together."

"My first watch on the ship, he told me he would acquaint me with the heavens."

I saw her smile in the darkness. "And he still will, once we've returned home."

I folded my hands behind my head. "I'd like that."

"The Six Nations see a Great Bear, too." She rolled onto her side, facing me. "That's what my father says. Only they also see three warriors hunting it. One with a bow, one with a pot for cooking, and one with wood for the fire."

The similarity struck me. "They see a bear, too?"

My father looked only for differences. He examined the Indians and others in the same manner that he examined plants, searching out the qualities that separated them from one another. But what about the things we held in common? What did we share? I rolled onto my side to face Jane. The night had turned her golden hair to silver.

"So we see the same thing as the Six Nations," I said. "The same sky. The same stars. The same bear."

"That's true."

"We look with the same eyes."

"I suppose we do."

I flopped onto my back. The stars glinted for me, just as they glinted for anyone looking at them in that same moment. "Ursa Major."

"Ursa Major," Jane said.

The Great Bear.

Thunder woke me. At first, I thought I was back on the ship during the storm, and I leaped to my feet. But as the woods came into focus, and I remembered where we were, I saw them.

Incognitum.

A great herd thundered by us, stampeding but feet away, a surging mass of brown fur, studded with tusks. The ground trembled. The sharp odor of their musk buffeted my nose. They lifted their trunks and bellowed with the deafening sound of a trumpet. They bumped shoulders and shook their heads and charged forward along the road.

"Stay in the trees!" my father shouted to all of us over the roar.

We didn't need to be told that, and I was grateful we hadn't camped in the road.

"There must be a hundred of them!" Mr. Godfrey said.

"God almighty," Phineas said.

Some of them appeared to be males, larger bulls with longer tusks. Most appeared to be smaller females, and as the stampede thinned, I saw younger *incognitum* among them, juveniles unable to keep up with the bulk of the herd. But they weren't alone.

"See how the young stay together!" My father leaned forward and pointed. "And the females surround them to protect them! Incredible!"

As he said it, one of the juveniles broke free, but it didn't fall far behind before one of the mothers came and rounded it up. Jane laughed next to me. I wanted to make a drawing of them, but I didn't want to look away to pull out my paper, quill, and ink.

After they had moved past us, the tail end of the herd came into view, the ones that moved more slowly than the rest. An old grizzled male shambled along, separate from the others, trying its best to keep up. Its massive tusks swung low.

Something darted in the corner of my eye and struck the old bull in the side.

An arrow. Hunters. The crack of gunfire echoed.

The beast bellowed and leaped forward, but a volley of new arrows caught it, lodging in its thick hide. More gunfire. The beast spun to face its attackers, unsteady and alone, the sounds of its herd fading in the distance. Indians emerged from the trees on both sides of the old *incognitum* and from behind it, perhaps a dozen of them. Some came out of the trees only a few hundred yards from where we now stood. They approached the animal slowly, bows drawn, rifles aimed, calling back and forth.

"It could still charge them," Andrew said. "This is the most dangerous moment."

I wondered if he had ever engaged in such a hunt.

The *incognitum* reared up on his hind legs, its trunk high in the air, and bellowed again, and in the sound I thought I heard its pain and anger and confusion. It brought its front legs down with a heavy thud, shifted and swayed on its legs, and I thought it might be preparing to run or attack. But a moment later, it settled. It planted its feet, held its tusks up proudly, and stood its ground as if waiting for something.

"Would you look at that?" Mr. Godfrey's voice cracked. "The old man is ready to die."

One of the hunters shouted a command, and then they all fired as one.

The *incognitum* jolted and rushed forward in the direction of its herd. But the beast made it only five of its long paces before it stumbled and crashed forward into the ground. Someone had made a killing shot.

A cheer arose from the Indians, and they rushed to the dying animal.

"We have found a hunting party." My father took a deep breath. "I should announce our presence."

"Wait," Andrew said. "Not yet. Let them calm down first. They've just risked their lives."

"And they are still holding their weapons," Mr. Faries said.

My father squinted at the Indians. "You are right. We will wait a short while."

So we watched as the hunters set about butchering the *incognitum*. So much blood. So much meat. So much skin and fur. But everything about the exercise, beginning with the kill and ending with bare bone, played out with efficiency and skill, and I admired the hunters for it.

Meanwhile, a few of the Indians built a very large fire, right there in the middle of the *incognitum* road. Then they cut saplings and stripped branches and lashed them into several racks around the flames for drying and smoking the meat.

"They'll camp here for several days," Andrew said. "Cooking and preserving the kill."

I took the opportunity to sit down and make some drawings. First I sketched the *incognitum* herd as I remembered it, the details still vivid in my mind's eye. Then I sketched the old bull, rearing up, and I drew the Indians approaching it. I made a third sketch of the scene before us now, the aftermath of the hunt. Jane watched over my shoulder as I drew, and she smiled.

After I'd finished, my father looked at the drawings, and his face showed no reaction, pleasure or displeasure. A moment later he pulled a white handkerchief from his pocket. "I am loath to approach these Indians. I do not trust them." He put on his coat and straightened it. "But we have no choice. I want you all to remain here."

He took a step toward the hunting party.

"Would you like me to interpret?" Andrew asked.

My father turned. He appeared caught, snagged on the thorns of his own thoughts. He didn't trust Andrew. Hated him, even. But he needed an interpreter.

"My son saved your life," he finally said. "And four of us carried you for three days. I hope that counts for something."

Andrew limped forward. "You can trust me, Mr. Bartram."

"Then let's go."

My father held the handkerchief aloft and stepped from the trees. Andrew followed. The two of them appeared small and exposed in the road. They had not gone but a few yards when a cry of alarm went up among the hunting party.

I rushed to the tree line, still concealed, and watched.

My father marched forward, the white handkerchief fluttering, as the Indians grabbed up their weapons and came at him. When he was halfway to their fire, my father halted. Andrew stood next to him, and I marveled at their bravery.

The Indians reached them a moment later and surrounded them, guns aimed.

Andrew held up his hands. I heard his voice, but could not quite discern the words. Was that French? One of the Indians came forward. His loud voice sounded angry. Andrew's remained calm. Their exchange lasted a few moments, during which my father stood still. And then the Indian spoke to my father. Andrew leaned toward my father, translating, and then my father replied to the Indian, which Andrew also translated.

This pattern repeated itself several times. Those of us in the trees waited and watched. Jane came up beside me and took my hand in hers. It distracted me at first, but I found myself squeezing it a moment later.

And then the Indian said something to his companions, and the gun barrels came down. My father turned and waved to us in the trees.

Mr. Godfrey cleared his throat. "Well, I think that means we should go to him."

So we gathered up our packs and hesitantly stepped out from the trees. Mr. Faries lagged behind. I turned to see him reach back and tuck the leather bag containing his glass lenses in the crook of a tree.

"One can't be too careful with these," he said. "I'm ready now."

CHAPTER 21

Demons

They were Osage, as Andrew had predicted. *They were all very tall,* much taller than any of the Society members, with heads shaved back to the tufts of hair at the crowns of their heads, and tattoos and paint on their bodies and faces. Beads and bones hung low from their ears, and they had shaved off their eyebrows.

Only one of them spoke French, and I assumed him to be their leader. He wore a white cotton shirt, embroidered with shells, and tattoos crawled up his neck from beneath his collar. He refused to give his true name, but asked us to call him Louis. Through Andrew, he told us they were on one of their three annual hunts. Their homelands lay farther to the west, and it was normally in the endless plains beyond where they found bison and *incognitum* and lions.

His small group had come east after deer, but found the herd of *incognitum* we had just seen.

"We weren't well armed or prepared for such a hunt," Louis said, and Andrew translated. "But we decided to attempt it."

I looked around us, meat sizzling and smoking to one side, the *incognitum* carcass hulking on the other. I tried to imagine the bravery attacking such a creature called for, even with the proper weapons.

"We watched you from the trees," my father said. "And we were astonished. None of us had ever seen such a thing."

Louis smiled, said something to his companions in his language, and they smiled and nodded. He then asked, "What are you English doing here?"

"We were sent by our king." My father's voice carried authority. "We have come to trade."

"We do not trade with you." Though Louis spoke through Andrew, his eyes never left my father's face. "Our treaty and alliance are with the French. You know this."

My father nodded. "We do not ask for your furs. Those are for the French. But does your treaty with them include the exchange of information?"

Louis leaned back. He said something to the men at his side. They murmured with him. Louis leaned forward. "What kind of information?"

"We are seeking a people in these parts." My father looked at the rest of us. "They would not be English or

French. They would be something else, but not Osage or Indian. They are the people of Madoc."

As he said the name, some of the Indian hunters reacted. Their eyes opened, they shifted, and I sensed that though they did not understand my father's words, they had heard the name Madoc before.

Andrew began his translation, but Louis held up his hand to silence him.

"We do not speak of Madoc," he said.

They knew about Madoc's people.

I could see the other Society members thinking the same thing, looking back and forth at one another, nodding, smiling. We were close to achieving the purpose of our expedition.

My father's voice pitched higher with excitement. "Then you know —"

Louis held up his hand again. This time, I heard anger in his voice. "We do not speak of Madoc."

"You do not understand," my father said. "They are our kin. We have been searching for them."

Louis stepped closer to my father, right up to him, their chests but an inch or two apart. He said the same words in his tongue again. "We do not speak of Madoc."

My father, to my amazement, did not back down. "We only wish to find out where they might be."

As he spoke, several of the Osage warriors moved to the sides of our group, flanking us. Their mood had changed. They gripped their weapons, and though they had not yet raised them, they looked ready to. They appeared frightened.

"You invoke an evil name," Louis said. "I have given you a warning. If you press this matter, it will go hard for you."

"Be reasonable," my father said.

"John." Mr. Faries took hold of my father's arm. "Be prudent."

My father glanced at Mr. Faries's hand and then at the Indians surrounding us. "I'll not be silenced by savage superstition. Madoc is no more evil than —"

Louis shouted a command.

The warriors rushed us. One seized my arms from behind. I thrashed against him, but couldn't break free. I looked for Jane. They had her, too. She tugged, jaw clenched, but couldn't move. The Society members shouted and cursed, grappling with the Indians. And then a gunshot froze us all.

Louis held his smoking rifle, aimed up at the sky. He yelled something at us.

Andrew, himself restrained by one of the Indians, said, "He asks you all not to struggle and promises you will not be harmed."

My father shouted. "We did not mean to offend you! And I did not think to ask something of you without offering something in return. We have brought goods to trade!"

Louis tipped his head. "Let us see what you have brought."

They let go of us and gathered us together. Louis and a few of his men stripped us of our packs and sat us down. With rifles and spears pointed at us, we watched them empty our supplies out on the ground.

"Take what you want," my father said. "But let us go."

The Osage claimed almost everything, the goods we had brought to trade, as well as our food, blankets, and knives. They seemed especially pleased with Andrew's rifle. They didn't seem to know what to make of Mr. Kinnersley's Leyden jar, though. I cringed as they touched it, waiting for the lightning within to burst free and shock them. But it never did, and they let it roll harmlessly to the ground. And then they opened my pack. They took the ink, my paper, and my quills. Then they found my drawings.

I leaped to my feet, enraged. "Leave those alone!"

"Billy, be still!" My father yanked me back down.

I watched, helpless, as Louis thumbed through my work.

When he came to the drawings of the *incognitum* and his Indian hunters, Louis looked up at me. "You made these?"

At first, I just glared at him. "Yes."

He looked at them again. He showed them to his companions. They talked, pointing at the pictures and one another. When Louis gathered the drawings back, he gently shuffled them together and slipped them into my pack with care. He then placed my pack with the other supplies and provisions they had taken, which they hauled away and set with their own possessions. Louis stood before us, conferring with two of his men.

"Can you tell what they are saying, Andrew?" my father asked.

"I do not know their language. But I would guess they are trying to decide if they will take us, or some of us, as prisoners back to their people."

I looked at my father. So did the other Society members.

He looked back at Jane and me, his face pale. "Andrew, what do you think they will do?"

My father was afraid. And that made me more afraid than I already was. I had heard stories of Indians taking English children to raise as slaves in their villages. Were those stories true?

Andrew rubbed his leg. "Sir, I don't know what they will do."

"Why haven't they just killed us?" Mr. Faries asked.

"They know we've come on the king's business," Phineas said. "If they kill us, they have to worry about how their French allies will react. I suspect they will simply take us all prisoner and deliver us to the French." He spoke with a lightness in his voice, as though he wasn't troubled by this at all. But as a spy for the French, why would he be?

"They can't take us all prisoner," Andrew said. "They don't have enough men for that, with the *incognitum* meat they have to carry. But if they take *some* of us prisoner, they have to worry about what the rest of us will do, and whether the English will retaliate. In these circumstances, it may be easiest to simply let us all go free."

I chose to hope for that outcome.

So we waited to learn our fate.

A short while later, the Osage seemed to come to some agreement. Louis spoke to us. "Our French allies would expect us to take you prisoner."

Inside, I panicked, but kept my face and body from showing it.

"But I won't," Louis said. "It is more important that we take this meat back to feed our people. You are free to depart, if you go now."

My father stood, and so did the rest of us. As I had with my fear, I tried equally hard to keep my relief inside as we gathered up the few possessions the Osage hadn't taken.

My father turned to Louis. "I must —"

"Say nothing," Louis said.

My father bowed his head, then led the way toward the trees from which we had come. I didn't want to turn my back on the Osage warriors. I felt the threat in their eyes as acutely as from the points of their spears, which were still directed at us. The muscles in my neck and shoulders tensed as I walked, the tree line too far away.

We covered several yards. Then Louis shouted something.

I winced.

"Oh, Lord," Mr. Kinnersley said. "He's changed his mind. They're going to kill us."

"No." Andrew looked at me. "He wants Billy."

Me?

"What for?" my father asked.

"We must go find out," Andrew said.

I took a deep breath. What could he want with me? Would I alone be taken captive? I gathered what bravery I could. If they wanted me, then I would do what was necessary to save my father and Jane and the others.

"Stay here, Billy." My father looked back at the Indians. "Let me go."

Louis waved at me, motioning me toward him.

"No, Father. He wants me."

"I don't think he means to harm him," Andrew said.

"We'll go together," my father said. "The rest of you continue on to the forest."

So the three of us trudged back toward Louis, and as we approached, the Indian held up my pack. "Your pictures are very good."

His statement surprised me, and I didn't know how to respond. But as I looked at him standing there, smiling with my things, I grew angry again. He had taken my drawings. He had taken what I was most proud of.

"What will you trade for them?" I asked.

Andrew didn't translate. He just stared at me. So did my father.

Louis looked at me, his hairless brow wrinkled in confusion. He turned to Andrew, and when Andrew translated, the Indian's brow lifted. He laughed. "What is your price?"

I hesitated.

Louis waited.

"This is my price. Tell us where we can find the people of Madoc." As soon as I said the name, I regretted it. The Osage warriors all took a menacing step toward the three of us. I hoped Jane and the Society members had continued on to the woods like my father had ordered, but didn't dare look.

Louis played with one of the bones hanging from his ear. He no longer smiled.

I waited.

"We do not speak of Madoc," he said at last. "But if you wish to find him, continue on in that direction." He pointed over our heads, just south of west. "After several days, you will come to a valley. In the valley, you will find what you seek."

"Thank you," I said.

"Do not thank me," he said. "My people do not hunt in that place. You should be more afraid of them than you are of us."

"Why?" I asked.

"They are . . ."

Andrew's translation faltered.

"What did he say?" my father asked. "They are what?"

"Demons," Andrew said.

"What did he mean, Father?"

We had put a mile of forest between us and the Osage before I dared to speak or ask the question. We moved quickly without the burden of our now-stolen supplies. Mr. Faries still had the lenses he had hidden, and Mr. Kinnersley now bore the heaviest load with his Leyden jar. But he refused to leave it behind.

I continued. "And he said, 'him.' When he was talking about Madoc, he said, 'If you wish to find *him*.' Why would he say that?"

My father's gaze plowed ahead of us. "As to your first question, you needn't concern yourself with savage superstitions. And as for the second, it must be an error in translation."

"I made no mistake," Andrew said.

"Then I would doubt the Indian's French!" my father said. "No more talking. Quickly, now."

He set a relentless pace.

Mile after mile passed of the same underbrush and trees through which we had carried Andrew. By the time evening descended, we were far from the *incognitum* road, and my father finally let us stop. We made a fire but had nothing to cook, and we had no blankets to make our beds. My father laid his coat out on the ground for Jane to sleep on. I was hungry but too exhausted to complain.

"Tomorrow morning," my father said, "we can spare the time to forage for food. Agreed?"

No one answered him.

We sat around the fire, warming our hands.

My father stood on the opposite side of the ring from me, obscured by sparks and smoke. "I must apologize to you all. It was I who decided to approach the Osage. Our present state is my responsibility."

"Sit down, John," Mr. Godfrey said. "This is no fault of yours."

My father sat.

I stared at him through the flames. I did not agree with Mr. Godfrey. But I understood what it meant to blame yourself. Jane did, too. As the expedition had faced a threat, we had each made choices that brought it into greater danger. But just because my father and I experienced something similar did not make us alike. It did not change anything.

"Try to get some sleep, everyone," he said.

We settled down as best we could without any bedding. I rolled onto my side, away from the fire, feeling its heat across my back. Hunger gnawed at my stomach, but it wasn't yet painful enough to keep me awake.

When we woke early the next morning, the fire still smoked. My father led our forage in the surrounding woods, searching for edibles. We didn't find much, so we began the day even hungrier than we had been the night before. We took water from the plentiful streams and creeks we crossed, traveling in the direction Louis had pointed. For a few moments, it gave our stomachs the sensation of fullness, but that didn't last long.

In midafternoon, we came across a wild blackberry bush bearing some fruit. The thorns stuck my hands and my arms as we stripped it bare, but it was worth it when I bit into my first juicy berry. The sweetness and tartness satisfied some of my hunger.

That evening, we camped near a stream that held some tiny silver fish, flashing like penknives under the surface. I snapped off several green, flexible branches from a small oak tree and wove them together into a lattice. Then I waded into the water and slipped my makeshift net down under the surface. I held my body still, and I waited. Before long, the fish began to approach. When two swam over my net, I heaved it out of the water, tossing them up onto the bank, where they flipped and rolled in the grass.

I did the same again and again, until my back hurt and my feet were cold and I'd caught a little fish for everyone.

They did not taste good. But they were food.

The next few days passed like the previous two. Except we were hungrier. We ate what we could find. A few mushrooms. More berries. Some nuts and some roots. At each camp, we laid snares overnight, but only once did we catch a squirrel. And with eight mouths to feed, there was never enough, especially with the heat and the physical exertion the dense forest demanded. Flies and midges tormented us, stinging and biting our necks and faces.

Mr. Kinnersley wasn't doing well. He muttered to himself, and if I tried to talk to him, he acted confused, as though he didn't recognize me. Mr. Godfrey had fallen into a sullen silence. Mr. Faries and Phineas seemed to be doing relatively better, but they were both younger and stronger than the rest. Andrew hobbled along, and I couldn't tell if the pain in his leg had lessened or if he had simply grown accustomed to it. Jane kept up, but her feet dragged. So did mine.

If my father felt exhaustion, he didn't show it. He led the way forward.

Always forward.

CHAPTER 22

Predator and Prey

"**M**r. Bartram?" *Jane sat on the ground while the rest of us rose* and prepared to move on. "How much farther, sir?"

"I do not know, Jane." My father offered her his hand to ~~he~~lp her up, but she only stared at it blankly. "Louis said it ~~i~~s several days away."

Jane finally took his hand and got to her feet. "It's ~~b~~een six."

"I know," my father said. "Which means we must be close. I know you are all tired, but we are nearly there."

"Unless the Indian lied to you," Phineas said.

Silence followed.

That wasn't something I had considered. What if the hunger, the fatigue, and the strain of the past several days were in vain? What if my drawings had purchased us nothing? I thought back to the exchange with Louis and I did not think he had lied. His fear was too evident.

"I believe he told me the truth," I said.

"I also believe that," Andrew said.

Phineas raised his eyebrows but said nothing more.

We pressed on.

Hunger stalked me the following day, and the heat made it difficult to breathe. I felt weak, drenched in my own sweat, and I crossed some kind of threshold. My thoughts became hazy, my mind unfocused and slow. All I could do was keep moving.

Keep moving.

I stumbled more, tripping over roots and rocks. My vision clouded at times, and I could barely rouse myself to swat the flies away.

Keep moving.

"How does the Indian survive in this pestilent land" Phineas asked.

"They survive," my father said. "They do not thrive And they will never be truly civilized, until they learn to subdue and cultivate this land for its better use. This soil is rich. This land is fertile. Imagine what could be done with it under better stewardship."

"*Your* stewardship?" Andrew asked.

"Why not?" my father asked. "I look at this land and I see wide, verdant fields and pastures. I see its potential."

Fatigue loosened my tongue. "Why is a field better than a forest? Why is our use of the land better than theirs?"

My father's expression showed more confusion than anger. He reached over and touched the back of his hand to my forehead. "You're too hot. We need to find some water."

A short while later, we came to a wide stream, and my father called a halt for the night. He had me drink, then take off most of my clothes and submerge myself in the water. The cool current washed over me and carried away the dirt and heat of the day. I looked at the sky, imagining myself up there again, among the clouds, flying without a ship.

My father helped me out of the water, back into my clothes, and set me down in front of the fire. I stared into it. The wavering dance of its flames lulled me, and deep in the embers, I thought I saw a small beetle. *A beetle.* I blinked.

It was still there, right in the midst of the fire, polished like a mirror, reflecting the flames, appearing made of them. It crawled from coal to coal, then out of the fire and down a tiny hole. I imagined I saw the inside of its den, a dark warren of roots and moist air, where time passed slowly. I saw the beetle leave its home. It traveled over the ground, and the armor on its back opened, unfurling translucent, humming wings. I lifted off with it into the air as it flew in search of leaves and fruit to eat.

The beetle thrummed over a river, grazing the water with its feet, where a spotted frog slipped between clutches of waterweeds, eyes turned upward. I spotted the beetle's tiny silhouette dancing on the river's surface. The frog floated up into the dryness, blinking its eyes, waiting, and in an almost imperceptible movement, flicked its tongue. It caught the golden beetle in its mouth, broken legs and wings sticking out, then swallowed it whole.

The frog hopped up onto the riverbank, croaked its satisfaction, then splashed back into the water, while overhead, in the dry world, I stood with a stick-legged heron in the mud, its dagger beak poised, black eyes waiting. The little frog darted between the heron's legs and the bird snapped and scissored the water.

It wobbled the frog down its gullet, legs last. Then the heron stepped among the reeds and cattails and came up on the bank, where an enormous cottonmouth coiled in the sun. The heron startled it awake, and the serpent reared. The bird squawked, spread its wings and flapped only once. The snake struck, fang through feather, and the bird crumpled. The snake's jaw unhinged and opened.

Then the cottonmouth, bulging in the middle, disappeared into the forest. I kept with it to the shadows and the cover of brush and leaves. It danced its tongue over the ground, tickling out the scent and flavor of the woods. It eased into a meadow of dry grass, a ceiling of open sky overhead where an eagle soared, watching. The great bird caught movement, tucked in its wings, and plunged to the earth. The snake writhed and died, skewered on talons.

I returned with the eagle to the sky, soaring, while down below human eyes envied golden eagle feathers and coveted the freedom to fly. Bullets reached upward and brought the eagle down. I fell with it, then walked with the hunter, trophy feathers in his pack. He carved a path through the forest, cleared the land, and all manner of creatures fell away before him. He marched supreme, but his scent wafted away from him into the nostrils of another.

The bear-wolf erased the hunter's footprints with its paws as it stalked him to the edge of the wood. I felt its power as the animal charged, roaring, and though the hunter raised his gun, it was too late. And so the hunter fell. The bear-wolf sniffed at the body and rumbled under its breath.

It ate and then faded into the trees, leaving some of the hunter behind. The golden beetle reemerged from the ground. It and its brethren, the low crawling things, ate what was left until there was nothing but bleached chips of bone. The beetle returned to the fire, crawled from coal to coal, and disappeared into the heat and the ash.

"Billy."

Someone shook me, and I opened my eyes. The sun was up. The fire was cold.

I had been dreaming.

My father gripped my shoulder. "Do you feel better?"

"I'm hungry," I said.

"Here." He handed me a charred bit of meat on a skewer. "We caught three squirrels in our snares and a frog in the river. Eat up, and then it is time to go."

Before I took a bite, I asked, "Did everyone get a share?"

"Yes," he said.

I ate, and in a few mouthfuls it was gone. I was still ravenous but felt better. More clear in my thoughts. But the dream I'd had lingered. It felt important, somehow.

Jane came up to me. "Are you sure you're feeling better?"

"Yes, much."

"Good. I was worried."

Mr. Faries came trotting out of the trees. "There's a shallow spot to the north where we can ford the stream."

"Excellent." My father looked at the group. "Is everyone ready? Let's be off."

A distant roar sounded through the trees. I recognized it, and it raised the hair on my neck.

"No," Jane whispered.

Mr. Kinnersley clutched his Leyden jar tighter. "How could the beast have found us?"

My father snatched up his coat and shook it. "It must have been drawn to the scent of the *incognitum* kill. If we are lucky, it will pursue the Osage, but it may have picked up our trail. We must hurry."

"Hurry?" Phineas asked. "What is the use?"

My father spun on him. "If the bear-wolf is hunting us, our only chance for safety now is to find the people of Madoc!"

The bear-wolf roared again, an echo of my dream. I remembered the beast galloping toward us, and down here on the ground, I felt completely exposed and vulnerable. I looked around for something, anything to use as a weapon. All I saw were rocks and sticks.

Andrew appeared to be doing the same thing. He found a large, dead branch, planted his boot against it, and snapped off a piece. It broke away with a natural, sharp point. He did the same thing again, and again, handing out his makeshift spears.

He gave one to me. "It is something, at least."

Effective or not, I felt better having that something in my hands.

We set off. The place Mr. Faries had found to cross was shallow most of the way, just below our waists at the deepest. But the current was slow, and soon we were all on the other side. I looked back once across the river.

"*Isanthus brachiatus!*" my father said.

Was he collecting specimens? *Now?*

"Pardon, John?" Phineas asked.

"False pennyroyal." My father rushed to a plant with small blue flowers, growing along the riverbank. "This may help disguise our scent." He ripped off a handful of small leaves and shoved them into my hands. "Take some and rub them on your clothes."

The leaves were hairy and sticky, and they smelled strongly of mint. But I did as he asked me, and so did the others. Then we continued on.

The forest changed little: dense, humid, and hilly. But we moved quickly, no longer called by what lay ahead of us but driven by what stalked us from behind. We heard the roar several more times, and with each, it sounded nearer.

"I don't think it followed the Osage," Mr. Faries said.

"Keep moving," my father said.

We traveled another mile. Perhaps two. The strength I'd felt upon waking soon drained away, and my legs threatened to buckle. Each time we started up a hill, I doubted if I could make it to the top. But hope fueled me. Each time, I imagined that when we reached the summit and looked down the other side, we'd see Madoc's valley below. A land of fields and farms and a fortress. But each time, I saw nothing but another wooded ravine. I started to doubt what I'd said about Louis. Maybe he *had* lied to me. Maybe there was no valley, and we were just pushing deeper and deeper into an endless wilderness.

If that were true, the bear-wolf would eventually catch us, and I couldn't let myself think about what would happen then.

We started up another hill. The roar behind us was so loud, so close. The sound of it iced my skin.

"Perhaps —" Andrew said. "Perhaps we should look for a place to make a stand."

Make a stand? Against the bear-wolf? With toothpicks for weapons? I didn't know if I had the strength to climb the slope before us, let alone fight the beast.

My father twisted his spear in his hands. "Let's get to the top of this hill."

I steeled myself, and some moments later, we reached a clearing at the summit. This had to be it. I rushed to the far side and peered through the trees, down into the valley.

I saw nothing.

It was over. Our last hope was gone.

Andrew scanned our surroundings. He pointed at a formation of weathered stone perhaps fifteen feet high. "We could use those boulders."

"The beast can climb that." Mr. Kinnersley tapped his chin with an index finger. "We could use my Leyden jar as a weapon."

Phineas snorted. "What are you going to do? Throw it at the bear-wolf?"

"It is charged with lightning!" Mr. Kinnersley said.

"Then what is your plan, old man?" Phineas asked. "One of us holds the bear-wolf still, while you walk up and shock it?"

"Do not mock me!" Mr. Kinnersley stamped his foot. "Electrical fire is —"

"Now is not the time, Ebenezer!" my father said.

While they argued, I looked again at the valley. It was beautiful. Mountains rimmed three of its sides, a wide, shallow bowl filled with trees.

Wait. What was that?

There, in the distance, I spotted a gray smudge hanging just above the trees.

Smoke.

And near it, I saw more smudges. Several more. It had to be a settlement.

"Father, look!" I pointed. "It's Madoc!"

He squinted. "It can't be."

"It could be," Mr. Faries said.

"But that's nothing more than an Indian village," my father said. "Where are the fields? Where are the people?"

"I see a few breaks in the trees," Mr. Godfrey said. "There, and there. They could be small fields."

My father readjusted his stance. "What do you think, Phineas?"

"Hard to know," Phineas said. "But the bear-wolf is getting closer. We should try for it."

"We won't make it," Andrew said. "Listen. The forest has gone quiet."

It had.

An eerie silence enveloped us. No insects. No birds. Nothing.

"It's here," Mr. Faries whispered.

"To the boulders, quickly." My father pushed Jane and me toward the formation Andrew had spotted. "You two, up there."

Jane and I scurried to the top. My father, Andrew, and the Society members formed a defensive perimeter below us. Even Mr. Faries held a spear in his one good hand.

Fear filled the space left by my exhaustion. My own electrical fire. I trembled and looked at my feet. Around us were several rocks the size of apples and plums. I set my spear down and gathered up a handful. To my right, Jane watched me and did the same.

"When we throw these," I said, "make as much noise as you can."

She nodded.

We waited.

Every movement, every wind-tossed branch and snapped twig caught my breath. The beast was out there, somewhere, perhaps circling us, out of sight in the trees.

"Come on," Phineas said. "Come on, you devil."

Some buzzing insect sounds returned, but I didn't know what that meant.

"Where is it?" Mr. Faries asked.

"It's out there," my father said. "Billy, when the bear-wolf attacks, I want you to —"

The beast exploded from the trees. Its paws tore the ground. Its maw opened wide. Its speed and ferocity stunned me. I watched it charge us for a moment, and then remembered the rocks in my hand. I threw the first, shouting as loud as I could. So did Jane. We missed and kept throwing. It was almost upon us.

The Society members shouted and held up their spears.

Over them, I heard my father's voice boom. "STAY BACK!"

The bear-wolf skidded to a halt a few yards off. It stood up on its hind legs, at its full height, towering almost as tall as the rocks I stood upon.

"Steady, all!" my father shouted.

I threw another rock, and it bounced hard off the monster's muzzle. It blinked and roared. I kept throwing and shouting, "Back! Stay back!" while the men below brandished their spears and whooped.

The bear-wolf dropped back on all four paws, and circled around to the left side of the rock formation, then to the right, sniffing and huffing. It seemed to be sizing us up, looking for weaknesses or dangers.

"Keep at it!" my father said. "We've given it pause!"

More yelling. More rocks. They glanced off the animal's shoulders and sides. I scored a couple more hits to its head. Jane was nearly as good a shot as I was. But though the bear-wolf seemed to be hesitating, it wasn't retreating.

It moved to the right again. It stayed there. I pulled Jane over to the opposite side, placing myself between her and the beast. Phineas stood below me.

He glanced over his shoulder. "Stay behind me, Billy."

The other men angled their spears toward the bear-wolf as it swung its head low, back and forth, emitting a rumbling growl.

Someone shouted, "It's getting ready to charge!"

And then it did.

It came right at Phineas. Somehow, he held his ground.

The bear-wolf's paw caught him in the side and sent him flying through the air. My father and Andrew both lunged toward it, and my father's spear caught the bear-wolf in the shoulder. The animal roared and swatted, but both men dove clear. The bear-wolf looked up at me. I held my arms out in front of Jane.

It leaped toward us, halfway up the boulders in a bound. I couldn't look away from its open mouth. That mouth was going to close on me. And there wasn't anything I could do.

Something hissed through the air over my shoulder. The bear-wolf cried out and slipped on the rocks, an arrow sticking out of its neck near its shoulder.

Three men advanced toward us out of the trees. Two had bows drawn, while the third pulled an arrow from his quiver. The two men fired, one missed, one found its mark in the bear-wolf's side. The animal roared, but it sounded different this time. Pained.

It hurtled from the rocks to the ground, facing the bowmen, but backed a few paces away from them. The three men aimed their arrows. The bear-wolf let out a low moan and bolted into the woods from which it had come, disappearing into the trees.

The bowmen watched it go and then turned toward us. They had white skin, thick dark hair cropped short, and wore leather leggings. One had a cotton shirt, but the other two went bare-chested, their torsos and arms covered in intricate, swirling tattoos. Metal coils of bronze and silver twisted around their arms.

The one in the shirt wore a stiff braid of heavy golden wire around his neck. It was open in front, ending in two wolves' heads that snarled at each other across his collarbones. I couldn't tell how old he was, nor the other two. They had a few white hairs, and though the skin of their faces was tough, it was not wrinkled, and they moved with strength and speed.

The shirted one stepped toward us. *"Pwy wyt ti?"*

"Welsh?" Mr. Kinnersley dropped his spear. "Is he speaking Welsh?"

The stranger looked at him. "You are English?" He spoke with an accent I didn't recognize.

My father approached him, his hand on his chest. *"Rydym wedi dod fel eich brodyr, ap Madoc.* We come as your brothers, son of Madoc."

"Your *cymraeg* is bad," the stranger said.

"Your English is good," my father said.

The stranger smiled. "My French is also good."

"John!" Mr. Faries waved frantically over by the trees. "Phineas is hurt!"

We all rushed to him and found Phineas lying on his back, unconscious.

Mr. Faries knelt beside him. "It looks bad."

The shirt and coat on Phineas's left side were rent and soaked in blood where the bear-wolf's claws had raked him and cast him aside.

"We will take him to our village," the stranger said. "We have men who can help him there."

My father nodded, and the stranger's two companions lifted Phineas by his shoulders and legs. They set off down the hill, toward the smoke I had seen earlier.

"Thank you," my father said.

"We will do what we can. I am Rhys ap Morfran, and I welcome you."

"I am John Bartram." My father bowed. "And we are honored and grateful."

Rhys turned and led us in the direction his companions had gone. My father motioned to Jane and me, and we followed after him, while Andrew and the Society members came behind.

As we hurried through the trees, Jane took my hand and squeezed it. "We have found it," she whispered. "The Kingdom of Madoc."

CHAPTER 23

Annwyn

When *we reached the bottom of the hill, Rhys directed us to a* well-beaten path. It was narrow and winding at first, but as we walked along, it straightened and widened into a road, leading toward the middle of the valley. Trees lined the edges, their canopy of branches reaching overhead. And then the trees backed away from the road, replaced by a kind of wickerwork fence made of long wooden stakes, with thin branches interwoven between them.

"We must hurry," Rhys said. "For your friend. Can all of you run?"

My body had not yet lost its fire from the bear-wolf attack, and everyone else agreed, too. We trotted down the road at a brisk pace, but had not gone very far when Mr. Kinnersley slowed to a walk.

He bent in the road, hands on his knees, breathing hard. "I'm an old man. I can't."

"Neither can I," Mr. Godfrey said.

Andrew favored his wounded leg, but said nothing, even though I was sure he couldn't run well, either.

My father gazed down the road. "We'll walk, then. We stay together."

Rhys nodded.

A short distance later, my father pointed at the fence. "You keep livestock in these woods?"

"Our pigs forage wild during the summer."

"I see."

"It is a better use of this land than pasture."

That furrowed my father's brow.

We followed the road for another half mile and then we did see a field. But it wasn't a cleared field. The trees had died, their leafless skeletons standing a silent vigil over clusters of corn, squash, and pumpkins planted at their feet and in the spaces between them. I noticed a band of bark had been stripped from each tree, all around their trunks near their roots. That was the reason they had died, and without their leaves, sunlight found its way down to the crops. It was also why we hadn't seen larger fields from the hill.

My father nodded toward the dead trees. "We sometimes use the same method."

"We learned it from the *pobl cyntaf*," Rhys said.

"Who?" my father asked.

"The First People. That is what we call them."

"Do you mean the Indians?"

"I think that is what you call them, yes."

My father shook his head. "In what regard are they first?"

"They were here before us."

The obvious way in which he said it, and the simplicity of thought behind it, almost stopped me in the road. My father had no reply.

We passed many more fields, cultivated in a manner similar to the first. But as we progressed, the trees dwindled, having dried and fallen down and rotted, giving way to open ground.

Soon, I caught sight of the first farmhouse. It was a small hut built of tight-fitting limestone, with a low door, narrow slits for windows, and a peaked roof shingled with overlapping strips of bark, similar to the longhouses we had seen at Aughwick. A Welsh foundation covered by an Indian roof. A woman dug in a small vegetable garden out front. She wore a simple deerskin dress but also an old-fashioned wimple that covered her hair, neck, and chin.

Mr. Godfrey spoke quietly from the side of his mouth. "The style of her headpiece is centuries old."

She waved to Rhys, and he waved back. She said something in Welsh while pointing down the road, and Rhys replied. She nodded, and we moved on.

"They brought your man past her cottage, and she was worried for him."

"I am worried, too," my father said.

We passed a few more farms, and then rounded a curve in the road. I caught sight of the village up ahead, a cluster of buildings like those we'd already seen but longer and wider. One in the center seemed taller than the rest but built of the same materials. Limestone walls and Indian roof, surrounded by forest and small fields of corn.

"Welcome to Annwyn," Rhys said.

"Ah, named after your Paradise, correct?" my father said. "It is a modest and pleasant village. How many live here?"

"Three hundred and fifty-four."

"An exact figure," my father said. "How far away is the seat of your kingdom?"

"The seat of our kingdom?"

"Yes. Where is your king's throne from here?"

"Our prince is here. We have no other place."

My father stopped in the road. "Does that mean . . . Is this village your only settlement?"

Rhys rolled his shoulders back and straightened his neck, his necklace glinting in the sun. "It is."

I couldn't read my father's expression. Disbelief? Disappointment? I think he was trying not to show it, though I felt that way, too. There were no grand castles here, no vast lands or armies. This was not the ally Mr. Franklin and my father had hoped for, nor the frontier kingdom we had gone in search of.

My father resumed walking. "Please. Take us to our wounded."

Rhys led us into the village, down the main lane between the buildings. We passed houses and barns, stables and sties. A blacksmith and a baker's shop. The villagers had come out of their homes to watch us pass, and, like the farmwoman, their disjointed appearance confused me. Their clothing and their homes, both Indian and old Welsh. Some of them nodded to us, some waved, and some stared. I smiled and returned their gestures, looking for someone my age among them. But all I saw were adults of the same indeterminate age as Rhys. We crossed a small village green and arrived at the taller building I had seen from a distance.

"Your companion is here." Rhys stood before the door. "This is the hall of Prince Madoc, and you are welcome to enter."

"The hall of Prince Madoc?" I whispered to my father. "How could that be?"

"A ceremonial title, I'm sure," my father said.

Rhys stepped aside, and we entered a dim and lofty great room. In the center, a fire burned in a hearth without a chimney. Phineas lay near it on a blanket, his shirt removed, while several men surrounded and attended to him. The gashes in his side were deep, ragged, and still bleeding.

The sight of him worried and confused me. He was a spy for the French. I was still sure of that. But up on the mountain, he'd put himself between the bear-wolf and me. He had protected me.

One of the men turned as we entered. He wore a finer shirt than the others, stitched with writhing, knotted dragons in red thread and Indian beads across his chest, and around his neck a heavy twist of golden wire with dragon mouths at the ends. His hair was longer than Rhys's and the others', and he had a thick mustache that reached his jaw.

He waved for us to approach, and Rhys led us before him, then backed away to the side of the room.

"I am Madoc ap Owain Gwynedd," the man said. "You are welcome to Annwyn."

My father bowed. "We are grateful to you and your men, Prince Madoc. I am John Bartram. With me are my son William, and my fellow philosophers. This is Jane Colden, and this is Andrew Montour."

I noticed Andrew hanging back from us, his head bowed.

Madoc craned his neck to look at him. "Welcome, all of you. Your man is gravely injured. My adviser, Myrddin, is skilled in medicine and will do his best to heal him."

A man kneeling by Phineas looked up. "The night will bear it out." His pale blue eyes had the color and quality of the ice that forms over the edges of our pond in winter. "I am about to stitch the wounds. Is there a healer among you?"

My father nodded toward Phineas. "He is our physician."

Myrddin went back to work.

"And now," Madoc said, "Rhys will show you to a house where you may stay."

"You are very generous," my father said. "But if I may —"

"There is nothing more you can do here." Madoc summoned Rhys with a flick of his hand. "I am sure you have questions, as do I. But now is not the time for answers. Eat, rest, pray for your companion, and then we will talk."

My father's mouth opened, then snapped shut.

He bowed again and allowed Rhys to lead us from the hall, back out onto the village green. We crossed to a nearby cottage, and Rhys let us inside. There were several beds and a table bearing trenchers of dried meat, corn, bread, and the vegetables we'd seen growing along the road. My eyes widened and my stomach came alive at the sight and aromas of so much food.

"Prince Madoc will speak with you this evening," Rhys said. "For now, this house is yours."

"Thank you, Rhys," my father said.

"I can take the young woman to her cottage, now."

Jane shot me a worried glance.

My father put a hand on her shoulder. "Her cottage?"

"Yes." Rhys cocked his head. "She does not sleep with the men, does she? We have arranged another place for her."

Jane shook her head, and my father cleared his throat. "I think she will stay with us," he said.

"With you?" Rhys glanced at Jane, then around the room at the rest of us. "Very well. If that is your custom." Then the Welshman left, shutting the door behind him. Through one of the narrow windows, I watched him stride back to Madoc's hall and go inside.

My father sat down on one of the beds and squeezed the bridge of his nose between his thumb and index finger. "This is a disaster."

"Agreed," Mr. Kinnersley said.

I was also disappointed in what the lost Welsh kingdom had turned out to be, but I did not find it to be the disaster my father did. The French attack, the spying, the loss of the *de Terzi*, the bear-wolf. Those were disasters. Madoc and his people were . . . strange. They were supposed to be like ourselves. But they had found a different way to live out here in the frontier.

"In what way is this a disaster, John?" Mr. Godfrey stood over the table. "We have found what we came to find." He picked up a strip of meat and tore off a bite with his teeth. He looked at the ceiling as he chewed. "I wonder if this is the flesh of an *incognitum*."

"Francis!" My father stared at him from across the room.

Mr. Godfrey took another bite. "One must eat, John."

My father stood. "Explain how this situation is *not* a disaster."

Mr. Godfrey reached and ripped off a hunk of bread from a large, round loaf. The crust crackled, and my mouth watered, but I didn't dare eat.

"Very well." Mr. Godfrey addressed the room. "When we left Philadelphia, who among you thought we would actually be able to strike out into the vastness of this New World and find what we were looking for? Be honest with yourselves. How many of you harbored doubts? Because I doubted. And yet here I am, against all probability, stand-ing in a Welsh-made cottage eating Welsh-baked bread." He took a bite. "And it's very good, I might add."

My father walked over to the table. He stood next to Mr. Godfrey, looking down at the food. "Billy, Jane, eat. The rest of you, too."

So I ate. Ravenously. Meat, bread, corn right off the cob that stuck in my teeth, and roasted vegetables. Jane and I both giggled like little children. I ate until my stomach hurt and couldn't hold any more.

My father didn't take a single bite. He watched us all eat, and after a while, he said, "I recognize that simply finding this place has been a tremendous feat, and you are all owed honor and glory for that alone. But that isn't enough."

The others put down their food and listened to him.

"Look at these people." My father pointed at the door. "Look at this place. They're practically Indians. We came seeking allies, but these backward Welsh are far from what we needed or hoped for. They have nothing to offer, strate-gically or militarily. Quite frankly, I'm surprised the French haven't found them here and driven them out."

Mr. Kinnersley brushed a kernel of corn from his chin. "Why *haven't* the French routed them?"

"I doubt they know they're here," Mr. Faries said. "Remember, the Osage in this territory do not speak of them."

My father pounded the table. "That's because there isn't anything to speak of!"

All of us froze, except Mr. Godfrey.

He licked his fingertips. "John, I'm afraid you must give up what you hoped to find and, instead, look for what you may have found."

"And what is that, Francis?" my father asked.

Mr. Godfrey shrugged. "I don't know. That is the reason you must look."

My father cursed and withdrew from the table. He went to one of the beds, sat, then lay down and closed his eyes. Watching him, I wanted to do the same thing. The food in my belly had put out the fire that had kept me going since the fight with the bear-wolf.

But something nagged at my thoughts.

Louis's manner had suggested he and his fellow Osage were frightened of the people of Madoc. He had called them demons. My father had dismissed that as superstition, but here in their village, in the demons' lair, I could not help but worry.

Across the table from me, Andrew stared with a vacant expression, rubbing the locket he wore around his neck. I realized he had not said a word since we had met Rhys atop the mountain and come down to this place.

"Are you well, Andrew?" I asked.

"Hm?"

"Are you well?"

"I am."

"What are you thinking about?"

His smile had a sad angle to it. "My mother."

*   *   *

We rested for the remainder of that afternoon. As the setting sun peered in through the cottage windows, my father rose from his bed and asked if I'd join him for a walk outside.

I didn't want to. I didn't want to be in his company, and nothing he had done since our falling-out at the ship had changed that. If anything, his reaction to Madoc and this village only confirmed what I had already said to him. But he was the elected leader of our expedition, and I was a Society member.

"Yes, sir."

Outside the cottage, the air smelled of woodsmoke and the fields glowed. Madoc's people walked the lanes of their village, coming in from their day's labor. They smiled and nodded, and we nodded back.

My father strolled with his hands clasped behind his back. "First, let me say that I do not hold you responsible for what happened to the *de Terzi*. That was Mr. Kinnersley's doing. You should not have slept on your watch. But to quote from Alexander Pope, 'To err is human; to forgive, divine.' I cannot blame you under the circumstances."

"Thank you for that." My voice came out flat.

"But things are still not right between us?"

"No. They're not."

"I would like for them to be."

"So would I."

"And how do you see them being made right?"

It was a fair question. It deserved a fair answer. I stopped in the middle of the street to face him. "Admit you were wrong about Andrew."

"But I was not wrong about Andrew."

I almost laughed at him but walked on instead. I had nothing more to say.

He caught up to me. "Even if I entertain your theory, and Andrew isn't guilty of spying, he is still half-Indian and not to be trusted."

I wanted to get away from him, but where? Back home, I would have gone down to the river, among the wild irises, to watch the fishermen out on their boats. But here, strangers surrounded us, and a wilderness surrounded them. I decided to turn back toward our cottage, toward Jane and the others.

"Billy, where are you going?" He followed me.

"I'm going back."

"I'm not finished."

"But I am, Father." I kept walking. "I am finished."

I reached the cottage and went inside. Madoc stood in the center of the room, flanked by Rhys and the adviser, Myrddin. Around them, the Society members looked somber. Jane and Mr. Faries had tears in their eyes.

"What is it?" I asked.

No one answered.

My father came in behind me. His eyes swept the room. "What has happened?"

"It's Phineas," Mr. Faries said. "He is dead."

CHAPTER 24

A Broken Peace

Annwyn had no churchyard. It had no church. Madoc said no priest had been willing to cross the ocean with their people. But the village had a graveyard in a grove of oak, and they agreed to let us bury Phineas there. Each of the Society members took hold of the shovel for a time as we dug a grave the proper size and depth. We had no coffin, so we simply laid his body in the earth and gathered around.

"I will make no great speech," my father said. "Phineas would not have wanted that. Instead, I will quote but one verse from the Gospel of John. 'Greater love hath no man than this, that a man lay down his life for his friends.'"

I looked down into the grave, the freshly turned dirt mixing into Phineas's blond hair. In the fight with the bear-wolf, he had laid down his life. Whatever else he had been guilty of, he had done that. In that moment, and for that reason, I forgave him.

My father stepped aside, and Myrddin gave what I thought to be a prayer in Welsh. Then each of the Society members took hold of the shovel for a time as we buried him. When that was done, we piled stones upon that spot as a marker and returned to the village.

As we approached our cottage, Madoc shook his head. "Come. We must talk."

We followed him to his hall and entered the chamber where I had last seen Phineas lying on the floor. The hearth was cold, but a haze filled the dark space between the timber rafters. Along one wall, I noticed a table lit with candles, and upon the table rested a silver chalice and a bottle. At the far end of the room stood a massive wooden chair. Carved animals leaped, crawled, and flew up its legs, over its arms, and down its back. What must have been years and years of smoke had darkened the wood to a rich umber, and the armrests bore the smooth polish of many hands.

"So you do have a throne," my father said.

Madoc took his chair and leaned back into it. His mustache accentuated the hard line of his frown. "Why are you here?"

My father glanced at Mr. Kinnersley, Mr. Godfrey, and Mr. Faries, the only other members of the Society remaining besides myself. Then he stepped forward.

"We have come to extend a hand of friendship to your —"

"YOU LIE!" Madoc's shout rang in the hall.

My father blanched.

The prince pounded the arm of his throne. "You come to wage war!"

"Prince Madoc." My father held his empty hands out before him. "We —"

Madoc pointed at him. "Before you say one more word, Englishman, there is something you should know."

"What is that?" my father asked.

"My scouts have learned that a French army marches toward Annwyn."

A murmur passed among the Society members. *The French?* I thought we had escaped them back at the Forks of the Ohio. But they were here? How had they found us?

"They are three days away," Madoc said. "At least five hundred men. They are led by a man named Marin."

My father nodded. "He attacked us once before, but with a greater number of men. Their march has taken its toll." He stepped closer to the throne. "Prince Madoc, I apologize for not being more forthright with you. It is true that we have come to seek an alliance with you, both political and milita —"

"Why would Annwyn want an alliance with you?"

"Well, I —" The question seemed to fluster my father. I think he had assumed an alliance as a given. "That is, we —"

"If I may ask a question." Mr. Godfrey stepped forward. "How is it you and your people know English?"

"We learned it from you," Madoc said. "Our spies have been among you since the first of your fur traders and missionaries reached us."

The revelation detonated among the Society members, leaving an aftermath of confusion. Madoc's people had been among us? When? Where? Were they in Philadelphia now? And why had they not announced themselves?

Mr. Godfrey held up a hand. I thought he was about to make a point, but he just sputtered. "How — I don't — But —"

"Our people had been in this New World, as you call it, for more than four hundred years when your people landed on these shores. If they had been there at Jamestown or Plymouth to greet your ships, they would have welcomed you and formed a quick alliance." Madoc leaned forward on his throne. "But by the time they learned of you, you had already gone to war many times against the *pobl cyntaf*, and they wanted no part of that."

"But you have seen your share of war, have you not?" my father asked. "We found one of your fortifications on the Ohio River."

"You found Gwynedd." Madoc rose from his chair and walked to the cold hearth. "One of our first cities. In the beginning, my people did as they had always done. They claimed land. They built walls and they defended them. But soon that land was not enough, and they sought to conquer more. But they were small in number, and the *pobl cyntaf* were numerous. Many from both sides lost their lives on the walls of Gwynedd, and the stones drank up their blood."

I remembered the echoes I had heard in the wall, the cries of anguish, fear, and rage.

"It took them many years, but my people finally found a way to live peacefully in this land." Madoc turned to my father. "We have observed you long enough to know that an alliance with you would make peace impossible."

He was right. We had come *because* Mr. Franklin feared that war with France was imminent. We were here to bring the Welsh into our conflict. And I think my father had assumed they would go willingly.

"I am sorry you have traveled so far." Madoc returned to his throne. "And at such great cost to you. But we cannot give you what you seek."

The hall was silent. My father put his hands on his hips and looked at the floor. He shook his head. "We came seeking something that doesn't exist."

"It may have existed once, long ago," Madoc said. "But no more. And now the French are here." He paused. "You English. You wanted me in your war. So you brought your war with you."

"Prince Madoc, believe me," my father said. "We did not intend for that to happen."

Madoc smirked. "Of course not. But you cannot help it. It is your nature."

"To err is human, sir," my father said.

To forgive, divine.

"Look at my village." Madoc made a sweeping gesture. "We have no wall. I have one hundred and seventeen men who can carry arms. But their weapons have not been used for anything more than hunting for more than three hundred years."

"We will leave your village." My father looked to the Society members, and they nodded their agreement. "Marin came for us. Perhaps he'll follow us."

"It is too late for that," Madoc said. "The French believe this territory to be theirs. Now that they have learned of us, they will not let us remain here. But we will find a new place and we will rebuild. As we speak, Rhys is spreading my order for our people to prepare themselves to leave. You should do the same. Go now." He dismissed us with a wave.

My father bowed and motioned the rest of us toward the door. We all shuffled from the hall out onto the green and were met there by several dozen men and women. They stared at us and glared at us, but said nothing. It seemed Madoc's order had already reached them, and they were angry with us. I couldn't blame them. They had to leave their homes and their farms because of us.

We had to thread through them to get to our cottage. Their gazes followed us as we walked among them and did not lift until we were inside and had shut the door.

"Now *this* is a disaster," Mr. Godfrey said.

"That isn't helpful, Francis." My father lowered his voice. "How could we have been so wrong?"

Mr. Kinnersley checked on the Leyden jar he had left in a corner of the room. "What I want to know is: How could Marin have found us?"

"Why don't we ask his spy?" My father turned to Andrew. "How many messages did you leave for Marin before we discovered you?"

I wanted to step between them and challenge my father. Andrew still hadn't said much, but he spoke up then.

"With respect, Mr. Bartram, it does not matter what I say. You will believe what you choose to believe."

"Not to mention," Mr. Godfrey said. "It's entirely possible that Marin followed the sightings and the evidence we all left behind. It's not as though the *de Terzi* was a covert vessel. Our conspicuous flying ship, the speed of the river upon which Marin traveled, and our own delays on foot could easily account for the French presence here."

"And they are still three days away," Mr. Faries said.

"Exactly," my father said. "Which is why we should prepare to leave at once."

"It is a shame, though, isn't it?" Mr. Godfrey said. "Peace is a precious thing, and they have enjoyed it here."

Peace *was* something rare and precious. I didn't know much about politics or war, but I knew that. Conflict never seemed to leave the colonies — fighting with the Indians, the French, the Spanish, and even with one another.

But not here.

Annwyn.

Paradise.

And we had shattered its peace by our mere presence.

"It is regrettable," my father said. "But it does not change the fact that we must leave. Are we in agreement?"

"No." It may not have been my place to speak. But that no longer concerned me. "This isn't right."

Everyone turned to look at me. Jane, Mr. Faries, and Mr. Kinnersley appeared surprised. Mr. Godfrey seemed amused. The weight of my father's stare bore down on me, but I continued under its burden.

"How can we leave knowing what we have done?" I said. "We had no business coming here, and now that we've drawn the French here, we owe more to these people than to run." I made eye contact with each of the men, and then with my father. "Before we left home, my mother told me that you had all done much for the protection of Pennsylvania. Is that true? Is that what this society does?"

Mr. Kinnersley lifted his chin. "That is *exactly* what this society does."

I took a deep breath. "Then shouldn't you protect these people?"

They made no answer. I looked at Jane. She beamed at me.

"By God," Mr. Godfrey said. "The boy is right."

Mr. Faries and Mr. Kinnersley agreed.

"We must decide on a strategy and course of action," Mr. Faries said.

"You'll do nothing yet." My father crossed to the cottage door. "Billy, come with me."

And he left.

I cast one more look at Jane, and then I followed him. Out on the green, most of the crowd had cleared away. My father strode in the direction of Madoc's hall, and I quickened my pace to keep up. He stopped when we reached the door.

"You are right, son."

"About what?"

"Our responsibility."

He entered the hall, and so did I.

"John Bartram!" Madoc's voice from his throne carried anger. "Our hospitality and patience have limits. What do you want now?"

My father approached him. "Prince Madoc, forgive my immodesty, but you have in your village four of the greatest minds in all the colonies. We have three days to prepare for Marin. Let us defend you."

"Defend us?"

"Yes." My father came before the throne and folded his arms. "We are the American Philosophical Society. And that is what we do."

Mr. Faries, Mr. Godfrey, and Mr. Kinnersley stayed up with my father late into the night, formulating their plans by the strips of moonlight that fell across the table from the windows. I tried to listen but wasn't able to understand most of what they were saying, and eventually I fell asleep.

They were still going when I awoke the next morning.

"They're doing this because of you," Jane said during breakfast. "And I must say, I was quite impressed with you yesterday."

I felt my face warming. "Thank you."

"What is their plan, do you think?"

"I couldn't venture a single guess."

"Nor I. But I'm looking forward to finding out."

After bolting down their breakfasts, Mr. Faries and Mr. Kinnersley left on some errands in the village, while my father and Mr. Godfrey continued to murmur back and forth. Mr. Faries came back a short while later, darting about with excitement, saying something about his glass lenses and bronze shields. When Mr. Kinnersley returned, he spoke about irrigation and seemed pleased. Then more planning and discussion, right through supper.

Jane and I grew bored and went for a walk around the village, where the residents all seemed hurried, running about with purpose and urgency. At the edge of town, silhouetted by the setting sun, rose a wide wooden tower still under construction. Dozens of men labored over it, and I wondered what it would be used for.

"Do you think it odd that we haven't seen anyone our age?" Jane asked.

"I wondered about that same thing. And, yes, I think it's odd."

"I wonder where all the children are."

"Perhaps they have none."

"Hm. Perhaps." But she sounded skeptical.

When we returned to the cottage, we found a dinner of bread, butter, and milk waiting for us. No one had touched it, so Jane had to direct the Society members to stop and eat, after which we all went to bed.

As I lay there, looking up at the ceiling, I realized that one of the three days had just passed. Marin was one day closer. There wasn't any chance of getting to sleep after that, so I was awake when, several hours into the night, Andrew rose from his bed.

He crept across the room, shoeless, opened the cottage door, and slipped outside.

I wondered what could pull him from his bed in the middle of the night, and I peeked through a window to see where he was going. He stole across the village green and entered the grove of oak trees where we had buried Phineas.

What could he be doing at this hour?

Clearly something he didn't want the rest of us to know about. And when I added this to the oddness of his recent behavior, I had to wonder if perhaps I had been too ready to trust him. Questions and doubts rose up through me like specters. I thought back over what I knew about him. Why had he been so ready to come on this expedition? Croghan had tried to discourage him, but he came anyway. Why? What purpose drove him?

My father's voice intruded on my thoughts. *He is a spy.*

No. He isn't.

But what if he was? Perhaps I had so wanted my father to be wrong that I turned my eyes from the truth. Even so, I resolved not to say anything to my father until I knew more.

It was some time before Andrew returned. I held still in the darkness and watched him steal back into his bed as quietly as he had left it. I was awake long after that, trying to decide what I would do.

CHAPTER 25

The First Battle

The next morning, after breakfast, my father told Jane and me that he had a duty for us to perform. We went outside and found a dozen large bronze shields leaning up against the cottage in the shade next to a pile of rags and a bucket of clay. The shields varied in size and shape, but each wore embossing on their faces, the same kinds of intricate patterns found in Rhys's tattoos.

"You will polish these," he said. "But I want you to polish the backside."

"The backside?" I asked.

"Yes, the smooth side." He showed us how to dab some clay on a rag and then rub the shield with it.

"After you have treated the entire surface with the clay," he said. "Rinse it off and then polish the shield with one of these."

He handed us each a satchel made of supple deerskin, packed tightly with sand.

"Yes, sir," I said.

He handed me the rag he'd been using. "When you are finished, each of these must be a mirror."

"Yes, sir." I set down the deerskin and dipped the rag in the clay. "Where is Andrew today?"

"He's helping Mr. Kinnersley out in the fields."

"What are they doing out there?"

"Concern yourself with this task," he said. "And after this, take these shields to Mr. Faries. You will find him at the tower Madoc's people are constructing for him. Assist him in any way he asks."

"Yes, sir."

He nodded and left us.

Jane and I set to work, following his instructions. The first two shields went easily. By the time we were done, I could look into them and see a monstrous and distorted image of myself staring back. And we had to be careful how we held them, because at certain angles, we could sear each other's eyes with the reflected sun.

Two shields later, my elbows started to ache, and by the fourth, they throbbed. I looked at Jane. She gritted her teeth, rubbing, rubbing, rubbing. But she didn't complain.

"I can finish these last ones," I said. "Give your arm a rest."

"No." She kept rubbing. "Thank you."

Some time later, we stood back, flexing and cradling our

elbows, facing an array of polished shields. The clay had softened the skin on my hands.

"I suppose we should get these to Mr. Faries," Jane said.

So we each took a shield and carried it through town to the tower I had seen the villagers constructing the day before. It had changed much since then. It stood perhaps fifty feet high. Mr. Faries patrolled around it, calling up directions to the men working at its peak.

I walked up to him. "Mr. Faries, my father wanted me to bring this to you."

He took the shield from me. "Ah, excellent, Billy." He turned his back to the afternoon sun and held the shield in front of him. He adjusted the angle, and a bright flash of reflected light lit up his face. "Excellent, indeed! Bring them all here."

"Yes, sir."

Jane and I made the trip to and from the tower several more times, and each time we returned, the wooden structure had changed a little more. By the time we brought the last two shields, a long and narrow platform balanced at the summit.

Mr. Faries walked around a wooden framework he and several of the Welshmen had built on the ground. It had a slight curve to it, like a shallow saucer. He took the shields one at a time and lashed them to the framework at regular intervals — three shields high, four shields wide — creating an almost continuous surface of bronze.

Mr. Faries cupped his hand to his mouth. "Raise it! And mind your eyes over there!"

A team of Welshmen heaved one edge of the shielded frame up to their chests and then over their heads. Then they walked the frame upright, hand over hand, until it stood vertical.

"Hold it there!" Mr. Faries ran some distance out in front and faced it. He walked a pace or two one way, then the other, eying the giant mirror. He jogged in a few times to make adjustments to the angle of the shields. "That's it, you can set it down!"

"What are you building, sir?" I asked.

Mr. Faries smiled. This was the happiest I had seen him during the entire expedition. "I am attempting to build a type of cannon."

"What kind of cannon?" Jane asked.

"A cannon of light," Mr. Faries said. He turned back to the Welshmen. "Gentlemen, let's get this up there in position."

They dropped ropes down from the top of the tower, through a network of pulleys, and tied them to the shield mirror. As Jane and I watched them hoist the framework off the ground, Mr. Godfrey appeared at my side.

"Archimedes himself could not have done better under the circumstances."

"Sir?"

"This device is not without precedent. A similar weapon set the ships of Rome afire as they laid siege to Syracuse. But Mr. Faries has the benefit of modern optics."

Several moments later, they had the shield mirror mounted vertically at one end of the platform. Mr. Faries slung his leather bag over his shoulder, the one in which he'd brought his glass lenses.

"Care to join me, Billy?"

"Up there?"

"Of course."

He walked to the base of the tower and took hold of a ladder. I did the same, and we climbed. It felt higher than I thought it would, and I took every rung with great caution. We reached the platform, where Mr. Faries sighed over the vista below us. To the north lay the village, and I could see our cottage and Madoc's hall. Mountains rose up behind and to either side of the settlement. To the south, the land opened up into fields with fewer trees, cut through by a river. Welshmen worked out there, but I couldn't tell what they were doing. It did not look like farming.

Jane and Mr. Godfrey waved to me from below, and I waved back. A wooden rib arched over us, with an iron ring at its peak. There were four of these arches along the length of the platform, descending in height by degrees until the final one rested just before the level of our eyes.

"Before I arm this cannon," Mr. Faries said, "let's aim it somewhere harmless. Take those two ropes there on either side."

I stood to the rear, near the shields, and grasped the two ropes he indicated.

"If you pull on one, the platform will move in that direction. Try it."

I leaned to one side and pulled. The planks under my feet shifted, and I widened my stance to keep my balance as the entire platform rotated, facing us away from any people below.

"Pull the other rope, and we swing the other way. And now . . ." Mr. Faries brought the leather bag around in front of him. He pulled out one of the glass lenses, polished it with a cloth, and carefully lifted and clamped it into the first iron ring. He did the same with the remaining lenses, until each ring held one. "Those bronze shields will catch the sun's light, and when I pull this rope, the trigger, they'll shoot that light down the barrel of these lenses, firing a highly concentrated ray out of the end."

"A cannon of light," I said.

"Exactly. I had to make do with the materials available, but this will be serviceable, I should think. Shall we test it?"

"Yes, sir!"

"Be ready. This will be bright." He shielded his eyes with his hands and pointed. "Let's aim for that bush there, by the river. You see it?"

"Yes."

"Move the ropes like I showed you."

I pulled the rope on the right and swung the light cannon around.

"Now, those ropes there, the two running up and down near your shoulder, those will raise and lower the barrel."

I found the ropes he referred to and pulled on one. The end of the platform lurched upward.

"Whoa, not that one," Mr. Faries said.

I pulled on the other rope, and the barrel pivoted downward. I let go when I could see the intended bush through the farthest lens.

"Ready?" Mr. Faries asked.

"Yes."

"Give the order to fire."

I watched the bush. "Fire!"

He pulled the trigger. I heard no sound, but I felt an instant heat on my neck, and a blinding flash lit up the bush. He let go of the trigger.

The bush had burst into flames. It had taken less than a second.

Welshmen rushed to put out the fire with water scooped from the river. I watched them, stunned by what had just happened, almost disbelieving it but for the smoke I smelled in the air.

"Aim us somewhere safe, Billy," Mr. Faries said.

"Oh." I pulled on the guide ropes, and the cannon lifted and swiveled, the barrel pointing at the distant horizon.

Mr. Faries looked around at his device and nodded. "Yes. This will do nicely."

*   *   *

On the morning of the third day, reports came in from Madoc's scouts that Marin's army would be at Annwyn that evening. We were gathered in the prince's hall. Madoc sat upon his throne, Rhys to his right and Myrddin to his left.

"Are you ready, Ebenezer?" my father asked.

"I am," Mr. Kinnersley said.

"Your wisdom exceeds my own," Myrddin said. "Cannons that shoot light. And you say your fire burns through water?"

Mr. Kinnersley held up a finger. "Electrical fire, yes."

"So are we ready to flood the fields?" my father asked.

"When Prince Madoc gives the order," Mr. Kinnersley said.

My father turned toward the throne.

Madoc stood. "You have the order."

Mr. Kinnersley bowed and left the hall.

"Rhys," Madoc said. "Are your men ready?"

"They are, my prince. Swords and spears sharpened."

"I want everyone not fighting to go to the forest. They should be ready to flee if things go badly for us."

"It will not go badly," my father said.

"I trust not." Madoc resumed his throne. "The only other matter I would like to address before the battle concerns this man you call Andrew Montour. I would speak with him alone."

My father looked at Madoc askance. "Why?"

I wondered if this was somehow connected to Andrew's late-night wanderings.

"That is not your concern. Andrew, please come forward. The rest of you may go. I will meet you on the field of battle shortly."

Andrew glanced at each of us and stepped forward. We all lingered a moment and then filed toward the door. My father stayed where he was, and I wondered if he would refuse to leave. It would be intolerable to him to think of Andrew, the spy, in a secret conference with Prince Madoc.

"Go now, John Bartram," Madoc said. "Let me remind you that you are still a guest in my hall."

My father glowered, but he came with us. Outside the hall, he milled around the green, waiting. We waited with him, and I wondered if I should report what I had seen Andrew do the previous night. Before I could decide, Andrew emerged from the hall, heading toward our cottage.

My father stepped into his path, blocking his passage. "What happened in there?"

"Please let me pass, sir." Andrew's eyes were red, as though he'd been crying.

"Not until you tell me what happened. What did you say to Madoc?"

Andrew tried to walk around, but my father stepped back in his way.

"What did you do, Andrew?"

"That isn't your concern," Andrew said.

"This expedition is my concern!" My father shook a fist in Andrew's face. "What? Were you trying to make a deal for Marin? Trying to ally Madoc with the French?"

"You're insane."

My father slapped him. "What did you say, half-breed?"

Andrew touched his reddening cheek. And he punched my father in the face.

I stepped toward him as he stumbled backward. Jane gasped, while Mr. Faries and Mr. Godfrey rushed to restrain Andrew.

My father spat blood. "If you ever touch me again —"

"What?" Andrew threw off the Society members and opened his arms wide. "What will you do? You want to know what Madoc said to me? You want to know why I'm here? It's because these are my mother's people! She came from this place. Madoc sent her out to learn about all of you, and to do that, she became an interpreter. And out there, she married my father, Carondawanna, and she bore me. She couldn't come home before she died, so I came for her, to lay something of her to rest in the Annwyn grave-yard among her kin."

I noticed the locket was gone from around his neck, and it all made sense. That was what he had left in the middle of the night to do. There wasn't anything sinister or secre-tive about it. It was a moment Andrew had simply wanted to have in private.

"I was right," my father said. "You've been lying to us since the moment you came aboard our ship."

"No, Father," I said. "You were wrong. You accused him of being a spy for the French. You accused him of dropping messages for Marin, when it was Phineas, all along. You were wrong about that, and you were wrong about Andrew."

"But I was right not to trust him!" His outburst carried across the green.

Mr. Faries and Mr. Godfrey shook their heads. They stepped away from Andrew, and though they didn't apologize to him, they looked at him in a way that expressed sympathy.

Andrew nodded to them. "Since I want to be honest with all of you, there's something else you should know."

"And what is that?" my father asked.

"Madoc offered me a drink from the chalice," he said.

"The chalice?" Mr. Godfrey asked. "They offered you a drink? What does that mean?"

"It means they were offering me a place here. They asked me to come home."

He left then, returning to the cottage.

Mr. Faries followed after him, ushering Jane with him, but as they passed my father, Mr. Faries put a hand on his shoulder.

"You should listen to your son, John." And then they were gone.

Mr. Godfrey muttered to himself, "The chalice . . ." and shambled away, leaving me alone with my father on the green.

I took a step toward him. "Father, I —"

"You listen to me, William." His voice was strained, on the verge of breaking. "You said you were wrong to want to be like me. That is the prerogative of every son. But before you judge me, know this. I believe as I do for a reason." He looked at the ground near my feet. "You never knew your grandfather, with whom you share a name. He was a good man. An industrious, honest, and charitable ma —" His voice failed. He brought his fist up and pressed it hard against his lips.

I waited.

He cleared his throat. "He was a beloved father to me. When I was eleven years old, he left me in the care of my own grandparents in Pennsylvania, and he moved to North Carolina to establish a farm. I never saw him again. On the twenty-second day of September, Indians raided his farm and brutally murdered him in cold blood. My stepmother, and my precious younger brother and sister were taken captive. It is only by God's mercy that they were returned to us. But my father —" He pounded his chest, tears falling from his eyes. "My father was taken from me by those savages!"

I didn't know what to say. I had never seen my father in such pain. He had always seemed invincible. Impregnable. But in that moment, he was open and completely vulnerable, and I loved him for it.

"Father, I didn't know."

"Your mother didn't want you to know until you were older."

"Thank you for telling me."

He nodded. "I am what I am. Perhaps now you understand."

I did understand him better. But that did not mean I agreed with him. Andrew had not killed my grandfather, and I couldn't hate him for it, even if my father did.

"Is there anything you would like to say to me, son?"

I didn't know what he expected or wanted to hear. I wouldn't — couldn't — apologize, because I still believed everything I'd said. So I decided to give his own words back to him.

"To err is human, Father. To forgive, divine."

CHAPTER 26

The Engines of War

We didn't speak after that. The afternoon waned, and the village prepared for battle. Rhys formed ranks with his men at the southern edge of town. The warriors all went shirtless, armed with spears, javelins, swords, bows, and a few rifles. They had covered themselves in a nitrous ointment that made their skin shine and their tattoos writhe. The sight of them frightened me, but not as much as the thought of what was to come. I was preparing to climb up the light cannon with Mr. Faries when my father called to me.

"Come away from there, son."

I faced him. "I'm going to help Mr. Faries in the battle."

"No. I want you and Jane to go to the woods with the villagers."

He wanted me to run and hide. If I was honest, I wanted that, too, but I refused to give in to my fear. "I'm staying to fight, Father. Mr. Faries needs my help with the light cannon."

"Someone else can assist him."

"No. I'm staying."

"I can remove you by force."

"And as soon as you leave me, I'll just come back."

He seemed to be struggling inside.

"You can't keep me away. This is my choice, Father. Not yours."

"I promised your mother I would keep you safe."

"And I promised her I would find my own path."

Madoc appeared on the front line. Unlike his warriors, he wore armor. An ancient shirt of chain mail, and a helmet that covered his nose and his cheeks but left openings around his eyes and mouth. He carried a bronze shield like those we'd polished, a sword, and around him a mantle of strength.

"Any sign of the French?" he asked.

"No," my father said.

"Well, let them come. You've ignited coals in me I thought long dead and cold, John Bartram." He turned to me. "Where will you be during the battle, Billy?"

I looked at my father. "I'll be in the light cannon, assisting Mr. Faries."

"Good lad," Madoc said. "Is everything in order with Mr. Kinnersley?"

"I believe so," my father said.

"Excellent. May we all meet well on the other side." He marched away.

What he'd said had more than one meaning. I turned back to my father, the reality of what was about to happen just now occurring to me. This would be a battle of life and death. I might not see him again. "Where will you be, Father?"

"Assisting Mr. Kinnersley with his electrical fire." He shook his head. "I'd never have guessed that one day I would utter *that* phrase."

We chuckled together, more than we probably would have under different circumstances. I wanted to make peace with him. But I didn't know how, and there didn't seem to be time.

"Will you be safe there?" I asked.

He nodded. "I'll meet you on the other side."

I nodded back to him, and with nothing more to say, I climbed the ladder. But halfway up I shouted back down to him, "Make sure Jane goes to the forest!" He saluted me, and I continued up to the narrow platform. Mr. Faries was already there, tinkering.

"Ah, Billy. Good to have you." He looked at his arm in its sling.

"I'm here to assist you, sir."

"When the battle starts, you'll aim, and I'll fire. Between us, we'll burn Marin to a crisp."

Below, Andrew appeared at the edge of the village. He had taken off his shirt and carried one of the Welsh spears. Someone had drawn tattoos across his skin, and he looked like one of Madoc's warriors as he took his place among them.

I turned to the south. Out in the fields, I saw small ponds and puddles, patches of shallow water reflecting the blue of the sky. Mr. Kinnersley had flooded the low ground and turned it into one big water trough, through which his trapped lightning was supposed to burn. He was down there somewhere, safely perched up in a tree with his Leyden jar, wires connecting him to the water, waiting until the right moment to shock an entire army. If it worked. There had been no way to test it first.

The Leyden jar had but one charge.

Mr. Faries saw them first.

"The French!" he shouted, waving his good arm. "The French are here!"

I glimpsed them then, among the trees. They came from the open land to the south, avoiding the mountains, no doubt trusting in their superior numbers to obtain an easy victory. They stopped short of the flood plain and sent two emissaries ahead, one of them waving a white flag.

Madoc waited for them beneath the light cannon, safe on dry land, his armor glinting in the sun. Behind him, the glistening Welshmen leered. They presented a frightening image, even to me, and the white flag trembled in the emissary's hand. He actually dropped it as he approached, snatching it up so quickly it seemed he expected to be shot full of arrows the moment he was no longer holding it. Madoc's men laughed at him.

"I've read that barbarians laugh in the face of death!" the emissary cried. "And now I observe that to be true."

A cold silence fell over the Welshmen.

He drew near enough that I recognized him. He was the same man who had come with Marin to threaten and negotiate with Major Washington back at the Forks. And the man next to him . . .

"Mr. Colden!" I shouted.

Mr. Faries leaned outward. "Cadwallader?"

Mr. Colden looked up, his face battered and bruised. "Billy?"

"Silence," the Frenchmen said, and Mr. Colden flinched.

"You threaten us under the banner of the white flag?" Madoc asked.

"No, Prince Madoc," the emissary said. "I come with terms for your surrender to Captain Paul Marin." The emissary presented a sealed scroll.

Mr. Colden was alive.

I wanted to run shouting the news to Jane and my father, but I couldn't.

Mr. Colden raised his head, but his shoulders slumped in defeat. His hands were chained behind his back, his clothes were unkempt, and it was obvious they had treated him poorly. His eyes sought me out, then looked to either side of me. He seemed to be studying the tower. His eyes landed on the bronze shields, followed down the line of lenses to the end of the cannon, and then opened wide. His shoulders rose a little then, and his lips formed a barely concealed smile. He knew what this was.

"I do not even need to read that." Madoc looked at the scroll without taking it. "I reject his terms."

"That is unwise, sir." The emissary looked around. "You are on French soil. Captain Marin does not need to offer you terms at all. He is within his right to simply raze your little village."

"I do not recognize his claim to this land," Madoc said. "And if he attempts to drive us from it, he does so to his ruin. There is a reason the Osage name us demons."

The emissary sneered. "That may have kept you hidden until now. But you are outnumbered, sir. We are the *troupes de la marine*. And your men here, with your wooden weapons, your . . . telescope, and your pathetic attempt to flood us out, you have no chance of victory."

A telescope? Good. Let him keep thinking that.

"But you do not have to take this on my word alone. With me is one of the philosophers, a former companion to those here with you. He has come here with me to reason with you." He turned to Mr. Colden. "Speak."

Mr. Colden took a deep breath. "The Frenchman is right. You are outnumbered."

The emissary nodded along with him.

"But seeing you gathered here" — Mr. Colden raised his voice — "I know you will be victorious! Stand your ground, I say! Stand and fight —"

"English dog!" The emissary struck Mr. Colden so hard

the blow knocked him to his knees. The Frenchman spun back toward Madoc. "It matters not what this man says! It is certain you will lose this conflict. But if you turn over the other English philosophers to Captain Marin's custody, and leave French soil forever, your lives will be spared."

Marin had to know we no longer had the airship. But he still wanted *us*.

"Are you finished?" Madoc asked.

The emissary recovered his composure. "Yes."

"Good." Madoc removed his helmet. "Now that you have spoken your piece, I will speak mine. And here are my terms for Captain Marin's surrender to me. He will remove his army from these lands, swearing on his life that no Frenchman will ever return, or we will destroy him. He has awakened the Red Dragon of Wales, and we will rain fire down upon him."

The emissary's thin smile lasted only a moment and then vanished. "Then Captain Marin will see you on the field of battle."

He bowed and returned across the flood plain, waving his white flag high, dragging Mr. Colden with him. I watched Jane's father go, feeling that I should have done something more for him.

Madoc replaced his helmet. "Are you ready with my dragon, Mr. Faries?"

"We're ready!" Mr. Faries turned to me. "Bring us around, Billy."

"But, sir, Mr. Colden —"

"The best way to help him now is to win this battle. Are you with me?"

I tightened my grip on the ropes, and it helped to stop my hands from shaking. "Yes, sir." I swung us around, aiming the cannon down the flooded fields.

"I'll fire on your mark," Mr. Faries said. "Just as we practiced."

The emissary disappeared into a group of trees. A short time after that, the French soldiers formed up in the forest, in and among the trees. They appeared accustomed to wilderness combat. But that would not help them when the danger flowed beneath their very feet. They began their advance on the village.

"They're coming," I said.

"Oh no." Mr. Faries looked up at the sky, and I followed his gaze.

A heavy bank of clouds appeared to be moving in, deep and wide.

"Without direct sunlight," Mr. Faries said, "we have no ammunition."

Which way were the clouds heading? I watched their movement, and they seemed to be coming directly toward us.

Mr. Faries pointed at the trees. "Let's show them what this telescope can do. Quickly, before we lose our sunlight."

"But, Mr. Colden —"

"He saw this cannon, Billy. He'll know to stay clear. Now are you ready?"

"Yes, sir." I pivoted and turned us, aiming for a distant group of trees on the far side of Mr. Kinnersley's flood plain, at the backs of the French. If I burned the right places, the flames would drive them forward into the water. "Ready."

"Then let's breathe some fire."

I gave the order.

He pulled the trigger.

Light blasted from the cannon. Frenchmen shouted and scattered from the trees where it struck, shielding their eyes and their faces. The trees burned.

"Again, Billy!"

I repositioned the barrel. "Fire!"

He pulled the trigger.

This time, men burst from the trees with their clothes aflame and threw themselves forward into the flood-waters to extinguish it.

I aimed. "Fire!"

Another hit.

I aimed. "Fire!"

Soon, a line blazed across the fields and woods, just as I had planned, leaving the French without an escape route and pushing them forward.

I aimed. "Fire!"

He pulled the trigger, but the shadow of a cloud fell over us, shuttering the light from our weapon. We stood upon a useless platform, creaking in the wind, and I watched the skies, praying for an opening.

Mr. Faries let go of the trigger. "Let's hope we did enough. It's up to Ebenezer now."

The Welshmen had taken up defensive positions. The bowmen crouched behind a few stone walls and peered from around buildings, ready to fire, but so far, no Frenchman had come within range. The light cannon had stalled them, perhaps frightened them, and hopefully given them second thoughts. They waited, ankle-deep and knee-deep.

"Mr. Colden is down there," I said.

Mr. Faries pulled a telescope from his coat and stretched it open. "Let us pray he's behind the fire line, out of the water."

"What is Mr. Kinnersley waiting for?" I asked.

He peered through the telescope, his other eye pinched shut. "For my signal."

The French resumed their forward march.

"I see Marin," Mr. Faries said.

"Is Mr. Colden with him?"

"No."

The first French soldiers reached firing distance and halted. I could see them loading their rifles in the trees, pouring their powder and ramming their bullets.

"Mr. Faries?"

"Yes, it's time." He pulled a red cloth from his pocket and waved it over his head. I saw a matching red handkerchief flap a reply, and then a Welsh runner took off toward Mr. Kinnersley's position.

"Now." Mr. Faries tucked the cloth back in his pocket. "Let's see what these Frenchmen make of lightning in a bottle."

We waited and watched.

Nothing happened.

"Sir?"

"Give him time."

Still nothing happened. The French shouted orders back and forth. They seemed to be readying for their first assault.

Mr. Faries tapped his foot on the wooden planks. "Come on, Ebenezer."

And then it happened.

It had no sound. No flash. But the electrical fire burned. Every Frenchman I could see jolted upright in the exact same moment. I knew how they felt. I knew how it felt to have your whole body slammed from the inside. Men cried out. Some of them fell forward into the water among the corn and other crops. Some of them staggered and fell against the trees.

Mr. Faries waved the red handkerchief again. "Now, Prince!"

Madoc raised his sword high. "*Dynion o Annwyn! Ymosod!*"

He and his warriors charged forward, hurling battle cries. I tried to follow Andrew with my eyes but lost sight of him in a dense patch of trees.

The sounds of battle reached us. Clangs, grunts, groans, and cries of pain. It was the sound of the ghost wall reaching up through the centuries. The first gunshot cracked in the distance somewhere. Then another. Madoc's men fought hand-to-hand, man-to-man in the trees and the fields, with spear and sword and shield, and on that footing, they were the superior force, pushing the French into retreat.

"The jar didn't contain enough lightning to kill them," Mr. Faries whispered. "Only stun them."

He was right. The farthest Frenchmen were regrouping in the fields and the trees. They loaded their rifles, those whose powder was still dry. The rest pulled their swords free of their scabbards. I looked nearer to us, at the line of battle. Madoc's men thought they were winning.

But they were still outnumbered. And in another moment, the might of Marin's army would fall upon them.

I looked upward, helpless. The clouds continued to roll over us.

"Please," I whispered. "Just a little bit of sun."

The rear guard French forces were drawing closer. They would soon be ready to ambush Madoc's men, who still fought hard and fierce, pressing their foes back into the trees.

"Look out!" I shouted. But no one could hear me over the clamor of battle.

I worried for Andrew down there. I worried for my father and Jane and Mr. Kinnersley. I hadn't seen Mr. Godfrey for some time. I didn't know what his assignment had been and hoped he was safe. Perhaps he had gone with the others into the woods.

Mr. Faries peered through his telescope. His voice was a whisper. "It's going to be a slaughter."

CHAPTER 27

The Chalice

The French behind the battle line had stopped and taken up positions behind the trees, surrounding the open fields. They loaded their rifles. Hundreds of them. Madoc's forces would be shredded. I had to do something.

I rushed to the ladder.

"Billy, where are you going?"

"I have to warn them!"

"You won't make it in time!"

"I have to try!" I stepped out onto the first rung.

"Billy, look!" Mr. Faries pointed skyward.

A gap in the clouds approached us, dragging a patch of sunlight across the ground below. I breathed a thank-you, and leaped back to the ropes.

"We won't have long," Mr. Faries said. "But it has to be enough."

I pulled us into range, sighting down the lenses.

"I'm going to hold the trigger open," he said. "It will be a continuous beam. You have to keep control of it and be careful of our men. We have to drive the French back before Madoc gets there."

"I understand." I took aim at the trees and visually scanned another burn line, planning the sweep of my shot. "I'm ready."

"Wait for the light, lad. Then give the order."

I squared my stance.

And then the sun reached us. Its warmth poured over me.

"Fire."

He pulled the trigger, unleashing my artillery of light. The French were still in the shade. But my burning ray found them. I ignited the first group of trees, scattering the enemy.

"Hurry, Billy!"

I pulled the ropes, swinging us left, to the next unit of soldiers, leaving a trail of flame and smoke behind me. They, too, fell away before the power of the sun. I pulled down on the ropes to my side, lifting and dipping the ray at the same time that I rotated the platform, carving a track of fire.

"We're going to lose the light soon!" Mr. Faries said.

"Where was Marin?" I blasted another group of soldiers.

Mr. Faries, holding the trigger rope, tried pointing with his wounded arm. "There, by that tall sycamore!"

I couldn't see the French captain. But I brought my weapon to bear on that spot, torching the ground all around. And then the opening in the clouds passed over us, and my weapon died. Mr. Faries released the trigger. Below us, two lines of fire now burned; the first we had lit, and now this second one. Smoke billowed into the sky.

"You did it," Mr. Faries said.

The enemy line had broken. Marin's men now found themselves trapped between the two fires. They were scattering in any direction they could to escape. Moments later, Madoc's men reached the first blaze, driving the French before them. After that, the enemy fell into a full, chaotic retreat.

"The day is ours," Mr. Faries said.

"Thanks to you and Mr. Kinnersley," I said.

"We simply provided the engines of war. Your father devised the whole strategy."

I felt pride in my father as he said it, something I hadn't felt in some time.

Mr. Faries looked at me, then reached over and tousled my hair. "And let's not forget our eagle-eyed gunner."

I smiled a little. And then I returned my attention to the field of battle. I wanted to make sure everyone was safe. My father, Mr. Kinnersley, Andrew. And I worried about what had happened to Mr. Colden.

"I'm going to go find Jane," I said.

He nodded. "Go. I want to keep my eyes on those fires to make sure they're not spreading out of control."

I crossed the platform to the ladder and descended. On the ground, I turned toward the village and ran, past the hall, until I reached the forest on the far side.

"Jane!" I called. "Jane!"

I wandered a few paces into the trees, shouting her name through my cupped hands. A few moments later, I heard her calling back, and then she came into view.

She ran toward me. "Is it over?"

"We won! But you have to come with me. Your father is here!"

"What? Where?"

I pointed toward the battlefield. "The French had him."

"We've got to find him."

I nodded, and we took off running back through the village. When we reached the light cannon, I called up to Mr. Faries.

"Have you seen Mr. Colden?"

He clutched his telescope. "I thought I caught a glimpse of him. That way!"

We left in the direction he had indicated, and even though I knew there was no longer any danger from the electrical fire, I still hesitated for just a moment before I plunged into the water. It soaked my boots and came up to my knees in the deepest places, making it difficult to be sure of my footing. It slowed our pace as we slogged ahead.

Though the battle was over, we still heard the sounds of clashing off in the trees: Madoc's men taking on the stragglers left behind as Marin's forces retreated. There were bodies in the water, mostly Frenchmen. I didn't want to look at them, but I had to make sure Mr. Colden wasn't among them.

"Father!" Jane called beside me.

"Mr. Colden!" I shouted.

We pressed onward, stumbling and supporting each other through the drowned fields and stands of skeleton trees. Both of us fell into the water more than once and came up soaked to our chins. But we called to Jane's father every few steps.

The air became hazy and stung my eyes, while the sharp smell of smoke clawed at my nose and my lungs. "We must be getting close to the first fire," I said.

Jane stopped. "First fire?"

"We burned two lines in the trees."

"Was he . . . ?"

"I don't know."

She turned away. "Father! Father!"

"Mr. Colden!"

The smoke grew thicker, tinged with orange ahead of us, and I started to feel heat on my face. I could hear a distant roar, like a rushing river. We were getting too close to the flames. I took hold of Jane's arm. "We should turn back!"

She shook me off.

But if the fire was moving toward us, we needed to get out of its path. "Jane, it's too dangerous!"

"Father!"

I didn't know how I was going to be able to pull her away. And then —

"Jane?" came a faint reply, off to one side.

We turned toward it. A shadowy figure staggered

toward us through the smoke, and as it drew nearer, we saw that it was Mr. Colden. Mr. Faries had pointed us in the right direction.

Jane rushed to him. "Father!"

"Jane," he said. They embraced, tightly, and for a long time. "I thought I'd never see you again."

Jane was crying. "I'm so sorry. I'm so sorry I left the ship."

"Shh, there now." He stroked her hair. "None of that. It wasn't your fault."

I was still worried about the fire. "I think we should head back to the village."

Mr. Colden looked up. "Quite right. Lead the way, Billy."

And so I turned away from the smoke and the heat and led us through the trees and fields. Jane and her father came behind me, leaning on each other. I offered to help, but Mr. Colden waved me off. Before long, I could see the tower with the light cannon from the perspective the French would have had. It didn't look dangerous at all, from here. I could see Mr. Faries, and he seemed to be looking through his telescope. I waved to him, but didn't know if he could see me.

Soon we reached the edge of the fields and emerged onto dry land. Jane and her father sat down on the ground.

Mr. Faries called down from the tower, laughing. "Welcome back, Cadwallader!"

Mr. Colden waved back. "You've outdone Archimedes himself!"

Then Madoc strode out of the battlefield toward us. He favored one of his legs, but appeared otherwise unharmed.

Soot blackened his armor and his face, and blood streaked his sword. Rhys and Myrddin walked beside him. Rhys had a gash on one of his arms, and Myrddin bled from several places, but none of the wounds appeared mortal.

Madoc gave Rhys an order in Welsh, and he sprinted back toward the battle. Madoc then said something to Myrddin, and the man trotted off in the direction of the village.

Then the prince saw me.

"Hah! My dragon!" He came over and draped a heavy, jangling, mailed arm over my back. He kissed his free hand up at the tower. "From up there, you couldn't see the looks on their faces, could you? It was glorious. A battle befitting the days of old!"

When we first arrived here, Madoc had wanted nothing but peace. A peace that had lasted for hundreds of years. And here he was now, in his armor, smelling of blood and smoke, a different man.

"I've ordered Rhys to harry those French to the ends of the earth. Offer them no quarter, no rest, until they are wiped out. And Myrddin just went to bring in the others from the forest. Tonight, we celebrate our victory!"

He had no idea how close his men had come to defeat, that without Mr. Faries and the light cannon, they would have been massacred. "Have you seen my father?" I asked.

"No. But I owe him and Mr. Kinnersley my thanks. That electrical fire gave my men the chance they needed to break the enemy line."

"Billy!" Mr. Faries shouted down from the tower. "I see them!"

I forgot about Madoc. "Where?"

"There!" He pointed. Then he craned his neck forward. "Wait. Something is wrong."

"What do you mean?"

"I think one of them is hurt."

I raced off in the direction he had pointed, splashing through fields and trees. *Please, not Father. Don't let it be Father.* I entered a newer section of crops, the trees still thick and looking half-alive. And then I heard them.

"Hold on, Andrew." That sounded like my father.

"He's not going to make it, John." That was Mr. Kinnersley.

"Father?" I called.

"Billy?"

I followed his voice, and they came into view. My father and Mr. Kinnersley were soaked to the waist, faces and clothes smeared with ash, but they appeared unharmed. Andrew staggered between them, his arms around their necks, bleeding from his shirtless chest.

"Billy," my father said. "Help us."

I rushed to them and bolstered Andrew, taking Mr. Kinnersley's place. We stumbled forward, dragging Andrew between us, his head lolling forward.

I looked across him at my father. "What — ?"

"Not now, son. Let's — let's just get him to the village."

Mr. Faries must have watched our progress, because he and Madoc met us with a few Welshmen and conducted us to the main hall. Inside, Myrddin pointed at a table. "Lay him there." He retrieved a leather roll from a chest in a corner of the room and opened it to reveal his medical tools. Blood poured from the wound as he examined it. The image of Phineas came to my mind, lying there wounded. "He was stabbed," Myrddin said. "Knife?"

"Bayonet," my father said.

Andrew moaned and mumbled.

My father stepped closer to him. "Mr. Kinnersley and I, we were trying to make it back to the tower." He glanced at me. "Andrew found us. Apparently he'd been searching for us, and afterward we made our way together. But then we encountered a group of French soldiers. Andrew fought them. Bravely. He saved our lives."

"The wound is very deep." Myrddin turned to Madoc. "I can do nothing for this."

Jane covered her mouth.

My father noticed Mr. Colden standing next to her. "Cadwallader? It's good to see you, old friend."

"You, too, John."

Madoc unbuckled his sword and set it down. He pushed my father aside. "Let me speak with Andrew." He bent down close and laid his hand on Andrew's brow. "Lad, open your eyes." His voice was tender. "Can you hear me? Andrew?"

Andrew's eyelids fluttered. "Wha —" His face contorted in pain. "I —"

"You must listen to me," Madoc said. "And then you must answer me. Do you want to drink from the chalice?"

323

The chalice? I looked across the room at the candlelit table. The chalice was there, but the bottle that had stood next to it was gone.

"What is this?" my father asked. "This is your medicine?"

Madoc ignored him. "You must agree to it, Andrew. I need you to nod your head. Quickly, now. Before it's too late."

"Too late for what?" Mr. Kinnersley asked.

Andrew swallowed and jerked his head forward, attempting to nod.

"That's enough, Andrew." Madoc looked up at Myrddin. "Go. Get it."

Myrddin turned in the direction of the side table and jolted to a halt. "It's gone."

"What?" Madoc stood upright. He ran to the table and, after a brief search, faced my father. His face showed more rage and hate than he had directed even at the French emissary. "What have you done?"

"Pardon me?" my father asked.

Madoc flew at him from across the room, grabbed him by the throat, and slammed him up against a wall. "What have you done?"

Jane let out a surprised scream.

My father choked, "I — I don't . . ."

"Stop it!" I leaped at Madoc and wrenched at his arm, but I couldn't break his hold on my father. "Let him go!"

"My prince!" Myrddin shouted. "I do not think it was one of them!"

Madoc cocked his head. He released his hold on my father's neck. "Then who?"

Myrddin folded his hands in front of his chest. "Who is missing?" He returned to tending Andrew's wound.

I surveyed those gathered with us. "Where is Mr. Godfrey?"

My father rubbed his neck. "What is —" He coughed. "What is it you accuse him of?"

Madoc stared at him for a long time before answering. "He stole the Water of Life."

"The what?" Mr. Kinnersley asked.

I remembered a conversation between Mr. Godfrey and Phineas as we had left Philadelphia. They had spoken of the Fountain of Youth, its waters that grant immortality. *Could it be?*

Mr. Colden chortled, then stopped. "You don't mean . . ."

Something had never felt quite right about this place. The ageless quality they all shared. The odd customs they adhered to. Madoc's ancient armor. The absence of children.

Demons.

"Impossible." My father stepped closer to Madoc. He looked him over with the familiar scrutiny I'd seen him direct at his plants countless times. "You're not —" He took a step back, as though to find a better angle. "You can't be —" And gradually, I saw the scrutiny give way to awe and admiration. "You're him?"

"I am Madoc ap Owain Gwynedd," the prince said.

"Five hundred and eighty-three years ago, I sailed from my country to this land."

"The Fountain of Youth?" my father said. "But . . . where?"

"We do not know." Madoc gathered up the bottom of his chain mail shirt and stripped it off. It fell to the ground with a heavy metallic rattle. "Everything I told you about our history was true. After the fortress at Gwynedd fell, we fled, and along the way we stopped to take rest in a small dale near a spring. We drank, we filled our skins, and we moved on. By the time we realized what had happened to us, we couldn't find that place again, and we had but one skin remaining with some of the water left in it."

"And the chalice?" my father asked.

"It is symbolic. We preserved the last of the water in a bottle. There have been rare times, very rare, where we have poured it into the chalice and allowed someone to drink from it."

Mr. Kinnersley chewed on his lower lip. "You've granted them eternal life."

"It is not something we do lightly." Madoc went to Andrew. It seemed that Myrddin had slowed the bleeding from his chest. "I have a question they must answer first, and they have to want immortality without doubt."

"Who wouldn't want it?" Mr. Kinnersley asked.

Madoc regarded him. "I, for one, do not want it. And you would be wise to consider why you wish for it."

His voice carried a burden of sadness, and it made me wonder about the cost of living forever. The pain, the loss, and the grief of life that would never end. "Is the water why you don't have children?" I asked.

"Yes," he said. "No child has been born since we drank it. Except one. There was a woman among us who was already with child when we found the spring. When that child was born, she was most precious to us. We raised her, assuming she would have our immortality. But in the end, she merely lived a long, long life. And that life was all she wanted. Though I offered it to her many times, she never drank from the chalice. Your people knew her as Madame Montour."

Jane touched her neck. "Andrew's mother."

Madoc smiled. "To protect us, she never told anyone where she came from. Not even her own son. But she left him hints and clues, and I think she always hoped he would somehow find his way home."

"Just now," I said, "you offered him the water, and he accepted. Would it save him?"

"It would have," Madoc said.

"Could it have saved Phineas?" Mr. Faries asked.

"No." Myrddin used a rag to wipe Andrew's blood from his hands. "We tried, but it was too late for your companion. Everything has a limit, even the healing power of the water."

I wasn't sure I wanted to ask my next question. "Is it too late for Andrew?"

"What is the point of that question?" Myrddin threw the rag to the floor. "The water is gone."

"What if we can get it back?" I asked.

"What makes you think there is anything to get back?"

Mr. Kinnersley sounded impatient. "Francis will have drunk it all by now, surely."

"No, he won't." Mr. Colden's smile was half-smirk. "I know Francis, and he'll conserve every single drop."

I watched Myrddin lay a bandage over Andrew's chest. What time we had to save him was slipping away. Every moment had worth. "If the water can heal Andrew," I said, "we need to get it back. And we need to hurry."

Mr. Kinnersley frowned. "What do you think, Cadwallader?"

Mr. Colden shook his head. "I defer to John."

I faced my father, my posture defiant. He had threatened to leave Andrew for dead once before, and I expected him to do the same again. Especially now that I knew where his anger came from. The reason for his hatred of the Indians had deep and tangled roots.

"I think . . ." He was talking to everyone, but he looked right at me. "I agree with Billy."

Though neither of us moved, his words closed some of the distance between us.

"If you're going after him," Madoc said, "then I'm coming with you."

Mr. Faries took a few steps toward the door. "He must have stolen it during the battle. Which means he has been on foot only a matter of hours. If we can find his trail, we can easily catch him. My apologies, Ebenezer, but Francis is an old man, after all."

Madoc took up his sword. "Not anymore."

CHAPTER 28

The Eyes of the Bear-Wolf

Out on the village green, we discussed which direction to search. Everyone agreed Mr. Godfrey would not be heading west, deeper into the frontier, nor south, along the retreat of Marin's forces. That left north and east, and between the two, my father decided that east seemed more likely, as north would take Mr. Godfrey closer to the French forts at Kaskaskia and Saint Louis.

"I think I'll wait here," Mr. Kinnersley said. "You were right about old men, Mr. Faries. I'll only slow you down, and Andrew doesn't have the time to spare."

My father looked at Mr. Faries's arm in its sling. "You should stay as well."

Mr. Faries frowned but nodded. "Find him, John."

"We will."

Mr. Colden shifted on his feet. He looked at Jane. "John, I —"

"Stay, Cadwallader. Stay with your daughter."

Mr. Colden nodded.

So my father, Madoc, and I set off at a run down the same road out of the village that had brought us in, then climbed back up the mountain. Though I had no idea what signs to look for, it did not take long for my father to spot evidence of Mr. Godfrey's passing.

"He's choosing speed over secrecy and keeping to the trails."

"How do you know?" Madoc asked.

"The plants tell me all I need. And they never lie."

We raced along, moving quickly through the forest, scattering birds from the trees. My father led the way, and I came next, followed by Madoc.

My father called over his shoulder. "How long until the water takes effect?"

"He'll feel younger right away," Madoc said. "But the full transformation takes days."

"Not Godfrey," my father said. "Andrew."

"Oh." Madoc paused. "Once he drinks the water, he will heal quickly."

We covered what I guessed to be several miles. My father still found regular signs of Mr. Godfrey. We knew we were on his trail. But we had no idea how far ahead he might be. After an hour or more of running, my father called a brief halt to rest.

I breathed hard and spat. A slight pain jabbed my chest.

"I thought we'd have overtaken him by now," my father said.

"What is your plan when we find him?" Madoc adjusted the sword on his belt. "I know what I would do, but he is your man."

"I haven't decided yet."

We rested a few moments longer and set off again. The pain in my chest stabbed deeper, making it difficult to breathe. But the thought of Andrew silenced any thoughts I had of stopping. We ran several more miles, and the sun began its evening descent at our backs, lighting up the forest before us. It reminded me of being up in Mr. Faries's cannon, the bronze shields behind me.

Not long after that, my father slowed and stopped. He glanced back at me and Madoc, his finger to his lips, and we crept forward silently to the edge of a bluff.

Down below, at the bottom of a steep incline, spread a field of *incognitum* bones. Acres and acres of jumbled skeletons rested together. Their ribs and tusks jutted upward in all directions, the single, empty eye cavities in their skulls staring endlessly.

"My god," my father whispered.

"I haven't been here in many years," Madoc said. "We found the bones before we saw the living animals, so we called them *cewri*. Giants."

"What happened here?" my father asked.

"Whatever it was, it happened long before my people

came." Madoc leaned out. "I think something drove the herd off the edge and they fell to their deaths. But sometimes the living *cewri* come here. They use their long snouts to gently move and touch the bones. Sometimes, they stay for days. They *know* what this place is."

Movement caught my eye. There was something down there.

"Father, look!"

It was Mr. Godfrey, crossing the bone field.

"Quickly!" My father charged right over the bluff, down the hill.

Madoc and I looked at each other, and then we both followed him.

I took the slope half sliding, half running. Mr. Godfrey saw us coming down and increased his pace, but he seemed to be having a difficult time picking his way over the skeletons.

We hit the bottom of the hill and continued after him.

"Stop, Francis!" my father yelled. "It's no use running!"

"I'll circle around him." Madoc split off from us to the right.

"Let me go, John!" Mr. Godfrey said. "You don't understand!"

The three of us moved more quickly than he did. The bones slipped, rolled, and cracked under my feet. I grabbed hold of them to steady myself, their white surfaces smooth in my hand. And as we drew closer, I saw that Mr. Godfrey did look younger. His hair wasn't as gray, and his wrinkles not as deep. But he wasn't quite young, yet.

"You don't understand, Francis!" my father said. "We need that water for healing! Andrew will die!"

"I'm sorry, John!" Mr. Godfrey kept going, clawing his way forward, his movements frantic.

Madoc had almost made it around him. Just a few more feet and he would cut him off.

"Francis!" my father shouted.

"No, John! No! I won't — !"

Madoc's sword rang as he pulled it free of its scabbard. "Halt, old man."

Mr. Godfrey stopped. "Old man." He was panting, and laughing, or crying. I couldn't tell which. "Old man."

"It will go hard for you, Francis." My father stretched out his hand. "Unless you give me the bottle."

"No!"

"Mr. Godfrey!" I stepped toward him. "Andrew is hurt. I know you don't want him to die."

"Of course not!" He looked skyward. "But there isn't another way, Billy. I've searched, and there isn't. I'm dying!"

"Of course you are," my father said. "So are we all."

"No, John. I am *dying*."

"I don't understand," my father said. "How could you do this, Francis? After all we've done together, I thought I knew what manner of man you were."

"Oh, you know me very well." He pulled the pack off his back. "A monk, a magician, and a madman, isn't that what you said?"

What? My father had used those words to describe . . .

"Kelpius?" My father's footing slipped, but he caught himself.

Mr. Godfrey opened the pack and pulled out the bottle. It caught the fading sunlight, and I could see its contents sloshing inside. Mr. Faries had been right. He hadn't drunk it all yet.

"I had the philosopher's stone!" Mr. Godfrey stared at the bottle in his hand. "I've lived countless lives, under countless names, until one of my half-wit followers decided to throw my possessions into the river! He threw away the philosopher's stone!"

So the stories about him were true.

"Without it," Mr. Godfrey said. "I began to age. I began to die!"

"That was why you came on the expedition," my father said.

"Yes." He looked up from the bottle. "The Fountain of Youth."

"Enough of this!" Madoc raised his sword. "Let me strike this madman down."

Mr. Godfrey raised the bottle over his head. "Strike me and you shatter any hope that Andrew has!"

Madoc lowered his sword.

"Francis." My father calmed his voice to a conversational tone. "Be rational. You already drank the water. You don't need it any longer."

"Oh, but I do. I can't take any more risks!"

"Mr. Godfrey, please!" I shouted.

"I'm sorry, Billy." He turned back to my father. "Why do you care about that Indian, anyway, John? I thought you hated him."

My father fell silent. I had wondered the same thing — why was he doing this for Andrew? — and I waited for his answer. "To err is human, Francis."

"Pope was a hack!" Mr. Godfrey laughed. "And his translations were abominable. Do not quote him to me, sir."

But I'd heard my father say it. Perhaps he had listened to me, after all, as we stood upon the green.

"Answer me this, madman," Madoc said. "It is a question I ask of everyone before they are allowed to drink from the chalice."

Mr. Godfrey waited.

"Do you seek immortality because you fear death, or because you want life?"

The question appeared simple on its surface. But it grew deeper by looking at it, and it seemed to penetrate Mr. Godfrey's thoughts. In that moment of distraction, my father lunged at him, grasping for the bottle.

"No!" Mr. Godfrey wrestled him for it.

And suddenly the bottle flew from their hands.

It tumbled through the air.

I ran and dove for it, my arms and hands and fingers stretched as far as they could. I caught the bottle before it hit the ground, but I went down, and my shoulder slammed into an *incognitum* skull.

"The bottle!" My father let go of Mr. Godfrey and rushed toward me.

"I have it!" I held it to my chest. "It's safe."

"The madman flees!" Madoc said.

Mr. Godfrey scrambled away from us over the bone field.

I got to my feet, careful of the bottle, and handed it over to my father.

"Do we pursue him?" Madoc asked.

My father watched him for a moment. "No. No, we have what we came for."

"Are you certain? My sword still thirsts."

"Can it ever be quenched?" my father asked.

Madoc looked down at the blade in his hands. Something flashed in his eyes, some recognition, and then they softened. "How easily it is lost," he whispered.

Mr. Godfrey reached the edge of the forest and turned back to look at us. In spite of what he had done, I was sad for him. His madness —

Suddenly, the bear-wolf erupted from the trees behind him, and an instant later had Mr. Godfrey's neck in its jaws. It lifted him into the air and shook him violently, his legs and arms flying wildly, and then it dropped his limp

and lifeless body to the ground. Broken stubs of arrows
jutted from the bear-wolf's neck and side. It was the same
beast, and it must have been mad with pain and fear. We
watched, motionless, as it sniffed what was left of Mr.
Godfrey and then lifted its head toward us.

It roared.

"Run!" my father shouted.

We tore across the field toward the forest, tripping
and stumbling, chips and splinters of bone flying behind
us. My father and I raced shoulder to shoulder. But fear
burned in my body, a familiar fire, and by degrees, I pulled
ahead of him.

I glanced back. He was running hard, grimacing. And
behind him came the bear-wolf. It was gaining on him fast.

I could not beat my father to the trees. I could not leave
him behind.

I slowed my feet, and the distance between us vanished.
And then my father was beside me again, shouting, "Go,
Billy! Leave me and go!"

But I stayed with him.

Madoc reached the trees ahead of us. He spun around,
gripping his sword with both hands extended before him,
shouting a battle cry. *"Dewch â'ch brwydr i mi, cythraul!"*

We were almost there.

But then what would we do? The trees offered no safety,
no escape.

The bear-wolf roared. It jolted me, close enough to feel
on the back of my neck. I lost track of my footing, tripped

over a tusk, and crashed off to the side into a pile of bones. The bear-wolf slid to a stop. I rolled up onto my knees to face it as it turned back toward me.

"Billy!" my father shouted.

The beast's breath rattled. I could hear a gurgling sound deep in its chest from where I knelt. And it swayed on its long legs, the fur around its wounds matted with blood. It was dying. And padding closer to me with its teeth and its claws. I had no weapon. I couldn't run. It was over. With that awareness came calm assurance.

I bowed my head, my hands in my lap. I thought back to my animal dream, the one in which I had lived and died several times over. "It's all right." I spoke to it calmly, but also to myself. "I don't hate you. I am what I am, and you are what you are. And though we are different, we are connected."

Its front paws stepped into my view, directly before me, the size of wine casks. Its head had to be right above mine. Was it looking at me? Smelling me? What was it waiting for? I barely breathed, but I raised my head and looked into its rich brown eyes. It stared back into mine.

"For Annwyn!" Madoc cried.

He came from the side and rammed the bear-wolf hard, driving the entire length of his sword up into its chest, just behind its front legs. A heart wound. The bear-wolf staggered sideways. It lifted its head and moaned, then huffed and tottered.

"Get out of the way, Billy!" my father shouted.

Madoc grabbed my arm and pulled me up and away as the bear-wolf collapsed onto the bones. Its chest rose twice more, then stilled.

My father rushed up, his mouth agape. Then he threw his arms around me in a hug.

I just stood there. In my mind, I saw the memory of the bear-wolf shaking Mr. Godfrey's body, breaking it. That could have been me. It could have done that to me. A trembling started in my legs and moved up through my chest, into my arms. I realized I was crying.

My father hugged me tighter.

I lifted my arms and hugged him back.

Back at Annwyn, in Madoc's hall, we all stood around Andrew as Myrddin emptied the contents of the bottle into his mouth. Every last drop. Andrew choked and swallowed it down, and within a matter of moments, the rictus of pain faded from his face.

"It is working," Myrddin said.

Sighs of relief turned to tears and laughter.

Madoc crossed the hall and collapsed onto his throne. "That a man should live to see such times." He shook his head. "Cannons that shoot light and men who stare down bear-wolves."

He had called me a man.

My father went before him. "The fires destroyed most of your crops. I would like to offer the aid of the Philosophical Society in helping you replant and rebuild."

Madoc said nothing.

"We can begin work right away," my father said.

"When I sailed from my country," Madoc said, "all those years ago, I did so to find peace. My father had just died. Four of my brothers fought for his throne, and I did not want to be drawn into their wars. Even so, it took us hundreds of years to find the peace we sought in this land, and if we had not been immortal, we never would have. And I see now how fragile a thing it is." He stood. "I appreciate your offer of assistance, John Bartram. But we will not rebuild. The French will only return."

"What will you do?"

"We will do as we have always done. We will leave. We will go and find another place, farther west, and disappear into the frontier once again. And this time, no rumors of us shall reach you."

The next night, Madoc held a banquet in his hall for the whole village to celebrate our victory and honor those who had fallen. Annwyn had lost twenty-eight men in the fight with the French, and they had each gone into battle knowing there wasn't enough of the Water of Life for all their wounds.

"Before the fight, each of them forswore the chalice," Madoc said in Welsh, with Rhys translating for us. "For none would take the Water from his brother. We honor them and pray they are speeding swiftly across the seas to the lands of our fathers."

After that, the prince listed the names of the dead, and he counted Phineas among them, buried among Madoc's people.

"And now," Madoc said, "we are also honored to welcome home the son of one who left us long ago." He lifted his goblet. "To Andrew."

The assembly all raised cups and mugs. Andrew, who had healed almost completely overnight, bowed his head, seated next to us.

"And now it is time to eat!" Madoc said. "Drink! Tell tales of glory and days gone by."

With a cheer, everyone turned to their food and companions. Next to me, Jane sighed. Her father and mine were laughing and talking across from us. But Mr. Colden winced every so often, still quite bruised.

"Has he said anything about his time with the French?" I asked her.

She shook her head. "He won't talk about it. It makes me sad."

"You don't still blame yourself, do you?"

She shook her head again. "People are saying you stood up to the bear-wolf. Is that true?"

"At the time, it felt more like I was *giving* up. Or maybe just accepting that I couldn't beat it. That there wasn't anything I could do."

"Either way, that was very brave."

I shrugged. It hadn't felt brave, either.

"But I don't think that's the bravest thing you've done," she said.

I smiled. "No?"

"No."

"Then tell me, what was the bravest thing I've done?"

She looked across the table. "Standing up to your father."

I didn't know what to say. I followed her gaze and watched my father for several moments, a man I had thought I knew before coming on this expedition. A man I had learned more about in the last few days than I had in my whole life with him on the farm. And in spite of that, or perhaps because of it, a man who felt more like a stranger now than he ever had. But Jane was right. Those moments when I had refused to accept my father's words, the times when I had argued with him, and the moment when I had even defied him, had been even harder for me than when I had looked into the eyes of the bear-wolf.

A week later, we stood upon the green, healed, refreshed, and ready to begin the voyage back to the colonies. We had taken down the light cannon and its tower, and Mr. Faries had his lenses stored safely in his pack. Madoc had supplied us with new provisions. Food, blankets, and all that we would need to hunt and fish our way back home.

Mr. Colden had resumed command of the expedition. "And I expect a full report of the events that have transpired in my absence," he'd said. "Beginning with how you shocked an entire French army and myself!"

But there would be plenty of time for that on the journey.

Madoc, Rhys, and Myrddin stood before the door of their hall.

"Safe travels," Rhys said.

Andrew stood with them. He was one of them now, the last who ever would be, and he had chosen to stay with them. But before we departed, he asked to speak with my father, privately, and the two of them stepped away from us. I wondered what they were saying, especially as my father extended his hand, and they shook. Perhaps I would ask him one day.

"Farewell, philosophers," Madoc said. "Men of wisdom and action. May you all return to your homes safely."

"And may you find yours," my father said.

Madoc nodded, and we started down the road. The villagers had all gathered in the streets outside their homes. They waved to us and slipped extra cakes into our hands as we passed them. But soon we'd left the main village behind and followed the road east that carried us by their farms.

"I know this might seem strange to mention," my father said. "But in the fall, I am planning an expedition into the Catskill Mountains."

"Just you?" I asked.

"Just me. But I was wondering if you would join me."

Before coming on this expedition, I knew what my answer would have been. But was that something I wanted anymore?

I thought back to what my mother had said before I left. About finding my own path. I thought about the things I'd said to my father since then, some of which I still meant, and some of which I didn't. We were alike, he and I, in so many ways. But so different in others. There were parts of him I admired, and parts of him that still shamed me. Parts of him I wanted to distance myself from, but parts of him I wanted to emulate.

He was what he was, and I was what I was.

He was my father, and I was his son.

"Yes, Father. I'd like to join you."

"Excellent," he said. "Excellent."

We reached the farthest farmhouse, the first one we had seen. The same woman stood outside in her deerskin dress and wimple, hoeing in her garden. She waved to us, and after we'd passed her, it felt as though she might still be waving to us in the road.

I smiled.

And I turned to wave back.

AUTHOR'S NOTE

In telling Billy's story, I set out to write an American fantasy. Though the names of its characters and settings may be recognizable to many, even iconic, *The Lost Kingdom* is not a work of history. I have made extensive changes to the facts, some of which will be obvious, some less so. Where I have deviated from the record, in every case I have done so in service to the story. Though it may remove some of the mystery and magic in the book, the historian in me compels me to list some, though not all, of these changes.

William Bartram and his father, John, were real-life American naturalists, each respected and renowned in his own right. Their relationship was a very complicated one, rooted in the tension between their similarities and differences. For a wonderfully sensitive and human portrayal, I recommend *The Natures of John and William Bartram* by Thomas P. Slaughter, a work I relied on heavily while writing *The Lost Kingdom*. I have attempted to remain as true to their individual characters as I could. Sadly, John Bartram's father, Billy's grandfather, was killed by Native Americans, and John harbored a lifelong prejudice. Billy, on the other hand, held startlingly progressive views and attitudes toward the Native Americans for his time.

As for the other people on the Madoc expedition, there really was an American Philosophical Society in Philadelphia, founded by John Bartram and Benjamin Franklin. The Society exists to this day, but had fallen into a period of apparent inactivity by 1753, the year in which *The Lost Kingdom* ostensibly takes place. I took advantage of this gap to create my own secret history of the organization, based on the patriotism expressed by many of its earliest members. The men who I portray in the book are largely my creations, although, with the exception of Mr. Godfrey, I did base them on actual Society philosophers and their respective disciplines and accomplishments. Cadwallader Colden had a daughter named Jane, who was a talented artist and the first female botanist in America. It was even suggested in passing by a mutual friend of Colden and John Bartram that Jane might be a suitable match for Billy. In reality, she was not the young woman portrayed in the book, but fifteen years Billy's senior. Andrew Montour and his mother were prominent colonial interpreters, and Madame Montour's true identity remains something of a historical mystery today. Johannes Kelpius, the Wissahickon mystic, was an eccentric historical figure. Described as "weird as a wizard" by the poet John Greenleaf Whittier, Kelpius was rumored to have possessed the philosopher's stone, while his alter ego in the novel is a fabrication of mine. The aeroship in the novel is based on an actual concept by

Francesco Lana de Terzi, and I tried to remain true to his design. Captain Paul Marin and his *troupes de la marine* were marching through the Ohio Valley in 1753, and George Washington was at the Forks of the Ohio, though not until much later in the year than when I place him there. In 1754, the young major would be involved in the skirmish that ignited the French and Indian War.

The purpose of the Society's expedition is grounded in colonial American beliefs. Rumors of a tribe of "Welsh-speaking Indians" were widespread. Governor Dinwiddie of Virginia offered a five-hundred-pound reward to anyone able to bring back proof of their existence, and at the beginning of the nineteenth century, President Thomas Jefferson instructed Meriwether Lewis and William Clark to make contact with them as they crossed the continent on their famous expedition. It is likely the story of Madoc began as a political fabrication to bolster England's claim to territory in the New World. But it soon took on a life of its own, and folklore surrounding Madoc persists to this day, including legends about several ruined stone fortresses like the one that appears in *The Lost Kingdom*.

With regard to the mastodons and bear-wolf (a beast inspired by the prehistoric *Arctodus simus*, or short-faced bear), into the nineteenth century, fossils in hand, many believed mastodons still existed somewhere out in the American frontier. I chose to take that belief at face value. And once you've found mastodons, who knows what else might be lurking.